MOONLIGHT AND MAGIC SERIES

MOONLIGHT AND MAGIC SERIES

MINA CARTER

Blue Hedgehog Press

Editor
Craig Kim
Cover Artist
Mina Carter
This is a work of fiction. The characters, incidents and dialogues in this book are of the author's imagination and are not to be construed as real. Any resemblance to actual events or persons, living or dead, is completely coincidental.

This book was produced using PressBooks.com, and PDF rendering was done by PrinceXML.

Contents

Moonlight & Magic

Chapter One

Boredom was a fucker. He needed to get laid. That, or try to kick himself to death with rubber boots on.

Daelas sighed and tried to concentrate on the paperwork in front of him. He wasn't doing so well. The club accounts had never been particularly riveting, but he normally had less trouble keeping his attention on them.

The numbers swam past his eyes as he chewed on the pencil in his hand. The wood cracked under his teeth, snapping him back to the present. He grimaced at the ruined end of the pencil and dropped it back into the pot, picking a metal barrelled pen, instead.

He *really* needed to get laid. He was an incubus, so the need for sex went without saying, but he hadn't seen any action between the sheets for months. Too many other things to take care of, or his brother's latest madcap scheme to clear up. Anyone would think he was years older than Jaren, rather than just fifteen minutes. Sighing in resignation, he shook his head to get rid of the buzz trying to settle behind his eyes.

He flopped back in his chair and turned it to face the club below, the one-way glass allowing him to see, but not be seen. Like most weekends, it was busy. Packed to the rafters. The throng of humanity below all seeking something—be it amusement, companionship, or darker needs, conducted deep in the shadows.

Pen tapping against his thigh, he looked down over the club, a brooding expression on his face as he tried to isolate the cause of the buzzing. No one brooded as well as a demon, and no demon brooded as well as Daelas. Apart from his twin, Jaren. Apparently, the staff had a running argument going, as to which brother brooded better.

The cacophony of human thought rising from the packed club below battered at his mind. Used to the sensation he ignored it, like a horse would a fly. If he felt the necessity, he could filter through the noise and latch onto one set of thoughts, reading the emotions and desires of the human they belonged to. It was the way the incubi hunted, drawing their victims into their web to play on their thoughts and needs, then seducing them to feed off of their sexual energy.

Some, like Daelas, were so adept at it, so skilled at weaving their web around their victims, that all they had to do was crook a finger, and their prey would fall at their knees. Which was wonderful for stroking his male ego, but it got lonely after a while.

Just once he'd like a woman to see him for himself, rather than have her eyes glaze over when he got within a foot of her.

Longing hit him.

To be able have a conversation with a woman without knowing he could click his fingers and have her under his spell, would be wonderful.

Daelas shook his head, his frustration a hiss between his teeth as he watched a young blonde gyrate on stage for the amusement of the men on the dance floor below her. The sight didn't affect him. Even from here he could tell she was human. Easy pickings, and therefore no challenge. Daelas needed a woman with some sort of paranormal blood, or even a female demon. He shuddered, the thought exciting him even as the reality repulsed him. Daelas didn't want a female of his kind anywhere near him. Even if the chances of Daelas and his brother meeting their soul-mate out here in the mortal world were slim, it was still preferable to getting saddled with a female sex demon for the rest of eternity. Beautiful and deadly, but with the morals of an alley cat, a succubus would only destroy everything he and Jaren had built, and laugh while she did it.

Absently, his gaze wandered over the already full dance floor, and then swept over the rest of the club. With an ease born of practice he picked out the trouble spots, noting they were all clear. Everything was running like clockwork down there. He sighed, a combination of relief and regret.

He was bored; he wanted something—anything—to happen.

Just as he turned away from the window, he felt it. Amongst the throng of humanity choking up the "airwaves," there was something else. The buzzing intensified, settling behind his eyes like a bad headache.

"Well heeellooo…what have we here?" he murmured, sitting forward with interest as he tried to isolate the feeling. It wasn't human, that was for sure. Whatever species, it was alluring, lingering on the periphery of his senses, like trying to catch sight of something out of the corner of his eye.

A haunting feeling—similar to the sense of loss after harp strings have been stroked and the music has died away—filled him.

"Where are you?" he whispered into the silent office, his sharp eyes riveted on the club below. "*What* are you?"

*

"Sheeerrri. I thought you said there were sex demons in here?" Sage giggled as she tried to open the cubicle door. She was tipsy, way past tipsy. In fact, she'd sprinted past tipsy like an Olympic athlete, and was heading into full-on "drunk as a skunk" territory.

Sage squinted at the door; alcohol and lack of her glasses, left off for reasons of vanity, not helping her any. Finally, with great concentration, she flicked the lock open and did a little victory jig right there in the cubicle. No lock would stop her.

Sherri looked over her shoulder and shrugged as Sage joined her, her friend's earrings sparkling as they caught the light.

"S'what the flyers said…about the waiters. I dunno. They're cute, whatever they are. Come on, slowpoke, I wanna dance!" Sherri urged as she washed her hands.

"Dance? You can barely stand up! Hold your horses, missy," Sage ordered, grinning as Sherri swayed on impossibly high heels. She had no idea how Sherri could walk, let alone dance in those things.

Sage checked her appearance in the mirror, an automatic reaction. A petite, rather curvaceous woman looked back at her. Always the critic, she pursed her lips and checked her eyeliner, then tucked a stray lock of hair behind her ear. Her hair had a mind of its own, always managing to escape, no matter what she did with it.

Quickly she checked her top, pulling the neckline up a little to cover her cleavage—oft repeated warnings about not showing herself off like a tart flashing through her mind. Shaking her head and ignoring the little voice—her ex's—in the back of her mind, she smoothed the top over her stomach and assessed herself. Not too shabby, she decided, and grabbed her bag to head toward the door. "Now, let's go dance."

They walked back into the club, giggling as they wove through the packed main room, heading for the stage. The newest hotspot in town, *Moonlight & Magic*, was a cut above the other clubs in town, with tasteful interior design, comfortable seating, and a large dance floor. It traded heavily on its paranormal associations, which wasn't to some of the clubbers' tastes, but Sage had to admit it made good business sense.

Anything paranormal was big, with a capital B. Since the paranormals had come out of the closet two years ago, fascination with anything paranormal had steadily increased to near fever pitch. Now, stick a pair of fangs or wings on something, and it was guaranteed to sell.

A lesson *Moonlight & Magic* seemed to have taken to heart, if the large number of people in the place were any indication. Still before midnight it was already packed, and Sage hadn't been sure they'd get in. She'd never been before, had avoided the place since it'd opened, but now she realised how much she'd been missing out. Not that Marcus had let her go out much, convinced all a guy had to do was look her way and she'd be off to his place or some back alley, panties around her ankles. She snorted to herself. Showed what he knew. She was well rid of the jerk.

Heavy music pounded through the speakers dotted around the walls, filling the room with a wild, sensual rhythm that had her feet tapping, as something inside her ached to join the writhing throng already on the dance floor. She didn't though, didn't have the chance to, as Sherri grabbed her hand and dragged her toward the stage.

She almost ran into Sherri's back as the other girl stopped dead, standing aside to let one of the waiters by, a grin on her face as her friend ogled the guy's ass. Sage couldn't blame her. The rotating overhead lights showcased a honed body displayed to perfection, wearing sheer black t-shirt and pants. Must be the staff uniform; she'd noticed all the waiters were dressed the same. Sherri sighed in rapture as the waiter noticed their attention and smiled, white teeth flashing in the semidarkness of the crowded club.

"Now, you can't tell me *he's* human!" Sherri hissed, leaning close so Sage could hear her over the loud music, her friend's stare following the waiter until he was out of sight. Or more specifically, followed his ass, until *it* was out of sight. Her friend sighed again and looked back at Sage, who shook her head in amusement.

"Well, he does have a bit of an exotic look..." Sage admitted, her tone noncommittal. Her gaze flitted around the club, checking out the rest of the staff. They did *look* exotic, with an indefinable cast to their features that spoke of bloodlines not completely Homo sapiens.

It was fake. Totally fake.

But there was no way she could tell Sherri that. If she did, she'd have to tell Sherri *how* she knew they were fakes. Friends since fourth grade, Sherri knew everything about Sage. From the first boy she'd ever kissed, right through to the complete disaster when she'd lost her virginity. She'd even told her about all the crap Marcus had put her through, albeit on pain of death, after Sherri had managed to get her out of the apartment for a while. It'd been such a relief to tell someone, to assure herself that she wasn't going nuts.

There was one thing Sherri *didn't* know about Sage, however. Something no one knew about her. A secret her father had drilled into her relentlessly to keep to herself.

Sage was part fae.

Quite what flavour she didn't know. Her mother had died when Sage was three, and her father refused to talk about it. So in the grand scheme of things,

Sage was a little out of touch with her fae side. Hell, for all she knew, she could've been descended from the Queen of the Fairies and she wouldn't have had a clue.

Her lips quirked. The chances of her being a fairy princess were similar to that of finding a snowball in hell. She'd seen Queen Mab on the news, and even though she'd like to think it, she couldn't claim descent from a woman who looked the way Mab did. Sage was far too short and plain.

Faery princess or common imp, Sage's instincts were strong enough to see through the glamour being used on the club's staff. A glamour that rendered them something extraordinary, something darker and sexier than the plain old humans they were.

"Sorry, but was that exotic…or erotic?" Sherri's chuckle drew Sage back to the present, her friend's dirty laugh making a few heads turn in their direction. Sage flushed, shushing her.

"Behave you," she giggled, feeling the unaccustomed effects of the alcohol surging through her system. The music changed, the heavy beat of a familiar song reverberating around the room. "Ooh! I *love* this one. Come on, there's a space on the stage!"

*

The haunting aura was driving Daelas insane. He'd tried to ignore it by concentrating on the club accounts, but it was getting to him now. He sighed, closing the laptop. It was no good. He had to go see what it was.

Leaving the office, he headed down the short flight of stairs leading into the club. As soon as he pushed open the door, the heat and noise of the club wrapped around him like a warm, wet blanket. He grimaced as his shirt stuck to his back. He should've taken his jacket off. His office had air conditioning, but even with the doors open and the AC units on, the club felt like a sauna. Just too many people in here, with the heat of their bodies and a myriad of scents—perfume, aftershave, shampoo, body lotion—all combining into a heady, cloying atmosphere.

Daelas took a deep breath, filling his lungs and feeling at ease. This was his world—the perfect hunting ground for an incubus.

Knuckles, the heavyset bouncer stationed at the door, turned in surprise when he saw Daelas, but then his face returned to its normal stoic expression, straightaway. Daelas didn't blame the man for the surprise. It was rare for him to venture into the club proper; this was more Jaren's domain. But if there was nothing else for it, he had to find the source of that buzzing.

Stepping into the crowd, he moved through it with ease. A touch of an elbow here, a quick thought there, and a path opened up before him, the human cattle moving as he commanded. A few, all female, turned, their eyes speculative, but Daelas ignored them, his mind focused. None were the woman he was looking for; he'd know her when he saw her.

But he knew that it was a *she*. It had to be. There was something intrinsically feminine about the impression which called to him, spoke to his soul and drew him in. But where was she?

Stopping in the middle of the dance floor, he scanned the room. Tall for any man, human or paranormal, Daelas had a good view of the club, turning as his gaze swept over the crowded floor.

He froze, his attention riveted on the stage.

There, dancing in the center, was the source of his problem. She was small...no, she was *tiny*...with a figure which would tempt a saint.

Daelas was no saint.

His mouth dried as he watched her, standing in the middle of the dance floor like he'd been poleaxed.

She was pure temptation, all smooth-skinned limbs and curves, a mass of dark hair pinned up to reveal the delicate line of her neck. A line he ached to run his hand along, curving it into the nape of her neck and tilting her head up so her lips—a perfect cupid's bow—were his for the taking.

"Shit," he growled, his body reacting to the erotic images burning themselves one after another into his brain. He needed to get laid, seriously needed to get laid, and as soon as he'd set his eyes on her, no other woman would do.

He had to have her.

Stalking toward the stage, he watched her every step of the way. She danced sensually to the heavy music, the sultry look on her face pure temptation. Daelas' mouth watered, his cock harder than he could ever recall, a growl sounding low in his chest.

His. She was his. She just didn't know it yet.

She must've felt his interest, turning to look at him as he approached, her hips swaying in a siren's call. Her lips curved, it was a smile of feminine mystery and mischief.

Daelas stopped in front of the stage, looking up at her, still watching. She was a mere foot away, her intense stare flirting with him. Meeting his gaze for a second, she turned, presenting him with the graceful arch of her back as she danced. Daelas bit back a groan, lust hitting him like a truck travelling at Mach 1. Her subtle aura wound around him, drawing him in, just as much as the quick, flirtatious glances and the undulation of her hips.

She turned back and he beckoned, his face tightening with the control he exerted under the darting lights of the dance floor, calling her to him. She lifted her head, little chin going up as if in challenge, her eyes assessing as she looked him over. His lips quirked a little as she pretended to consider his unspoken order. She would obey, he just knew it. *Come on sweetheart, you know you want to*. He waited for her to come to him.

Like a butterfly she flitted closer, a quick shimmy of her hips, until she stood in front of him. Daelas' smile widened. Even on the stage she hadn't been much taller than him. She didn't stop moving, her body still swaying slightly to the music as she tilted her head, watching him. Waiting for his next move.

He held out his hand, offering her the choice. To a certain point, Daelas was a gentleman. But it was just a mask that hid the primal creature. Strip away the civilized veneer, and there was pure demon beneath. He suppressed a shiver. No woman had ever brought out that side of him before. He'd always been in control.

Until now.

Chapter Two

Sage shimmied in front of tall, blond and gorgeous. She'd noticed him watching her, just standing unmoving in the middle of the dance floor like he owned the place, his light-eyed gaze fastened on her. His expression intent and dangerous.

Under normal circumstances that would've made her nervous. She'd have looked away, tried not to draw attention to herself. Marcus' fists had taught her that lesson. But, fortified by alcohol and the mood of the evening, she didn't. Instead, she danced to draw him in, every sway of her hips and arch of her back designed to entrance, to lure.

Then he stood in front of her, the demand in his eyes obvious. Sherri, dancing next to her and flirting with another dancer, grinned and winked at her, the silent message unmistakable: you go, girl!

So she did, hardly believing her own bravery as she put her hand in his with a small smile. A jolt of awareness shot through her at the first brush of her skin against his. Her eyes widened as she looked at him, seeing the same surprise echoed in his features.

He pulled her toward him, letting go of her hand long enough to help her down off the stage. He picked her up as though she weighed nothing, sliding her down his body in a movement so sensual Sage's heart stuttered right there in her chest as he held her against him for a moment, his larger frame wrapped around hers protectively. Or possessively.

Oh, god, is he going to kiss me? Her breathing shortened in anticipation, her lips aching for the touch of his as he lifted his hand. His touch was gentle as he tucked a wayward strand of hair back behind her ear.

His smile transfixed her, transforming his features from merely handsome to devastating, as his eyes, a shade of blue she'd never seen before, darkened. His fingers played with the lock of hair he'd tucked behind her ear, the tips transferring their attention from it to the skin of her neck. His thumb whispered across her collarbone before his hand ghosted down her arm.

He pulled her close and all her attention was diverted to the feel of the solid male body pressed against hers. The hard, very aroused male body pressed against hers.

Startled, her eyes shot up and found his. An amused, intense stare looked back at her, obviously watching the surprised expression on her face. She swallowed. Like he knew she could feel the hardness of his erection pressed into her stomach, he smiled at her, the glitter of his eyes hardening as she glimpsed the arousal in their depths.

"I don't even know your name," she pointed out, a fascinated smile playing over her lips. She'd never allowed a guy to touch her this way before. Certainly not without a few months and many dates between them. But this was different. He was different from the guys she usually dated. Try as she might, she couldn't imagine him as an accountant. Perhaps an actor or something...

"Daelas, my name is Daelas, little pixie," he murmured as the music changed, the beat slowing down to something softer and altogether more sensual. Then, he pulled her back onto the dance floor.

Awareness arced between them, his hand smoothing over her nearly naked back, lingering along the line of her spine as they danced. Less a dance and more a form of vertical lovemaking.

Sage closed her eyes for a moment, her head whirling. She couldn't believe this. Men who looked like Daelas didn't come onto women like her. They went for the leggy, supermodel types.

"You're just perfect as you are," he breathed into her ear, his lips just brushing the tender lobe. Sage started, bright banners of colour forming on her cheeks. She hadn't realized she'd spoken aloud.

"You didn't." His lips feathered down her neck. "You think you're the only nonhuman in here?" He pulled back and looked down at her. The blaze of desire in his eyes made Sage's breath catch in her throat, heat pooling in her abdomen at the sensual promise as he bent his head to claim her lips.

The kiss started slow and soft, his mouth feathering over hers. Exploring and caressing. His tongue flicked out, brushed along the seam of her lips as he tempted her to open her mouth for him, to allow him in. She sucked in a breath, tremors running hot and cold along her arms, which had somehow wound themselves around his neck.

Her lips relaxed and his tongue swept in, destroying what remained of her defenses as he deepened the kiss into something dark and deeply dominant. Her knees turned to jelly as she clung to him. She moaned when he broke away, a soft sound which brought a quirk to the corners of his lips.

He kissed her again, quick and hard. "Shall we go somewhere a little more...private?"

Her chin came up as she met his eyes, a sense of mischief running through her.

"You got somewhere in mind?" she asked, flicking loose strands of hair off her shoulders, naked apart from the thin straps holding up her sequined top.

"I just might have."

*

Daelas smiled, drawing her to the side of the dance floor as the music changed again. He opened his mind and probed hers, casting his lures to get her where he wanted her. Which was in his office, naked. But he met a resistance, a glass wall behind her eyes that his probes slid off. She stopped talking, shaking her head as though to clear it.

Shit, she'd felt his touch.

Wary, Daelas stopped, hiding his surprised look as he watched her. She shouldn't have felt a thing then, nothing at all. He was either losing his touch or she was something special; something more than a human with a smattering of paranormal blood.

She swayed again, just a little, but his hands snaked out, ready to catch her in case she fell. She grasped his wrist, steadying herself and looking up at him.

"What was I saying?" Her voice was light, puzzled but accepting, as though losing her train of thought was nothing new. He realised with a start that she *had* been affected by his mental touch, just not in the way he'd expected, and from the look in her eyes, she was recovering fast.

He moved in, taking advantage of the small window of suggestibility his instincts were telling him—that this was the only chance he was going to get. He smiled, crowding closer as though they were already lovers. His smile was intimate, teasing.

"You, little pixie, are drunk!"

She took the prompt, blinking at him owlishly for a moment before her body relaxed and she leaned against him, tipping her small, heart-shaped face up to argue. "Am not!"

"You bloody well are. You're not even standing up straight on your own," he pointed out, motioning to her death-grip on his arms. She stared back at him, her lips pursed, concentration written on her face as if she thought about framing her next words.

Daelas hid a smile. She was as drunk as a skunk and very cute with it.

"Pffft, of course I'm bloody drunk! How else do you think I got the courage to chat up a guy who looks like you?" She waved her arm in an all-encompassing gesture which could've been meant to indicate Daelas' tall, suited figure.

Instead, she knocked someone's drink off the ledge surrounding the dance floor. Stifling a chuckle, Daelas' hand shot out with nonchalant ease and half caught it, half righted it.

"You said, 'Am not' though, which usually means you're disagreeing with something," he replied, eyebrow raised. By now he was entranced; she was far more than she'd appeared to be, his subtle tests of her mental defences revealing a slippery wall he couldn't break through.

For a man used to getting what he wanted with a thought, having to work for it was a new experience. One that, to his surprise, he was finding enjoyable.

Daelas was a connoisseur of women. As an incubus, it was coded into his genes. Even so, he put a lot of time and effort into the study of women, and yet, this woman was turning the tables on him, weaving her web around and drawing him in with an ease only the most experienced succubi would manage. She wasn't a succubus though, so he didn't struggle to get away.

"I am not a pixie!" Her voice was forceful, her button nose wrinkling as she pronounced the word in a manner reserved for a word like "cockroach." "I'm a fae. A sidhe," she added, her tone proud as she met his eyes.

She was lying through her teeth. Oh, she was a fae of some description, but if that fae was a sidhe, he'd eat his hat. Daelas hid his ever increasing smile as his eyebrow winged up again. "Aren't you a little...short for a sidhe?"

She sniffed and ignored him. "Are you a sex demon? Sherri said there were sex demons here, but all we've seen so far have been humans *pretending* to be sex demons. I demand there be sex demons!" she announced, nearly stamping her little foot as she glared at him.

He'd lost the battle. His deep, rich laughter surrounded them as he led her through the club, shortening his stride to match hers, despite the haste gnawing at him. "*Demand* is it, little fae? Well, we'll have to see what we can do."

Minutes later he breathed a sigh of relief as he ushered his diminutive and very tempting companion into the office he'd recently vacated, closing the door behind them. Leaning back against the cool wood for a long second, he watched her.

Hell, even her walk turned him on. The subtle sway of her hips, not overdone like some of the man-eaters down in the club, held his eyes riveted. In fact, she wasn't like their usual clientele at all.

Deep chestnut hair with hints of red, it seemed untouched by a dye bottle. Her makeup appeared to be applied with a delicate touch, looking as natural as if she were wearing none at all. And her figure was built with the curves of a real woman, rather than the starved lines of the fashionable waif. Surrounding it all was a haunting impression which marked her as a fae, but mixed with enough humanity to make it unique.

So tiny and delicate, he virtually shook with the need to touch and kiss her. The quick kiss in the club had whetted his appetite, but now he wanted more. Much, much more.

*

"Nice office," Sage commented in a quiet tone, smiling over her shoulder. He hadn't moved from the door, still leaning against it nonchalantly. His pose was relaxed but he watched her like a hawk, glittering with intent. Like a panther about to strike.

She reached the desk, a large expanse of dark wood. Her small hand trailed along the smooth surface. Pushing some files out the way, she leaned back, her hands bracing either side of her hips and ankles crossed. Her small tongue flicked out and wet her lips, her gaze steady on his.

She felt wild and wanton. It was so unlike her usual self. She was a bookkeeper for heaven's sake. She didn't go around picking up random men in bars, no matter what her ex had thought. Even if they were as hot as Daelas.

It must be the wild fae blood her father had always warned her about. About time too, she decided, tilting her head to one side. "You planning on standing there all night or what?"

He pushed away from the door, stalking toward her. Sage's breath caught in her throat, attention riveted by the predatory grace in his movements. Even his walk oozed masculinity.

"Or what?" He towered over her, his larger body crowding her against the desk. So close she could feel the heat of his skin against hers. The scent of his aftershave surrounded her, carried on the warmth of his skin, teasing her senses.

"What or what?" she asked, not paying much attention to the conversation as his hand slid onto the nape of her neck. With gentle pressure, he tilted her head up. She sucked in a breath at the darkly feral expression on his face and the heat swirling in his eyes as he bent his head.

She sighed as his lips covered hers. Warm and firm, they coaxed her to open up for him. His free hand slid around her back, fanning over her hips as he pulled her hard against him. A moan broke from her as his tongue stroked along hers; the kiss turning hot and wild in a heartbeat.

Her back arched in response as she ran her hands up his arms. Her skin was too hot, felt too tight, her breasts heavy and full as heat pooled between her thighs. She needed to touch him rather than the suit she had ahold of. Her hands slid under the jacket, pushing at the fabric in silent demand.

He chuckled low in his chest and rolled his shoulders. The jacket dropped unheeded to the carpet. Sage sighed in satisfaction. Her hands roved over his broad chest, tracing the lines of his muscles, surprisingly heavy for his lean frame.

She shivered as he nipped her lower lip. If he could make her feel like this with just a kiss, what would happen if they were to get naked? Anticipation coursed through her, feeding the maelstrom swirling inside.

He moved from her lips, leaving a trail of fire down her neck. Her teeth caught her lower lip in an effort to contain the moan welling in the back of her throat. The soft brush of his lips across her skin, the heat of his hard body against hers, was utter torture. Especially with the thick erection pressing insistently against her soft abdomen; a hardness she ached to feel between her thighs, sliding into her, filling her.

*

God, she felt so good. Daelas groaned and dragged her into his arms, all but crushing her to his heavy chest. She wrapped herself around him, her arms sliding around his neck. Her small hands delved into the short hair at the nape of his neck.

He forced himself to relax his hold. His hand swept down her back in a long caress, revelling in the sensation as he felt a shiver—of pleasure, he hoped—run through her. His lips curved in a smile as he explored the satiny skin of her throat. She wasn't wearing anything under the strappy top. Candy from a baby, he thought as he urged her back onto the desk.

Spreading her thighs with a hard hand, he stepped between them and ran his hands over the flare of her hips. He held her gaze as he pulled her to him, letting her feel the raging hard-on he had for her.

"However pretty I think this is," he slid a finger under the thin strap on her shoulder, "I think it needs to come off now, don't you?"

He arched his eyebrow as he gave her the option. Much as he wanted her, he was done with taking choices away from women. He wanted her to want him for him, not because he was manipulating her.

He waited in silence, his finger hooked under the fabric as she looked at him. Her violet eyes were wide and dark. He still couldn't sense the thoughts behind them, the little bit of mystery turning him on more than he could ever recall being turned on before. This must be a little like having a soul-mate, he thought absently. No incubus was able to read their mate's thoughts; a failsafe to stop them from weaving their particular brand of magic around them and controlling the relationship. Was she his soul-mate? No, she couldn't be, she wasn't a demon, he'd stake his life on it.

She nodded. Triumph filled him, a grin spreading over his face as he drew the strap down her arm, inch by slow inch. His lips followed, a trail of butterfly kisses down the side of her neck, and then across. His hand slid around her back, nimble fingers making short work of the tie over her spine.

The cool draft of the air conditioned office whispered over her skin. Her breasts, free of their confinement, firmed, their peaks tightening as though begging for his attention. He pulled the top away, discarding it to join his jacket on the floor.

"Beautiful." The word was uttered in an awed breath as he gazed down on her half-naked figure. She leaned back a little, resting on her palms and arching her spine. The movement thrust her breasts higher, drawing his gaze downward. The dusky pinks of her nipples puckered tighter as the AC unit above them drew cold air down across her chest.

"You like?"

She shifted her position on the desk, arching her back and skimming a hand over her stomach. Her intense gaze held his as she trailed fingers up the centre of her ribcage, getting ever closer to the full curve of her breast. Her hand reaching its destination, her eyes half-lidded as she cupped the full weight and swept a thumb over the peaked nipple.

"Ohh, I like. I like a lot."

*

He leaned down to replace her hand with his larger one, his lips closing around her nipple, pulling the sensitive flesh into the warm cavern of his mouth. Pleasure shot through her as he suckled, sensation drawing a direct line from breast to the hot, heavy ache between her thighs, setting her on fire.

Her head dropped back, her back arching even more, offering the rounded curves of her breasts to his wicked mouth. He didn't disappoint, taking his time as he kissed and licked. Moving from one to the other, until Sage was almost out of her mind with pleasure.

His hands drifted to her thighs, pushing up the short skirt. His fingertips flirted with the tops of her stockings, a sound of appreciation low in his throat. "I wasn't sure women still wore these," he commented, kissing her neck as his hand moved higher.

Sage flushed, turning her head to the side to allow him better access. "Umm...I like pretty underwear," she admitted, hoping the lacy stockings and suspenders didn't make her seem like a slut. They were more pretty than racy, but she winced internally, worried what he thought.

"They are pretty, very pretty." His hand smoothed over her hip and found the little ties holding the satin thong together at the sides. "Now these I love," he whispered, pulling on the ribbons as his sharp teeth nipped her ear.

She sucked in a breath, her insides turning to jelly as his hand slid down between her thighs. His fingers, blunter and larger than hers, pressed against the folds of her body. They parted the soft lips of her labia gently, seeking the hard nub of her clit with an easy stroke.

"Oh!" Her hips bucked as he touched her, sliding a finger down into the wet heat that had already gathered, spreading it over her sensitized skin as he stroked.

"You're so hot and wet. Just perfect," he said in a low voice as he lowered her to lay on the desk. She shivered as the cool wood met the skin of her back.

She couldn't believe she was doing this. Couldn't believe she was spread half-naked across a desk with her legs open, as a guy she'd just met pleasured her with his fingers. Clever fingers that stroked over her body, teasing the arousal inside to fever pitch.

Just when she didn't think she could take more, he slid two fingers deep inside her. She whimpered, lifting her hands above her head to hold on to the edge of the desk. Her hips bucked as he thrust, pressing against the walls of her pussy in just the right place. She writhed, a familiar tension starting to build, until she was pushing against him, desperate for the relief her climax would bring.

"Oh, no, not just yet, little fae. I have more in mind for you," he whispered, sliding to his knees between her thighs. Sage half-lifted her head, a pout of frustration on her lips until she felt his warm breath on her thigh. A moan was all she could manage as he parted the folds of her lower body with his thumbs.

Her pussy clenched as the cool air from above blew over her warm, wet flesh. Then his tongue was there, in a long, slow lick over her until he found her clit. She cried out as he flicked the sensitive nub, circling and teasing relentlessly.

Her back arched, hips bucking against him as she writhed on the desk. His large hands gripped her, holding her still as he lifted his head for a second. "I'm going to make you come, then I'm going to fuck you senseless, little fae. And you're going to love every minute of it," he told her, his voice strained in the silence of the office.

Sage's reply was a moan, his crude words arousing her as much as the flicks of his tongue over her body. His fingers found her slit again, sliding deep before curling back to rub against the sensitive spot along her inner walls. She sobbed as her body contracted, ecstasy exploding within her as she tumbled over the edge.

Panting and shuddering with the force of it, she opened her eyes to watch him as he stood, towering over her. A feral grin spread across his face.

"Now, to fuck you senseless," he said, holding out his hand to pull her up from the desk.

Still weak-kneed from the force of her climax, Sage frowned at him in puzzlement. Then he spun her around and bent her over. His foot moved hers apart as the sound of a zipper dropping echoed in the room.

"Oh, my…"

She whimpered as his hand slid around her body, pinching and pulling her nipple lightly at the same moment the large, swollen head of his cock presented itself at her slick entrance.

"God, you're so warm and wet," he groaned, rocking his hips and pressing into her a little. She gasped as her body stretched around him. He was huge, bigger than any of her previous lovers. He waited, tension making his large frame tremble, until she relaxed. But then, her "grace period" was over.

His next thrust was hard and heavy, driving into her until he was seated up to the hilt. Ready as she was, the pleasure was incredible, surging through her as he set up a fast rhythm, feeding both of their desires.

"You like demon cock then, little fae?" he murmured in her ear, tweaking her nipple again and making her cry out in pleasure. His other hand slid around her, smoothing down her stomach and between her thighs, finding and stroking her already sensitized clit to match the tempo of his thrusts, until Sage was mindless and whimpering with pleasure.

Chapter Three

Jaren swept into the club in a swirl of black leather and drama, striding through the double doors at the front of the club. They hit the walls on either side with a crash, his habit of throwing them open the reason the glass panels had long since been replaced with wood.

He stopped just inside the club. Although he and Daelas were twins, identical in appearance when they were born, the similarity had ended on that day. Daelas was a born businessman and dressed the part.

Jaren, however, was born to be bad. A calling reflected in the ankle-length black leather duster swirling about him, layered over a silky black shirt and leather pants. He'd once tried a leather shirt, but preferred the sensual slide of silk over his skin. Hell, even his underwear was silk. The skin between his brows furrowed as he looked around. Something wasn't quite right. There was something…different about the place.

Interested, he stalked forward, ignoring the clubbers. His dark, brooding looks meant most left him alone. Most, but not all.

"Well, hello there, handsome, I didn't think you'd be able to make it tonight," a feminine voice purred as small hands wrapped around his torso from behind.

"Hey, Lana," Jaren replied, his hands gentle as he disengaged hers and turned to face her.

A real looker, Lana Burgess was one of the club dancers, a regular on the club circuits, and a veritable party animal. Jaren had watched her for a couple of weeks, coming in with her friends, before he'd made his approach and offered her a job with *Moonlight & Magic*. Then, one night in the backroom, he'd found out just how much of an animal she could be.

"There been trouble tonight?" he asked, ignoring the pouting lips and the hands on her hips. Lana was a drama queen, more so than he, which was saying something.

Lana shook her head and frowned. "Nothing unusual, other than Daelas coming down here earlier. Looked all mean and moody to boot. Sexy as hell!" She shivered, a hint of a mischievous smile peeking through.

Jaren's lips quirked. For some reason, they all found his brother, very reserved for an incubus, irresistible. Perhaps it was because he was *so* reserved. "Daelas was down here?" Surprise colored his voice as he turned to stride away, now even more intrigued.

He headed for the door to the office, nodding at Knuckles as he approached. Even more surprising was the huge bouncer clearing his throat to get his attention. It was rare for Knuckles to speak without being spoken to first.

"Boss's got company," the man announced, his low voice a mere rumble, almost lost in the background noise and music of the club. Luckily Jaren could lip-read well, an essential skill for anyone working in a place like *Moonlight & Magic*.

"Okay, thanks." He nodded and pushed the door open to head up the stairs.

Daelas had company? Company of the female and fairy kind, if the fading impression in the stairwell were any indication. Where had Daelas gotten hold of a fae? And just what was he doing with her in the office?

*

Daelas looked around as the door opened with a soft click, extending his senses to warn him of any danger. In the grand scheme of things, incubi weren't the most combat-minded of the demon kind, but they had excellent survival instincts, and fought dirty when cornered. A good kick in the bollocks was a wonderful tool for levelling the playing field in a fight.

The tension in his shoulders relaxed as he recognised the familiar chaotic swirl of energy that identified his brother, a second before his gaze fell on his twin. Too far gone to do more than nod, Daelas stroked a hand down Sage's naked back as his hips pounded against hers.

She was so hot and tight around his cock, the grip of her body so firm that he found his usual control slipping. He groaned as her hips bucked against him, her pussy clamping down on his rigid length. Milking his dick as her body stiffened, a cry escaped her lips as her climax hit her hard.

Two heavy thrusts later and he couldn't hold his own release back. His powerful body drove deep inside her as he groaned his pleasure. Every muscle locked, the edges of his vision blurred as his cock pulsed. Like most incubi though, he didn't ejaculate. A fact most of his long-term lovers appreciated. No wet patches to deal with.

He opened his eyes, widening them as he tried to focus. He'd never felt a climax so powerful, so intense. He leaned forward, kissing along her neck, his lips gentle.

Jaren had stayed out of sight, well out of Sage's limited field of vision as she was bent over the desk. But that wouldn't last long...and he wanted to prepare her before she went skitz on him.

"We have company, little one," he whispered, weaving suggestion into his voice as he did so. She'd been resistant to most of his usual tactics, but his voice seemed to work. "Just my twin...he thinks you're as gorgeous as I do," he added, his hands gentling her as she started, trying to push up from the desk and look around.

"Your twin? What...just like you?" Her voice was a little distracted as she stood, looking over his shoulder.

He moved a fraction, shielding her from Jaren's view in case she didn't want to take things that way. Probably not the scenery Jaren was after; Daelas could practically smell his brother's interest in the air, but at the moment, a view of his hairy arse was all Jaren was going to get. At least, until he was sure Sage was okay with this.

"Well, I'm better looking," Daelas boasted, his lips quirking a little.

"That's total bollocks. That's just his opinion. Everyone knows *I'm* the better looking one."

Sage peered over Daelas' shoulder, her eyes narrowing a little. Her lush curves pressing against him brought him right back to attention, his cock straining against her.

Sage's eyes widened as she looked down.

"What? You can't...not already," she whispered, shock on her face as her gaze flicked from his face to his cock, and back again.

Daelas grinned, but it was Jaren who answered, picking up Daelas' thought as naturally as breathing. "We're incubi, sex demons. We go on and on and on, kinda like the Energizer bunny," Jaren explained, reaching Daelas' side, holding his hand out in invitation as Daelas had known he would.

There was just something compelling about the little fairy that made a man want to touch her, taste her, get down and dirty with her as soon as he laid eyes on her.

"You can have two of us...all night. How's that sound, little fae?" Daelas whispered, kissing along her neck as she appeared to debate her decision.

If another male had approached her, Daelas would've ripped his limbs off and beaten him to death with the soggy ends. Jaren was different though. Incubi were born in pairs, two halves of the same soul. So sharing this delicious morsel of femininity, as they would their mate, seemed right.

She shivered against him, arching her neck as she kept her gaze on his brother. He could feel her thinking, considering the situation. She reached out and took Jaren's hand, moving to stand between the two men. Daelas released a breath he hadn't realised he'd been holding as she pulled Jaren down for a kiss.

*

This was fantastic. Unbelievable, but fantastic. She'd just had the best sex she'd *ever* had with the hottest guy she'd ever met, and he'd wanted *her*, not some skinny stick insect who complained about the fat on a lettuce leaf. Now there were two of them, both kissing and touching her, their attraction for her evident. She was still waiting to wake up, quite certain this had to be a dream.

Neither could take their hands off her, and then there were the massive erections; one tenting the front of Jaren's pants and one prodding at her hip in determination. She reached down and wrapped a small hand around it, her slow stroking eliciting groans from its owner.

She surrendered to Jaren's kiss, hotter and wilder than his brother's, with a hint of decadence that had her heart hammering in her chest. She moaned, sure she'd died and gone to heaven.

Daelas turned her in his arms, his hands caressing her full breasts as he buried his face into the curve of her neck. Warm lips honed in on the sensitive spot beneath her ear, making her knees go weak.

"You have a fantastic body. I want to lick and taste every part of it," Jaren whispered as he lifted his head, his eyes, *so* like his brother's, flaring with desire.

She swallowed as he slid to his knees in front of her, lifting her thigh, his attention focused on the secret delta between her legs. The skin there was slick with her feminine juices and he drew in a deep breath, his eyes closing for a second.

"Ambrosia," Jaren whispered, leaning forward.

Sage moaned as his tongue flicked across her clit, already swollen from his brother's attention earlier. Her hips bucked, the sensation almost too much to bear. She moaned and writhed against him as he feasted on her. Daelas' hands massaged her breasts, pinching and pulling her nipples, the two men working as a team to arouse her to fever pitch.

"You like this don't you, little fae? Two men touching you, caressing you. Licking you..." Daelas drew the tip of his tongue around the delicate curve of her breast. "Come for us, let Jaren taste you, and then we'll both fuck you. You'd like that, wouldn't you, two demon cocks filling you?"

The words were too much for Sage; hot and wild images of the three of them played in her mind as Jaren's clever tongue teased over her clit, his fingers buried deep in her body. She cried out as her body exploded, pleasure coursing through her.

Jaren groaned, his tongue lapping at her pussy as her hips bucked against his hold. "God, you taste so good," he murmured between gentle licks, the sound of his voice on the edge of Sage's hearing. Her heart pounded so loudly it was hard to hear.

"I want to watch you fuck him," Daelas whispered in her ear, turning her jaw to kiss her again. She didn't resist, their tongues meeting and dancing, sliding against each other's, adding fuel to the sexual tension already thick in the room.

She bit her lip, arousal racing through her as Jaren's hands slid around her thighs, lingering on their soft plumpness for a moment as he stood.

"Come here," Jaren whispered, pulling her to the large leather sofa that sat against one side of the room. "Ride me," he demanded, pulling her into his lap. Sage blinked. Somehow, between arriving in the room and now, he'd lost his clothes. She didn't remember him undressing. Of course, she *had* been a little preoccupied.

Then his hands were in her hair, its delicate style destroyed, and he was kissing her as if his life depended on it. She groaned as she straddled him, feeling the power of his lean body, so similar to his brother's. Jaren's hard cock brushed against her, settling in the grove of her cleft.

Sage gasped. Despite the amazing orgasms—four, or was it five so far—her body tightened in anticipation again, her pussy clenching at the thought of his rigid cock filling her to the hilt.

She rocked her hips against his thick shaft, biting back a moan as the friction against her clit—pulling the hood back to reveal the sensitized bud—threatened to send her over the edge again. Jaren wasn't faring much better, a low groan reverberating through his broad chest as his hands tightened on her hips.

"Fuck," he muttered, his eyes rolling back in his head as she did it again, rolling her hips and revelling in the sensation.

Hard hands lifted her hips and she reached between her thighs, encircling his cock and pumping twice slowly before she lowered herself over it. The swollen crown brushed against her pussy lips, already slick from his attentions and her climax. She bit her lip as her body accepted him with ease, the delicate flesh stretching to accommodate his impressive girth.

Hell, it felt *so* good. Sage gasped as she slid down on Jaren's cock, each slow inch stretching her further until her hips met his. She'd never felt so full. With a small sound of satisfaction she arched her back, grinding her pelvis against him.

"Little witch," Jaren chuckled, moving his hips in a long, slow rhythm, which stroked every nerve ending in her pussy.

She threw her head back, a murmur of pleasure in her throat as his hand slid between them, his thumb rubbing over her clit.

Sage needed to come. She needed to come so bad, but Jaren just kept bringing her to the brink, then would ease off until she wanted to hit him, rather than fuck him. Whimpering in frustration she approached her peak, but then he moved his thumb, slowing his rhythm until her body started to calm again.

"You're a wicked man," she panted, "that's just evil, you know."

"I know." He grinned, an unrepentant and sexy grin she couldn't help but return. "But you'll enjoy it more, I promise."

"Besides, it's not fair to finish the party without me, is it?" Daelas' voice sounded behind her. She felt the heat of his skin on her back an instant before he slid his hands around her body to caress her breasts. Daelas' lips whispered over her neck as she lifted her hands, linking them behind his neck. Offering her arched body to both of them. "Miss me?" Daelas asked, tweaking her nipples.

She murmured her assent, leaning against one brother as the other pumped his hips, hard cock driving into her, filling her pussy with each stroke. She'd definitely died and gone to heaven.

Jaren pulled her forward to kiss her deeply, his tongue tangling with hers as she sprawled over his large chest. Meanwhile, Daelas' lips trailed down her spine, sending shivers through every inch of her body. Even her toes curled in pleasure.

Jaren shifted under her, spreading his legs wider and taking hers with them. The change in position opened her up further and she gasped as she felt his hard cock slide into her another half-inch, pressing deeper inside her than any lover before. She shivered as Daelas' hands smoothed over the cello-like curve of her hips.

She hadn't realised what they'd planned until a cold wetness slid down between her buttocks, making her jump.

"It's okay, little fae, just a little something to help," Daelas murmured, his gentle fingers smoothing the lube down her skin, against the delicate, puckered rose of her ass.

She went still as he stroked, not sure about where this was going. She'd done anal before but not with two guys, not at the same time, and she wasn't sure she could take them both. She couldn't believe she was in this situation to start with. Two men that looked as gorgeous they did, treating her as though she were the only woman on Earth that mattered…it was as erotic as hell.

Jaren slowed his movements, his thumb stroking over her clit. Stroking then circling, reminding her of how much she needed to come, how close to the edge she was again. Sage moaned and bit her lip, her eyes rolling back in her head. It was too much, Jaren's cock inside her, her body aching for the next brush of his thumb, while from behind, Daelas' gentle fingers smoothed the cool gel against her ass.

It felt good, she realised in surprise, relaxing as a shiver travelled the entire length of her spine. Actually, it felt better than good as he rubbed the lube in, circling and pressing against her with the broad, blunt end of his fingertip. She gasped, her pussy clenching hard as Daelas' finger slid inside her just a little. Her breasts tightened, the nipples puckering.

Jaren groaned, his silver eyes riveted as he leant forward, drawing one of her tightened peaks into his mouth. He suckled hard; the sensation, with so much else going on, making Sage cry out, her pleasure-filled cry echoing around the room.

More, she had to have more. She rocked against the two men, riding Jaren's hard cock in a slow rhythm as Daelas worked her ass, preparing her. She shivered as he slid his finger a little deeper.

"Oh, god, that feels good," she moaned as he worked more of the lube into her heated flesh.

"It's about to feel a whole lot better," Daelas promised, sliding his finger from her. Sage frowned, feeling a sense of loss. It didn't last long as he moved behind her, replacing his fingers with the broad head of his cock. "Just relax into it, and everything'll be fine," he reassured as he pressed forward.

Sage tensed as the swollen head of Daelas' cock pushed into her ass. He wasn't going to fit. She hissed as a burning sensation—not pleasure, but not quite pain either—shot through her. But, the combination of the lube and Jaren's thumb stroking over her aching clit, eased things. With a grunt of triumph, Daelas slid past the initial resistance, sliding deep inside her body and pausing, as if waiting for her to adjust.

Sage panted, feeling fuller than she'd ever felt before, her pussy and ass both filled with cock. She shivered as Jaren moved a little, opening her eyes to see him looking at her in concern. The expression melted her heart, as she just knew it was mirrored in his brother's face, even if she couldn't see it, and that did it for her. They weren't just interested in their own pleasure, and that was the most sensual thing she could think of.

"You okay, little fae?" Jaren's kiss was soft and gentle, as if designed to reassure rather than arouse, and strangely platonic, considering their current activity.

She smiled as he pulled away, and nodded. "I thought you promised you were both gonna fuck me?" she challenged, mischief running through her. "But all I hear is a lot of talking here."

Jaren's grin matched hers. Daelas' chuckle reverberated against her skin as they started to move. Jaren slid out of her a little, then thrust back in as Daelas pulled almost completely out of her ass, just leaving the head of his cock inside her. Then they moved again, in perfect counterpoint to one another, a slow rhythm that had Sage moaning in ecstasy.

She could feel everything, the two of them taking her to places she'd never been before, and it wasn't long until she was straining against them. Urging the two men to take her faster, with soft cries and breathy little moans. It was hot and hard, and was going to be over very soon, she realized, as the first tightening of an impending orgasm blindsided her.

"Oh, god, I'm coming..." she cried out, the shudders of pleasure racking through her as she arched back against Daelas.

Her hips jerked, first grinding down onto Jaren's cock before pressing back hard against Daelas', his rigid length impaled deep inside her ass.

Her loud moans reverberated around the office as her inner muscles locked down like a vice around the two dicks inside her, milking them as she came harder than she could ever remember. Her world went grey around the edges as her heart pounded.

Her climax, the tightness of her body made tighter by her orgasm, tipped the twins over the edge. Their masculine groans mingling as the two thrust into her a last time, their cocks pulsed in unison, shoved deep inside her as they came.

Sage lay across Jaren's chest as she gradually came to, waiting for her heartbeat to return to normal as shivers of pleasure washed through her. The aftershocks of the incredible orgasm rippling through her as first Daelas, then Jaren, slid from her exhausted and satisfied body.

"That, little fae, was incredible," Jaren whispered, shifting her on his lap and enfolding her in his arms. "You're incredible," he added, kissing her on the tip of her nose.

She smiled in response, a smile which encompassed Daelas as well, as he offered her his shirt. "Oh, no, you don't get out of it that easily, handsome. You two promised me *all* night, and all night is what I want!"

Chapter Four

Sage woke slowly, warm and comfortable, curled up in a ball. Funny, but her bed seemed a little firmer than usual, and a bit smaller.

"I'm telling you, man…" A male voice filtered through her sleepy doze, causing Sage to wrinkle her nose as she cracked an eyelid.

Yup, that was right. She was still at the club. Blearily she pushed herself upright, the blanket someone had thrown over her slithering to pool at her waist. The air conditioner had been shut off at some point in the night, but still, her nipples peaked from the coolness of the room. A rush of heat came back to her as she recalled them doing the very same thing last night, right before or after one of the brothers had lavished his attention on them. She'd never realised her breasts could be that sensitive.

Well actually, she hadn't realised a lot of things until last night. Not the least of which was that she wasn't frigid, as Marcus had claimed, blaming his shortcomings on her. A small smile played over her lips. Oh, no, after all the attention she'd gotten last night from the two brothers—the two incredibly *hot* brothers—she wouldn't believe that one anymore. It'd been a dodgy accusation to start with; he'd swung between accusing her of being a frigid bitch to a slut, only waiting for a man to cock his eyebrow at her for her to go scurrying off.

There's one in your eye, Marcus. Amusement filled her. No cocking of eyebrows, just a helluva lotta cock, in every way possible.

She pushed her hair back off her face as she looked around. *Oh, my god, what time is it?* Guilt and shame hit her. She'd left Sherri on her own, down in the club without so much as a thought. A glance at the full-length windows across the office told her the club had emptied long ago, the darkness from the other side complete. No flashing strobe lights, no heavy beating of music. It was all quiet. Quiet enough for her to hear the soft conversation going on outside, on the small balcony attached to the office.

"She can't be. She's a fae."

Daelas' voice. How she knew she hadn't a clue, but somehow she could tell the difference between the two brothers. Probably from the rather intimate night they'd spent together, she decided, standing and starting to track down her clothes on silent feet.

She could almost hear the shrug as Jaren answered, "So? It's not like it hasn't happened before."

"Oh, come on, you can't count Barnabas and Vale's mate… She was a goat demon for heaven's sake!"

Goat demon? There was such a thing as a goat demon? Sage spotted her underwear beneath the desk and bent down to retrieve it.

"No, she wasn't. She just *looked* like a goat. I think she was a Talos demon. But that's not the point. The point is, a soul-mate doesn't *have* to be a succubus. Thankfully. Bloody tarts the lot of them," Jaren snorted, his tone laced with disdain.

Sage frowned as she slipped her underwear on, not bothering with the stockings and suspenders. They'd take too long to put on, and her head hurt too much. She'd just shove them in her bag instead. She knew the brothers were incubi, and she was fairly sure that succubi were the female versions of sex demons. Sounded like the genders didn't get on too well in their species. She wriggled into her shirt and skirt, looking about for her shoes. No surprise. In her experience, the males and females of any species tended to misunderstand each other. But the next words from the balcony stopped her in her tracks.

"So, you think Sage is our soul-mate, then?"

"I think so. I can't sense what she's thinking at all. You?" Jaren asked curiously.

"Nope, nothing…but it's sexy. And mysterious."

Sage blinked. Okay, so they couldn't sense her thoughts…that was a good thing, surely?

"It's as sexy as hell," Jaren agreed.

"But just because we can't read her thoughts doesn't mean she's our soul-mate. She could just have some fae mojo thing that stops us," Daelas argued, still unseen out on the balcony.

Yeah, what he said. Sage crept a little closer, close enough to grab her shoes from near the door. A one-night stand with a couple of hot men was one thing, but the paranormal equivalent of a shotgun wedding was a totally different matter. "Soul-mate" sounded a shitload more serious than a quickie wedding that could be sorted by just as a quickie divorce. It was more like "until death us do part," and possibly beyond.

She didn't wait to hear what they were going to say next, shoving her feet into her sandals and grabbing her bag from where it lay on the floor beside the couch. She headed for the door. It was time to pull her disappearing act before they decided to march her down to the demon judge or something.

Thankfully, the corridor outside was deserted, and Sage fled down the stairs as though her life depended on it; she'd heard about demon bonding ceremonies and the like. It didn't make for easy reading, and she was fairly sure it was hazardous to your health if you were a non-demon.

She poked her head through the door into the club, searching for a way out. The main entrance would be long since shut and locked, she was sure of that. Movement at the bar caught her eye and she smiled, recognising the bouncer on the door last night.

"Which way is out?" she asked sweetly, hoping he didn't go skitz on her and call the brothers from upstairs.

Some of her desire to flee must've been apparent on her face because he jerked his head toward the door at the back of the bar. "Staff entrance," he grunted. "Hurry up, before I lock up."

"Gotcha. Already gone. Thanks."

She slipped past him on swift feet, hoping she didn't look quite as dishevelled as she felt. Perhaps if she kept moving he wouldn't notice her clothing was definitely in disarray and her legs bare, possibly working out what she'd been up to with his bosses in the office.

Ha! He works here, so what else would he think I've been doing, shut up in an office with two men who virtually oozed sex? She nibbled her lip as she pushed open the back door, emerging into the early morning air, in an alleyway behind the club. The darkness of night was just beginning to pale to the faint light of dawn, and at the end of the alley, she could see the cabs were all still out and about, touting for business. Her heels tapped out a rapid beat as she headed for the road to look for a ride home.

*

Daelas leaned on the rail of the small balcony and breathed deeply as he considered Jaren's words. Even the air felt sharper, somehow more alive this morning, his senses razor-sharp instead of sluggish with boredom, as they had been recently. He always felt better after taking a woman to his bed, but this was beyond that. He felt invigorated.

He turned his head slightly and looked into the face that was identical to his. Even down to the frown. The only difference that distinguished them physically was the jagged scar that ran across Jaren's shoulder. The result of a run-in with a possessive shifter a couple of years back.

"You think she is?"

Jaren looked out over the city skyline, his posture a mirror of his brother's. He then nodded, a slow movement of his head. He turned slightly, looking directly at Daelas. The need and longing there took his breath away; he'd never realised Jaren was so lonely. He'd thought his troublemaker brother was happy with his lot in life, but the emotion rising off him like the scent of an expensive aftershave, told a different story.

"I want her to be, I think I need her to be," Jaren admitted finally, his voice low. "I've had enough of this...all this. The endless hunting, the searching. Meaningless sex with biddable women. I can't tell what Sage is thinking, what she's going to do next. It's exciting, new. Don't tell me you don't agree," Jaren added, pushing off from the balcony and turning to go back in.

Daelas stood upright, rubbing a hand along his stubble covered jaw. He did agree. There was no question of that. A couple of times in the night she'd surprised him, like making a move neither of them expected, or taken the initiative, whereas they were used to women acting passively while they waited for the next command or prompt. But was it just something new? A woman who they couldn't control? Or was Jaren right—that she was their destined soul-mate?

"Shit!" The expletive from inside the office was heartfelt and uttered violently. A lifetime's worth of frustration in one small word.

"What?" Daelas turned instantly, taking two short steps to join his brother inside. "What's wrong..." He trailed off, not needing the answer to that question.

The office was empty. Their little fae had done a bunk. "Shit!" he murmured, echoing Jaren's sentiment as he rubbed his hand over his bare chest.

Inside, around his heart, what felt like a thousand tiny ribbons, tightened, robbing him of breath for a moment as a sense of loss surrounded him. Bewildered, his eyes met Jaren's, then flicked down to where the other incubus was doing the exact same thing, his large hand over his own heart.

"You feel it too?"

"Yeah." Now, of all times, Jaren returned to his usual, less than eloquent self. "Convinced now?"

Daelas nodded, a grimace on his face as he strode over to the other side of the office, heading for the small bathroom and dressing room.

"Get dressed, we need to find her...and fast."

* * *

It'd been a long, slow Sunday, the sort of day that Sage liked. She hadn't arrived home from the club until about half past six, avoiding the gaze of the guy from the third floor as he left for his early morning shift, convinced he and everyone else knew what she'd been up to all night. Not that it made a blind bit of difference, she told herself firmly. She was an adult, she could do as she liked as long as it wasn't illegal. Pleasure like that *should* be illegal, though. She could still feel her body humming with it now, nearly twelve hours later. She'd never had that sort of a rush after sex, with any guy, and especially not with Marcus.

She moved lazily, uncurling from her small ball on the sofa for a full-body stretch that had her tight tee stretching over her bust. She hadn't bothered to get dressed properly after her shower this morning; she never did on Sundays. It was her chill out day, one where she didn't bother going out, instead getting her laundry done and catching up with her reading on the sofa. So this morning she'd just pulled on a faded tee and some yoga pants, before going about her usual Sunday routine.

She was just about to get back to her book and dive into the next chapter when the doorbell rang—a shrill demand for attention that was totally unwelcome. Her eyes narrowed as she looked up. No one bothered her on Sundays, because they knew it was her "me time." She opened the book again, determined to ignore it, but the bell rang again, the shrill note longer than before, as though whoever it was knew she was ignoring it and was purposely leaning on the button.

"Oh, for heaven's sake!" she hissed, marking her place in the book before putting it down to head for the door. "Whatever it is, it better be good," she threatened under her breath, her feet silent on the hall carpet.

She opened the door, her eyes widening as she recognised the tall male figure that stood there. Marcus. Instinctively, her stance became wary as she looked at her former fiancé. The one she'd dumped after finding him in bed with the blonde music student from two doors down, who'd then claimed it'd been her fault he had, that Sage was frigid, and that he'd needed a "real woman."

"What do you want Marcus? I'm busy," she said bluntly, not opening the door fully. Hopefully, he'd get the hint and leave.

"Sage. I wasn't sure you'd be in. How are you?" He smiled as soon as he saw her; his overused, well-oiled charm cracked up to the maximum.

"You knew I'd be in Marcus. I never go out on Sundays. What do you want?" she repeated bluntly, her fiery glare wandering over his face as she waited for an answer.

There'd been a time when she'd loved him more than she'd thought it possible to love anyone. Her heart had shattered into a thousand pieces when she'd found him in bed with Julia, a heartbreak so complete it'd been a long, slow road to recovery, putting her heart and her broken confidence back together. A process which had been completed last night, in the arms of her demon lovers. A fact she hasn't realised until now, as she looked on, wondering what the hell she'd ever seen in a jerk like Marcus.

Irritation flashed in his washed-out blue eyes, slightly red around the edges. Drinking did that to a man; it was no doubt responsible for the slight sagginess around his jowls and midriff as well.

"How's Julia?" she asked sweetly, sickly sweet. "You two getting on well these days?"

"I know what you are," Marcus blurted out, watching her face like a hawk for a reaction.

The bottom dropped out of Sage's stomach. He knew. He knew about her fae blood. He could've meant a thousand different things with that, but she knew he didn't. He knew she was a fae. Trying hard to hide her shock, she gave him her best "blank look."

"Bully for you. You've figured out the differences between little girls and little boys. Now, if that was all you wanted, I have things to do," she said, starting to close the door.

* * *

It'd taken a full day to track her down, a fact that weighed heavily on both brothers' shoulders. Now that they'd found their soul-mate, the need to claim her, to make her their own, was relentless. It gnawed at Daelas' insides as he sat in one corner of the cab, watching the streets pass outside with a scowl on his face.

Why had she run? If Knuckles hadn't been right behind her and seen which firm the cab she'd gotten into belonged to, they'd have been sunk. Without any idea where she was in the city, or even her last name, it would've been like searching for a needle in a haystack. A very large haystack. A shudder rocked his big, lean body. They would've been reduced to either combing the city to try to catch her aura, or having to wait until she came to the club again. Something Daelas was sure wasn't going to happen again soon.

The cab slowed and pulled up to the kerb. Jaren was out the door, looking up at the small apartment block before Daelas could utter a word, leaving him to deal with the driver.

"You're sure this is the place you dropped her off?" Daelas asked, the serious tone in his voice indicating the driver better not be leading them on a wild-goose chase.

The guy flashed him a nervous glance, as though there was something about Daelas that made the driver want to squirm out his seat and run for his life.

The man ducked down, looked quickly at the sign on the side of the building. "Yeah, this is the place. 'Apartment 4a,' she said, if that helps you any…" he trailed off, holding his hand out. His expression not changing, Daelas handed him a few notes, sliding his wallet back into his pocket as he climbed from the cab.

"Apartment 4a," Daelas announced to his brother, pausing as a wave of sickness washed over him. The green look on Jaren's face said he was feeling it too. "Sage—" They both broke into a sprint for the block doors.

The two demons sped up the stairs, the sound of their pounding feet loud in the stairwell. Daelas' heart hammered loud in his chest, his stomach coiling in nausea and fear. Next to him Jaren stumbled, a look of pain on his face as he clutched his chest. Instinctively, Daelas reached out and hooked a hand under his brother's arm, hauling him to his feet as they ran. The only thing that would affect them both like this was because of Sage—something bad was happening to their mate.

Their worst fears were confirmed as they burst onto the fourth floor landing. All but one of the doors were firmly shut. The sort of shut that said, "The occupants haven't seen a thing, officer." Inside the one that was open however, there was a struggle going on. All they could see was the broad back of a male as he backed someone else, a woman, in through the open doorway. Not just someone, Sage. Even though Daelas couldn't see her he knew it was Sage, a familiar buzzing settling in the back of his mind.

"Holding out on me, weren't you, you little slut? I know all about fairies…all about dancing naked and having orgies." His voice, laced with hatred, was interspersed with sounds of a large fist hitting flesh and the tearing of cloth that filled the small landing. "I figure you owe me a couple of years' worth of that fae lovin', you frigid little bitch!"

Daelas didn't need to look at his brother to know he was angry. The small space fairly crackled with energy as a wave of fury, so complete, hit the tall, normally sensible demon businessman, turning his vision red. This guy had Sage, and was hurting her.

Hurting *their* mate.

Jaren started forward, murder written on his face, but Daelas stopped him with a hand on his arm. His jaw clenched with rage as he shook his head. "Get Sage, this one's all mine."

With a roar, he propelled himself across the intervening space, barrelling into the tall figure trying to shove Sage back into her apartment. Hard hands dropped onto the human's shoulders, tearing him away from his victim and slamming him into the opposite wall. Incubi weren't generally known for their combat abilities; they were lovers, not fighters. But when the shit hit the fan, they were still demons, which put them higher in the pecking order than your garden variety Homo sapiens.

All the air left the human's lungs in a rush, the speed Daelas had used to throw the man into the wall winding him. The guy didn't have time to respond or even move, before the demon's fist connected heavily with his jaw. The man's head snapped to the side and he stumbled, going down on one knee. He then shook his head and blinked in surprise, dazed and obviously having trouble working out where the two furious looking men had come from.

"Who the hell are you?"

"Your worst fucking nightmare," Daelas snarled, reaching down for him. Ready to finish what he'd started, and put this worthless piece of human trash in a shallow grave.

"Daelas, no! Marcus isn't worth it!" Sage's panic-stricken voice stopped him, cut through the rage coiling in his body and clouded his vision. He dropped his hands, looking over his shoulder.

Sage was wrapped safely in his brother's arms, his jacket covering her torn clothing, preserving her modesty. Daelas' gaze flicked over her, assuring himself she was safe. She was pale, her large eyes wide and frightened; but *for* him, not *of* him. He sighed and looked back at the human cowering at his feet.

Marcus pushed himself upright, looking from one to the other. "You're some of her fairy friends, I assume?" he asked, a sneer on his face. "About right. You two are pretty enough to be fairies. Probably a pair of fairies doing each other. I heard you lot are kinky like that."

Daelas pinned Marcus to the wall by his throat with a hard grip. "Now, as an insult, that was poor. As a method of highlighting your prejudice and lack of intelligence, congratulations, it was spot on." The soft tone of his voice was totally at odds with the murderous expression on his face. "To answer your question, I'm the sort of fairy that does bad things to people that piss me off," he added, reaching out with his mind and sliding into Marcus'.

Like with most humans it was easily done, child's play for Daelas and his kind. Most of them learnt to read a human mind before they were out of the nursery, and by the time they hit puberty, most could do so without their subject being aware of it. Daelas didn't bother with stealth, with Marcus struggling in panic as he rifled through the man's mind.

Daelas shuddered, feeling sick at the images and dark desires he found in there, all centred around Sage and other women the guy knew. Christ, he was going to need a month-long bath after being inside there. Then he caught something, just the tail end of it, and followed it to its source. Grimly, he tweaked a few "settings" in the human's brain and withdrew.

"Gerroffme! What are you doing? What the fuck…?"

Daelas let him go, allowing the man to sag against the wall as he grinned in sadistic triumph and stepped back.

"What did you do to him?" Sage asked as Marcus whimpered pathetically, rubbing at his eyes as if trying to clear them.

Marcus dropped his hands and looked at the small group. Panic filled the man's eyes, and with a cry of terror he bolted past them, rebounding off Daelas' shoulder and fleeing down the stairs.

Daelas chuckled, unholy amusement running through him. "Seems our friend there is quite the homophobe. So I replaced your image, in all his sick little fantasies, with a twenty stone prison inmate named Bubba. Now, whenever he thinks about you, all he's going to see is Bubba. I shouldn't think you'll have any more trouble with him."

*

Sage nodded, shivering as she cuddled closer to Jaren. Tears welled in the back of her eyes. She'd never been so glad to see anyone as she had the two brothers. Even though this morning she'd done a runner on them, after all the scary 'soul-mate' talk, she could kiss the ground they walked on.

"Thank you," she whispered, "He...he..." She couldn't get any further, the tears in her eyes multiplying and spilling over onto her cheeks.

"Shush, shush," Jaren murmured, his lips gently against her hair as he rocked her soothingly. "It's over now. He's gone."

He looked up at Daelas, jerking his head toward the door as he guided her back into her apartment.

Sage wouldn't let him go, clinging to his strength as he settled her onto the couch, dragging him down to sit with her.

"I'm sorry," she murmured through her tears. "I'm not normally this pathetic. Honest."

Worried about how stupid she looked with both of them watching her, Daelas crouched down in front of the couch, and she struggled to sit up. She dabbed at the tears on her cheeks with the back of her hand, then took a deep breath.

"I feel a little better now." The comment had been meant for their benefit, but Sage was surprised to realise that she in fact *did* feel better. The horrible nausea that'd gripped her, making her stomach churn and bringing her out in a hot sweat when Marcus had touched her, had all but faded away.

"I felt sick, like really sick," she told them, a small frown of her brows as she tried to work it out. "I haven't felt that physically bad since I had appendicitis when I was twelve. But back then, it didn't go away this quickly."

Daelas smiled a little, nothing more than a quirk of his lips. She'd noticed that that was his way last night, and he was the more reserved of the two. Except when it came to doing something wicked to her. Sage shivered, a familiar heat coiling low in her belly. She felt heat coming off her cheeks. God, what was the matter with her? She'd nearly been assaulted in her own home, and now all she could think about was jumping her two saviours.

"I'm sick," she murmured softly, "really sick."

"You're not," Jaren said reassuringly, his hand smoothing down her back as she sat with her head in her hands. A comforting gesture that she appreciated. "Far from it. From what I understand, this is quite normal."

Sage's head came up slowly. "What do you mean normal? I don't know about you demons, but I can assure you, for me, that was certainly *not* normal!" Her voice rose a little on the end of the sentence, a shrill note of frustration and panic. Sage didn't like things she didn't understand, especially when it seemed as if other people knew what was going on, and were keeping her out of the loop.

Daelas' fingers under her chin, pulling her around to look at him, silenced her. His silver-eyed gaze was understanding, compassionate. She felt it again, that weird pull in her chest she'd felt back at the bar, and then just before they'd shown up to rescue her. Something she'd never felt before, but a feeling her instincts were telling her was important.

"Something's happening to me, isn't it?" Her voice was a bare whisper of sound, a sense of worry taking over as she looked at him. "Have I caught some weird sort of demon STD or something?"

The strangled snort from Jaren made her look around, finding him grinning and shaking his head in amusement. For all his "bad boy" image, he was actually the one who smiled the easiest. "No little pixie, we don't carry or contract STDs, but you're right, something *has* happened to you. You've—"

"Bonded to us," Daelas added, seamlessly picking up where his brother left off, his intense gaze looking her face over, as if searching for a reaction.

Shock coursed through Sage and she shook her head. "No, no. We couldn't have, not already. You said..." She paused, realising she'd just given herself away.

"I said what?" Daelas prompted gently, obviously trying hard not to push. Both of them giving her the time she needed to come to terms with this.

"I woke up and heard you talking. Something about soul-mates, about me being your soul-mate. It scared me. I ran. I was scared you'd haul me off for some sort of demon shotgun wedding," she admitted, biting her lip as her cheeks felt as if they were on fire.

She'd run out on them, and still they'd come to her rescue. Were it another time and place she might've been concerned that they'd managed to track her down, but instead, she was thankful. And something else. She was pleased to see them. Deep down, an ache in her very core eased, just being around them.

The sound of masculine amusement filled her small living room. "Sweetheart, we don't have weddings. We don't need them. As soon as we meet and touch our soul-mate, the bonding process starts," Daelas explained, an indulgent look on his face. "As soon as Jaren joined us in the office, I'm afraid you were done for. You bonded to us then."

Sage nodded slowly, feeling the truth of his words. She then blinked, looking at him in surprise. "What? To *both* of you?" she queried, not quite believing what she'd just heard. It'd been miracle enough that just one of them had fancied her last night, but to learn that both had, was something she was having some difficulty coming to terms with. But now, they were telling her that there was more…that she had them for good?

"Both of us, for as long as we live." They spoke together, their voices solemn. Sincere.

"Wow, okay. That I didn't expect!"

"And that's not all." Jaren shifted behind her, moving closer. She felt his breath on the side of her neck an instant before his lips touched her skin. A gentle caress that seemed to open the flood gates. Deep in her chest, she felt the bond tighten for a second as she accepted it, settling into a more comfortable fit as she smiled at the two brothers. The two incredibly hot brothers she just happened to be bonded to.

"Hmm?" she asked, tilting her head to the side as Jaren worked his way lower, Daelas' hands smoothing over her thighs. Parting them so he could press between them.

"We have lots of stamina," Daelas breathed against her lips. "More than enough to love you every second of every night."

Sage chuckled and pulled him closer, giving into temptation and kissing him deeply. "Now, a claim like *that*, you're going to have to prove. Starting right now…"

The End

Sunlight & Slavery

Chapter One

Saturday night had always been Neri and Jason's "date night." Some things didn't change. Their relationship was on the rocks, so far on the rocks it could only be described as a shipwreck. For Neri, at least, it had been over a while. She'd assumed they had a normal relationship, the sort where you could say, "I've had enough. I'm outta here." Except theirs wasn't a normal relationship. Here they were, out on the town on a Saturday night like normal, apart from one important distinction.

Neri didn't expect to make it to morning.

As though he could read her mind, Jason caught her eye from across the table and smiled. She suppressed a shudder and looked away. She'd tried to leave earlier but he'd stopped her. She looked up and to her right circumspectly. Neil, Jason's bulldog bodyguard, grinned down at her. This time she did shudder. She'd never liked the way Neil looked at her, as though he was undressing her in his head.

Neri reached for her drink with nerveless fingers, wrapping them about the glass and lifting it to her lips. Looking around the club she took a sip and tried to act as though nothing was wrong. That was the key. Jason was a stickler for appearances. If she played the game well enough she might be able to string things along, perhaps delay them long enough to find a way out.

There had to be a way out. Otherwise she'd end her life in a back alley somewhere with her body left in a Dumpster. The expression on her face didn't change as another thought occurred to her.

Neil.

She slid a glance at Jason. He wouldn't. Would he? Neil had some…unhealthy appetites. He would. Without a doubt he would give her to Neil. The numbness she'd been feeling since Jason had thrown her, half naked, into the bedroom and told her to get dressed for the evening burned away under her fear. She had to get out of here. Now.

Replacing the glass on the table she shifted along the bench seat.

"Excuse me… Oh, for fuck's sake, do you have to ask him for permission to take a piss as well?" she snapped when Neil looked at Jason to check.

"Let her go." Jason's voice was just audible over the heavy music of the club. He opened his mouth to say something else, but Neri grabbed her purse and slid past Neil before he could change his mind.

She fled through the club on swift feet. Moonlight & Magic was the biggest of the "paranormal" clubs in town. Neri didn't know much about paranormals. Sure, she knew they'd come out of the "closet" a couple of years ago, but she'd never really thought much about it. So the monster under the bed was real? Big deal. Neri had always known monsters were real, but in her world they went by the term *Homo sapiens.*

Still, perhaps she'd get lucky and Jason would piss off something big and mean that would tear his head off. Yeah, like she'd get *that* lucky.

Skirting the edge of the packed dance floor she made her way to the ladies' room. There had to be an exit out back somewhere, a staff entrance or something. She just needed a five minute head start. Just five lousy minutes and she'd disappear so completely even her own mother wouldn't be able to find her.

Her lips quirked as she paused to make way for a busboy. Of course, that would depend on her knowing who her mother was. Not information a brat left on the hospital steps twenty-four years ago tended to have access to.

Neri Jacobs. Unwanted by her own mother, shunted from foster home to foster home, and now the soon-to-be-deceased girlfriend of a sleaze like Jason Carrick, small-time wannabe crime lord. Just her fucking luck.

* * *

Knuckles, head bouncer, part-time barman and full-time resident badass at Moonlight & Magic, watched the group on the other side of the club out of the corner of his eye. Actually, standing at the bar and wiping glasses to keep his scarred hands busy, he watched everyone in the club, but he kept a special eye on the Carrick party.

Knuckles might have looked like a stereotypical thug, but he was far from it. For a start, he was the club owners' "right hand man"—a testament to his intelligence and diligence in his job. With Knuckles on duty, trouble was minimal. To all intents and purposes, his job was the reason he occupied the small apartment above the club, behind the offices. But the reality ran far deeper.

Knuckles was a gargoyle; admittedly one in human form most of the time but a gargoyle nonetheless. The club was his territory and nothing guarded a building better than a gargoyle. It was what they did, what they were.

And right at this moment Knuckles' "spider sense" was doing the quick-step about Carrick's party. He knew who they all were, of course. Daelas and Jaren, the club's owners, didn't pay him the big bucks to stand around looking pretty, which was fairly impossible when you were over six and a half feet with a face that looked like it had been carved out of rock. In all fairness, Knuckles' face *had* been carved out of rock, but that was beside the point. The point was

Knuckles made a habit of checking out all the regulars to the club to make sure there were no…undesirables amongst them.

Jason Carrick might not be an undesirable—being a vampire, a troll or an ogre put a person on the club's shit list automatically—but he was a nasty piece of work all the same. A human snake who profited on the misery of others, he'd earned a place on Knuckles' own personal shit list—right up there at the top, just under stonemason. The glass cracked under his massive hands as his lip curled.

"Yo, man, you got some serious leakage there." The voice brought Knuckles back to the present and he glanced down. Sure enough, blood dripped from his closed fist onto the floor.

"Great, just bloody great. *Jaaaac,*" he called out, attracting the attention of the willowy blonde the other end of the bar. "Grab the mop, would you? Need to clean up." He lifted his bloodstained hand in explanation.

"Sure thing, love. Want me to tell Jaren you're off the floor?" Jac replied in between ringing up a drinks order and pulling a pint. Knuckles had never figured out how she did so many things at once. One of the multitude of mysteries women held for him.

"Nah, won't be long," he said over his shoulder, and he headed for the toilets.

* * *

There was no way out. No back door and the windows in the ladies' room were jammed shut. What sort of bloody place was this? Didn't they know it was standard procedure to have a back door for desperate girlfriends needing to escape their asshole boyfriends?

Neri slammed her hand against the window frame in an effort to loosen it and succeeded in jarring the bones of her wrist.

"Shit, shit, shit, shit!" she cursed as she folded it under her arm. Small even for a woman, she weighed about the same as a wet kitten, so she just wasn't up to rigorous activities like trying to break out of a nightclub.

Climbing off the toilet, she considered her options. A snort escaped her. What options? She didn't have any bloody options—that was the problem. Her nerves were so shot that the door crashing against the partition as she barged out of the cubicle made her jump. She didn't have long. Any minute now Jason would send Neil in to find her, and she wouldn't get another shot at escape. It was now or never.

She barreled into the corridor with the force of a cannonball, intent on finding a back door or some other way out of here. Right at that moment even throwing something heavy through a window and cutting herself to ribbons on the glass was looking favorable. What was the worst that could happen to her if she did that? Some vamp would find her, make her immortal and she could go slap Jason around for a change. A grin split her lips. Yeah, she liked that idea.

All those pleasant thoughts of retribution came to an abrupt end as she turned the corner and ran into a brick wall...a warm, breathing brick wall.

* * *

Whatever Knuckles expected as he stepped out of the staff toilets, it wasn't to be trampled by a tiny woman on a stampede. She hit the middle of his chest, rebounded with a small *ooof* and started to lose her balance. Automatically his arms wrapped around her to stop her falling over. At the worst, she'd land on her backside, the rather pretty and lush backside filling his palm, but still a gargoyle did what a gargoyle had to do—namely protect humanity, even from a bruised ass.

"Hey, little lady, might wanna watch where you're going." Knuckles' lips curved in an approximation of a smile as he turned the woman the right way up. It never failed to amaze him quite how delicate humans were, especially female humans. Then she flicked her hair back from her face, and he lost the power of thought.

Large eyes the color of slate looked up at him, shadowed with fear. The fear hit him in the gut and his protective instincts rushed to the fore. The next instant the air prickled with power—power which crawled over his body, gathering under his skin and readying him for the change. Readying his body to drop the human mask and reveal his natural form. He gritted his teeth and held onto control like a bad-tempered terrier on a postman's pant leg.

"Hey there, you okay?" Concern crept into his gruff voice as she clutched at his arms, her little hands trying to get purchase on the heavy muscles under his work jacket. He wondered what they'd feel like against his skin, all soft and warm and... His body hardened, his cock leaping to attention in his pants.

What the hell?

Carefully he set her on her feet, hoping to all that was holy she hadn't felt his reaction to her nearness. What was that all about? He'd never had such a reaction to a human woman before, hell, to any woman, even the ones who had tried it on, eager to find out if what they said about his kind was true.

"Between a rock and a hard place...you don't know the half of it, sweet stuff."

Mentally Knuckles shook his head, the glib lines his brother Mac had used to pull the women in the past filling his memory. Family for gargoyles was an odd thing. Mac was his brother because they'd both been created to guard the same church. Where Knuckles had been a spire gargoyle, removed from the churchgoers, Mac had been a doorway grotesque. He had the gift of gab. He'd had centuries to listen to humans before they'd been freed, the church they'd guarded no longer holy ground. It was an apartment block now, for up and coming singletons.

"She's fine, aren't you, Neri?"

Another voice, an unwelcome voice, broke into their little reverie. The small woman next to Knuckles flinched, and he watched hope die in her eyes.

"Yes, I'm fine," the now-named Neri murmured and smiled at Knuckles before she walked to Carrick's side. The small expression turned his stone heart over in his chest. It was a smile of hopelessness and resignation, not of joy. Another question replaced the one about his reaction to her; what the hell was going on here?

"He hurt you?" Carrick flicked an accusing glance over Knuckles' massive frame. Knuckles bit back the snarl that rose to his lips and forced his normal stoic expression to remain in place. The fucking little weasel, like he would *ever* hurt an innocent, especially one as delicate and perfect as this one. But it was the sort of thing many humans thought him capable of based on the way he looked.

"No, not at all." She shook her head, flicking him another small smile over her shoulder. It was just a smile, more than he usually got from women, but why did he feel like she was saying goodbye as Carrick hustled her through the door?

Knuckles followed the two back into the club at a slower pace and resumed his normal post at the top bar. He tried to forget about his unusual reaction to the little female tucked firmly into the booth next to Carrick. She wasn't his type. Hell, Knuckles didn't have a type. The nearest he got was looking at stone angels on crypts or something. *Gargoyle porn...* The big man shook his head as Mac's voice came back to him again.

He missed his brother. Mac could be an irritating little shit but he was family. The place seemed empty without him, and to be honest, he could do with the backup at times. Particularly with the new vampire nest which had set up on the other side of town. They seemed to have gotten the message that vampires were unwelcome at Moonlight & Magic, but there was always one who got too involved in the hunt and found itself in places it didn't want to be, like in a back alley having a chat with Knuckles and his boys. Between a rock and a hard place. Vampire fangs were useless against gargoyle skin in any form, so the bites didn't bother Knuckles. They just pissed him off.

He sighed and leaned on the corner of the bar. From here he could see across the entire club, which was handy for noticing hotspots and marshalling the troops to stop them before they became serious trouble. In other words, before the human clubbers noticed anything out of the ordinary. Moonlight &

Magic prided itself on its unique status, on being a place where humans could "dip a toe" into the scary world of the Night Races, but not actually be in any serious danger.

Keeping half an eye on the group around Carrick, who was now loudly ordering the best champagne, the gargoyle swept a practiced eye across the club. They had at least two dealers they knew of in here tonight. Knuckles rubbed his nose with a large hand, just thankful they were human and dealing human shit. They'd had a Fae in last month peddling Faery dust. Knuckles had waded in and the shit had hit the fan big time. The rest of the staff were still making fun of Knuckles for the bright pink beak he'd sported until sunrise.

Movement caught his eye. One of the dealers, a short thin guy who was living proof humanity was descended from rodents, sidled off to the toilets. Knuckles waited, not wanting to send his guys in like the household cavalry if the guy was just taking a piss. Within a minute another youth had detached himself from his crowd and headed in after him. The big gargoyle nodded sagely, he'd had a feeling they were together.

Knuckles caught the eye of Tiny, one of the bouncers named for being the opposite and nearly as big as Knuckles himself. A quick jerk of his head had the other bouncer heading in after the furtive pair. Of course, it might all be very innocent and they might be trying to catch some "alone time," but Knuckles didn't care if there was the slightest chance they could stop a deal going down. One day, dealers of all races would learn not to piss about with his rules.

"Heya, Ugly, what's up? You got a face like a bulldog chewin' a wasp, and that's insulting bulldogs," a voice announced beside him.

Knuckles didn't flinch and turned slightly to nod at the tall slender man who appeared next to him. Jaren, one of the twin incubi who owned the place, was always light on his feet and often managed to sneak up on him. Knuckles was surprised to see him, considering the brothers had discovered their mate, Sage, a few weeks ago. They were still in the "seriously loved up" stage with no sign of them leaving it anytime soon.

He ignored the insult. Jaren always teased people, and it was considered bad form to rip your employer's arms and legs off. Not that the insults bothered him. He knew how he looked, and Jaren's words were affectionate, if that was the right word. Knuckles wouldn't have taken the same crap off of a stranger, that was for sure.

"Coupla dealers. Tiny's gone to have a chat," he rumbled in explanation. "Carrick's in again. Something odd going down. Don't like it."

The incubus' silver-blue eyes cut to the table Knuckles indicated and narrowed. None of the staff liked Carrick. Some of the girls had even gone so far as to refuse to serve him and his group—the men anyway. The woman they all felt sorry for. Carrick was a bastard and never passed up an opportunity for a piece of skirt, even with his girlfriend sitting next to him. If things got too intense, he just had his thugs take her home.

"No, me either. Jac… I'll take it over." Jaren easily lifted the tray from the barmaid's hands as she went to slide past them and headed over to the Carrick table in her place. The siren shrugged, patrons already clamoring for attention, and returned to her place behind the bar.

Knuckles watched as Jaren's tall figure wove through the packed floor, and not for the first time, admired the easy way he moved, like a dancer, always in motion, always graceful, never the clumsy lumbering oaf Knuckles was. Jealousy spiked in the middle of his chest as Jaren served the champagne, even managing to snag Neri's hand to place a kiss on her knuckles.

Knuckles gritted his teeth, unprepared for the wash of anger that swept over him at the sight of the charming and handsome incubus touching her. He looked away to get himself under control.

The last thing the club needed was a gargoyle on a rampage. It would knock the former big bad—vampires—completely off the top spot because there wasn't much that could stand up to over three hundred pounds of granite-hewn monster, even the brickwork.

You wouldn't like me when I'm mad. His lips quirked. Slap some green paint on him and he could have had a nice little career as a stunt double in Hollywood, if he could work out how to explain the wings.

Looking away from the group, Knuckles concentrated on the floor and his job. He didn't need to form an obsession with a human female. They were too easy to damage, especially for someone like him.

Within minutes Jaren was back at the bar, setting the tray of empties down. Knuckles cocked his head at the thoughtful look on his boss's face.

"Keep an eye on them," Jaren replied to Knuckles' look as though he'd spoken. All of the staff did that. They were used to Knuckles being less than verbose at the best of times. Hell, his little conversation with Neri in the corridor had been his verbal quota for the week. It wasn't that he couldn't talk, or hold a conversation, just that by the time he'd framed his reply the conversation had moved on.

"Problem?"

"Hmm, not sure. Bullyboy on the end's jumpy; all sorts of sick fantasies running through his head. So many it's hard to tell what's real and what's not. I don't think he knows himself." He shuddered. "After being in his head I need mind bleach. The girl's terrified and Carrick's…well, the less I have to do with him the better. Not thinking anything illegal at this moment. But keep an eye on them, okay? I don't like the atmosphere around them," Jaren ordered, nodding toward the table.

His eyes drifted out of focus for a second and a sappy grin covered his face. Knuckles sighed, recognizing the signs. For such a small woman, the twins' mate Sage sure had them wrapped around her little finger.

"I'm being summoned. Gotta go. Catch you later." The smaller man clapped Knuckles on the shoulder before disappearing through the door to the office suite upstairs.

Knuckles nodded but Jaren was already gone. Always watchful, the gargoyle settled down to wait. He didn't move. He didn't fidget. Only the slow rise and fall of his chest gave him away as a living being rather than the stone carving sunlight turned him into. In the darkness of his small corner only his eyes moved, glittering with purpose as he watched.

Chapter Two

Neri had gone past simply scared now, right through into all out terrified. The evening had slipped away faster than she could think of a way to escape, and she knew her time was almost up.

Panicking, and with no clue what to do next, she drained her glass. Perhaps if she got drunk—passed out drunk—then she wouldn't care what happened to her. Perhaps it wouldn't hurt as much. A hard hand removed the glass before she could signal for a refill, and Jason's cold eyes glittered down at her.

"Oh, no, sweetheart, no more for you or you won't be any fun for Neil, now will you? If you pass out, you won't be able to scream for him. And he does like it when a pretty girl screams for him. Doesn't much care why she screams though…" he whispered in her ear, nuzzling her neck to place a kiss. Neri flinched as bile rose, and his hard hand clamped around her throat.

"Shouldn't have tried to leave me, baby girl. You know better. *No one* leaves me, not ever." He pushed her away, a hard, angry shove which had her sprawling across the seat. A pair of pant legs appeared in front of her eyes, the crotch tented by a massive erection. She looked up into Neil's excited eyes and felt sick.

"She's all yours, Neil," Jason drawled behind her, his voice bored. "Just remember to clean up after yourself."

Neri opened her mouth to scream. There had to be someone here who would help her, get her to the cops… A hard hand clamped around the back of her neck and dragged her to her feet, Neil pulling her tightly against his body. Pain flared as his grip on her neck tightened, stealing her breath as his fingers ground the delicate bones against each other.

"Behave and things'll be easier on you," he warned, beginning to march her through the club. Then he giggled. The sound was wrong, so very wrong, from such a big man and struck fresh fear into her already terrified heart. "Then again, I wouldn't count on it. I've been waiting a long time for the boss to get sick of you so I can have you all to myself. So if you cause any trouble, I'll kill whoever tries to help you. Understand?"

Neri nodded mutely. The people here were innocent, with no concept of the sort of nastiness Neil was capable of. He wouldn't care who tried to help her. He'd hurt them anyway, then track down their families and hurt them too, just because.

He propelled her across the club, cutting easily through the crowds by sheer force. Her legs threatened to buckle, only the cruel grip he had on the back of her neck keeping her upright and walking.

Tears welled in Neri's eyes. She couldn't see a way out. Once out of the club she'd be bundled in a car and her life would be over. Well, not quite but she'd wish for death within minutes of the sort of attentions Neil lavished on his women. There was a reason he didn't have a steady girlfriend, and it had nothing to do with a fear of commitment.

They walked out the door and into the crisp night air. Neri locked eyes with the doorman for a moment, her eyes pleading for help. He looked at her, then looked through her, nodding at Neil.

"Lady's had a little too much." Neil's grip all but crushed her neck, warning her to stay silent.

The doorman nodded. "Best get her home then. Have a good night, sir."

"Will do. Come on, sweetheart. Let's get you in the car."

Neri couldn't help the whimper of terror which started in the back of her throat and bubbled over her lips like water from a fountain. Neil's grip tightened, and he all but dragged her unresponsive form down the street toward where they'd parked earlier.

"Come on, bitch, walk properly. You're embarrassing me." He yanked her up against his solid body, anger in his voice. He worked out obsessively and his muscles were rock hard. Neri shivered as he held her still, his ham-like hand stroking across her face in a sick parody of a lover's touch.

"You don't want people to think we have a problem, do you? Because then they might decide to come and help you, and I'd have to kill them. And it would be all your fault."

He paused to look down at her. "Unless…unless that's what you want. You wanna see me kill people? Does that do it for you, doll? Get you all hot and wet? God, yeah, I'm fucking hard just thinking about it."

His eyes glittered with excitement as he pulled her up harder against him. He ground his groin against her, the hardness of his erection pressing into her belly insistently.

Neri felt sick. He was unstable; she'd always known that—a total fruit-loop. Quite how he'd arrived at that particular conclusion she didn't know, didn't care, and she wasn't going to argue, not if it kept her alive a little longer.

"Sure, yeah…gets me hot," she lied through her teeth as she forced her body to soften, relaxing against him as she slid her arms up around his neck. "Carrick's a pussy. Too soft, not man enough to give me what I need. Are you man enough, Neil?"

He moaned at her seductive words, his hands groping at her ass as he pulled her backwards.

"Fuck, yeah, I'm man enough," he growled as he shoved her back against the wall. His large hand spread over her thigh, hauling her knee up in a rough gesture so he could cram his pelvis between her opened thighs. He thrust his hips against her. "Feel that, doll? That hard cock? I'm gonna give you a fucking you won't forget."

Tears streamed down Neri's face as his hands tore at her clothes, ripping them in his haste. There was no way out. She couldn't fight Neil off. If she screamed someone was going to die, and if she didn't, she would.

Rock and a hard place.

Without warning Neil's weight was snatched away from her and flung halfway across the alleyway. Off balance, Neri stumbled and clutched at the wall. In front of her stood the bartender from the club—the one she'd almost trampled earlier—with murder in his eyes as he glared at Neil.

"Hey! Fuck off, man, get your own piece of ass. This one's mine," Neil snarled, picking himself up from the pavement and rounding on the bigger man.

Neri gasped, terror running through her. Her rescuer was huge—way bigger than Neil—but Neil was a nasty piece of work. He wouldn't think twice about killing anyone, much less someone who'd thrown him clear across the alley. There was no way he would let such a blow to his male pride go; he'd killed people for less.

"No! Please, go! He'll kill you." She pushed her knight in shining armor...or black Armani...toward the entrance to the alleyway. It was like trying to push a cliff; he didn't take the hint.

"Baby, please...ignore him, come back to me," she cooed at Neil, desperate to divert his attention. She couldn't let him kill the bartender, not for trying to help her.

Neither man moved, each weighing the other up. Neil jittered slightly on his feet, like a boxer, in an attempt to intimidate his opponent. Neri's eyes flicked from one to the other. It didn't seem to be working. The big man stood as still as a statue, shielding Neri, only his eyes moving to track Neil.

"Should do as the lady says," Neil snarled. "I'll carve you up into itty bitty pieces even those filthy fucking vamps wouldn't touch."

The other man merely smiled and curled his massive hands into fists. His knuckles cracked, the sound like rocks crushing against one another. "You're assuming vamps scare me."

His answer, and the complete lack of emotion, made Neil pause. He stopped, his eyes shifting from side to side as he tried to work the situation out. "Everyone's scared of vamps. They're the top of the fucking food chain, man!"

A smile crossed the man's face. "Nastier things than vampires out here."

"Yeah, like what?"

"Me."

The fight was over in seconds. The human rushed him, and with a lazy backhand, Knuckles swatted him against the far wall. People saw him as ponderous and slow. Within the confines of the club where he had to at least *act* human, he was. But out here in the night Knuckles was something else. A guardian, one designed to protect the innocent, and the woman with the sad eyes and ripped clothing behind him was his definition of innocence.

"Wha...what the fuck are you, man?" the human whined as he tried to drag himself upright. He shook his head to clear it, his leg trailing as though motor control to the left side of his body was funky. Knuckles moved in for the kill.

"Retribution."

He stomped heavily on the guy's ankle as he answered, feeling the bones inside grind to dust. The human screamed, a sound filled with pain and fury. Another scream from behind him echoed it. A female scream. Knuckles whipped his head around, expecting to see another thug attacking her. But she stood alone by the wall with her eyes wide. Fixed on him.

Fear rolled off her in waves but she took a step forwards. Her hand, pale and slender, reached out toward him. "Pl-please don't kill him."

Confusion filled Knuckles, whirling in his head. "Thi...he was attacking you?" he said finally, his hand lashing out as the human tried to crawl away. Knuckles easily pinned him to the wall with one massive hand wrapped around his throat. Just one small squeeze...

He looked at her again. Was she saying the guy *wasn't* attacking her? Some humans liked pain; he knew that because they came on to him a lot. Knuckles felt sick. Had he attacked a couple in the middle of some freaky foreplay? Convinced she needed his protection because she was pretty and small and...he *liked* her?

He watched as she picked her way closer, reaching out to wrap her hand around his arm. The touch burned through his tough skin. Heat burrowed inwards and raced through his veins, heading straight for his groin, pooling there like molten lava as his body came to rampant life.

There was the problem...he wanted her.

"Please don't kill him. You don't need to; he's not worth it."

Relief hit him hard like a truck. He'd been hit by a truck once, the first time he'd seen one, and been too dumbstruck to move out of the way, so he knew what it felt like. They weren't a couple. His eyes cut to the whimpering human in his grip.

"He was hurting you."

She nodded as her other hand joined the first and tried to pull him away. "But you don't need to kill him. You're better than that. Please?"

Her last "please" did it for him. Humans saw him as a thug. They assumed he was capable of violence and killing, that he was more prone to it because of the way he looked. Hell, if he'd been able to go out in daylight, he was sure little old ladies would cross the street rather than walk by him. He was used to it now, expected it, but that she thought he was *better* than that? The words were a balm to his soul.

He dropped the human, his lip curling as he looked at the pathetic heap on the ground. "Your lucky day, bud. You should thank the lady."

Knuckles moved his arm, sliding her hands down until he could engulf her hands in one of his. She was shaking. He squeezed in reassurance as he leaned down to the shivering guy on the ground. "Never speak to her again. Never *look* at her again. In fact, never even *think* about her again, or I'll rip your arms and legs off. Understand me?"

Chapter Three

Neri shivered at the dangerous note in her rescuer's voice. She still couldn't believe the impossible had happened and help had arrived. Someone, somewhere, must have been listening to her desperate prayers.

Turning her away from the whimpering mess on the ground, he looked down at her. Dark eyes bored through to her soul, a dangerous, almost feral expression in them. Neri's breath caught in her throat. He wasn't human. Everything made sense now. Of course he wasn't human. No human would go up against a maniac like Neil with such confidence. No human could move like that.

She swallowed again. Moonlight & Magic was advertised as a paranormal club, but she'd assumed that was just hype and the staff were human. They looked human; they talked human. Well, apart from the silver-eyed guy who had served them earlier. There had been a buzz, a power, about him which screamed "non-human."

"Let's get out of here." Gently he herded her out of the alley, and Neri didn't look back to where Neil whimpered in his own pain-filled world. She didn't feel sorry for him. To be honest, she didn't know why she'd pleaded for his life; he deserved everything he got and then some.

Flicking a glance up at her companion, she studied him from under her lashes. She hadn't done it for Neil but for this guy. Something in his dark eyes, softer now without the flash of rage in them, had said he would kill if he had to but that he really didn't want to.

"Thank you," she murmured as a violent shiver racked her. With her hand still caught in his grip she couldn't wrap her arms around her body to warm herself up. Why was she so damn cold? A quick glance down gave her the reason, and her eyes widened in shock. She was almost naked. Her top was in tatters after Neil's mauling, and her skirt was ripped at the seams, clinging to her waist by a few threads.

"Oh, my God." Her cheeks burned as she realized the sight she must be presenting. She paused at the entrance to the alleyway; she couldn't go out into the street, not like this.

"Here. I'm Knuckles, by the way."

Heavy cloth settled around her shoulders as he wrapped her in his jacket. Neri looked up into dark eyes. They weren't brown, as she'd thought, but black.

57

Like an animal's eyes. She'd seen the sheen when he'd turned toward her earlier. They'd glowed like a fox's did in a car's headlights, the eyes of a night hunter.

"Neri. Pleased to meet you. Thank you."

Gratefully she snuggled down into the warm cloth, breathing in the masculine scent and sighing. The jacket still carried the warmth of his body and the faint scent of his aftershave. She burrowed deeper, trying to still the quakes going through her body.

"I'm sorry." Her teeth chattered as he steered her into the street and back toward the club. "I can't stop shaking."

"Shock," he replied, nodding as they passed the heavyset guy on the door, the one who'd ignored her earlier. "Thanks, Jon, I found her in time."

She looked up, a question in her eyes as Knuckles herded her, not into the club this time, but through a door hidden behind the main entrance. A door which led to a utilitarian corridor nothing like the opulence of the rest of the club.

"He told you? I didn't think he'd noticed anything w-w-was..." She broke off as her teeth chattered again. Stairs loomed ahead, and she stopped to cast them an apprehensive glance. Her knees were knocking together so much she knew she wouldn't be able to manage them.

"He noticed. We've been watching Carrick all night. He raised the alarm when he saw you leaving."

He noticed her distress and the next moment Neri found herself swept up into rock-hard arms. She squeaked in surprise. "You don't need to do this. I can walk!"

"Yeah, right, surprised you can hear anything over the sound of your knees." He chuckled, the sound reverberating through the massive chest she was being held against. His head turned, their faces mere inches apart as he climbed the stairs with her nestled in his arms. Neri felt safe, cared for. Her hands tightened on his shoulders, feeling the solid muscle underneath.

"You're not human, are you?"

He shook his head, the movement almost imperceptible as he opened the door at the top of the stairs.

"Nope. Not even remotely." His voice was low, a rumble almost on the edge of hearing. The deep tones wrapped around Neri, traveling through her body to settle low in the pit of her belly. She loved men's voices, particularly distinctive ones, and his was more than distinctive.

"What are you?" The question was soft, breathed in the air between them. To be scared didn't even occur to her. He'd rescued her from a very human monster. What could he do to her worse than the things Neil had planned? Somehow she didn't think he was into rape and murder.

He slid her down his body slowly, not breaking eye contact. Neri shivered at the sensation, feeling every hard, sculpted plane as she slid over them. He didn't answer her, a look of reluctance in his eyes.

What are you?

Knuckles froze, still holding her wrapped in his embrace with his heavy arms around her tiny waist. She was so delicate it made his teeth ache. The rage which had possessed him in the alley had leeched away, and he felt like a lumbering idiot again. An oaf not worthy of touching her, let alone harboring some of the hotter thoughts cramming themselves behind his eyes at light speed.

"A gargoyle," he admitted after a long pause. His hands loosed their grip around her waist and he stepped away. *The gentlemanly thing. Don't scare the squishy human,* he told himself. Bollocks, Mac's voice taunted from inside his head. *Putting temptation out your reach, you mean.*

Leaving her standing in the middle of the lounge, Knuckles moved into the small kitchen area and put the kettle on. "Tea or coffee?" he asked, looking over his shoulder. "It will help with the shock."

"Err, coffee, please. The stronger the better."

Knuckles nodded, moving around the tiny kitchen with the ease of long practice. Unlike some other paranormals, he didn't have weird dietary requirements. He didn't need to eat, but he liked to cook so the cupboards were filled with food.

He watched her out of the corner of his eye, automatically tracking her as she padded forwards. His jacket still swamped her. It hit her at knee length, and there was enough fabric in it to wrap around her a couple of times. He smiled to himself as he dumped instant coffee granules in the two mugs and waited for the kettle to boil. Cute as hell, she looked like a small child playing dress-up.

"A gargoyle?" she asked, fascination written over her face as she slid onto one of the stools at the breakfast bar opposite him. "Like you see on buildings?"

Knuckles' lips quirked as the spoon clicked against the side of the mug. He slid the coffee over to her and leaned back against the counter. Automatically he slouched, trying not to loom. It was an instinctive reaction, one he'd learned years ago. *101 ways not to make the squishies nervous.* "Yeah, like on buildings. Well, not the modern stuff you see. Traditional stuff, churches…that sort of thing."

"Oh."

One delicate hand emerged from the long sleeve of his jacket to clasp the mug, her slender fingers wrapping around the handle. Knuckles' eyes riveted to it. What would it feel like to have those fingers wrapped around his cock? Wrapped around his cock and slowly pumping the hard flesh?

He bit back a groan and forced his eyes away. This time they focused on her lips as she took a sip of the hot liquid. Full, pouty lips which would look just right... He cut the thought off—he knew where *that* one was going—and a bead of sweat trickled down his spine. He was going to hell, express route, baby.

"So...were you...?"

Gray eyes looked at him over the rim of her mug. Behind it he could see her biting her lip. He took pity on her and answered anyway. "On a building? Yeah. St. Michael and All Angels, just shy of Sherwood."

Her eyes widened. "So you're English? Bit far away from home, aren't you? What happened to St. Michael's?"

"Decommissioned and closed. Apartment block there now." He buried his nose into his mug. The scalding liquid burned his lip but he ignored it, savoring the pain; anything to get his mind off the cute little thing who sat on the other side of the bar. He should never have brought her up here. She was too innocent, far too trusting. With no idea of what he was, she'd willingly entered his "lair." He shook his head to himself. If anyone had told him this morning there were still such naive humans around, he'd have called him a liar.

"You don't look much like a gargoyle."

A snort of laughter escaped him. "Yeah, right, I'm an ugly bastard and I know it. Ain't nothing going to change that now."

Neri swirled her mug in her hands and watched the rich, dark liquid move. He wasn't ugly. At least, she didn't think so. He was huge, easily over six foot and broad with it, and his face...well, determined was one word. Undeniably masculine, with its strong lines and planes, was another. But ugly? No, she wouldn't say that.

"No, what I meant was you look..." She trailed off again and sighed. How the hell did she say this without sounding rude?

"Normal?" He said it for her, a weird look on his face.

"You get that a lot I take it?"

He nodded, setting the mug on the side next to him. The movement caused the fine fabric over his chest to pull, revealing a hint of the heavy muscles she'd felt there earlier. "Humans are always curious about us paranormals. Because I don't bother to hide it anymore, I get most of the questions; the other staff not so much."

It took Neri a moment to realize he'd spoken. All her attention riveted on the small triangle at his throat where the shirt parted to reveal the hollow of his throat. Would he be the same all over, that hard muscle and firm skin she'd felt under his jacket? What would that feel like against her softer, human flesh...

"Huh? What? None of the other staff are human?" she asked to cover her lapse. "They look human."

His lips, surprisingly full and sensual in such a starkly masculine face, curved into a smile. "Most of them are except for senior staff. And looking human... Well, that's sort of the point. Paranormals who couldn't hide what they were from lynch mobs tended not to breed much. Selective evolution."

Neri nodded. It made sense. But one thing was bothering her, and her curiosity, once unleashed, wouldn't leave it alone. "So, gargoyles look human. What about the ones that are all...weird creatures. With wings and stuff?"

Ahh, Knuckles understood what was puzzling her now. He shrugged, strong fingers gripping the edges of the granite work surface. This was where the curious look in her eyes, bright and innocent, turned into disgust, or even worse, fascinated excitement.

"We look different in the daylight. Sunlight turns us to stone as we sleep." Hopefully that would stop her and he wouldn't need to explain any further. No such luck. She slid off the barstool and padded around the counter until she stood in front of him.

"So do you have wings?" She tilted her head to one side, her eyes wide with interest, and the cupid's bow of her lips pursed a little as she waited for his answer.

"Do you ever stop asking questions?"

"Not usually." She shook her head and laughed. Her dark hair danced over her shoulders as the musical sound danced around the room. Just for that, that carefree, happy little sound, Knuckles would have done anything. Usually people ran screaming when they realized what he was.

Gargoyles weren't as sexy as vamps, even though there was less chance of them ripping your throat out for a snack. Still, humans tended to equate charm and good looks with good intentions, which was probably why they ended up as food.

"Yeah, I got wings. Claws, tail, the whole works." Why the hell was he telling her? He never usually spoke about this sort of stuff. Usually he told the curious to get lost in no uncertain terms whether they were asking invasive questions of him or another member of the club staff.

He watched her as she stood in front of him, arms wrapped tight around herself. She was so tiny and delicate he was scared to breathe on her in case she broke. Knuckles was not telepathic, or empathic. He couldn't read auras, and he didn't have freaky talents like some paranormals.

He could tell she was looking for something though. Perhaps proof that not everyone out there was a monster. After time spent with Carrick and his bully boys he didn't blame her. In fact, he wouldn't have blamed her if she was paranoid of anything vaguely masculine that drew breath.

Her hand reached out, touching his arm where it was folded over his chest. Knuckles stopped breathing. The first, tentative touch sent a wave of fire through his body. The second started the inferno low in his pelvis.

Her fingertips skittered over his forearm, pressing against him to test the firmness of his skin, tracing the line of the muscles. "Your skin is harder."

Ain't the only thing, baby. He was at full attention and harder than he'd ever been before. His nostrils flared. The temptation to boost her up on the counter behind her, strip her panties down her smooth thighs and bury himself balls deep in her softness nearly got the better of him. He swallowed and shifted position. *Just don't look down, doll, please. I'm not a fucking rat like Carrick, but you're a beautiful woman… I'd have to be dead not to notice.*

"Oh, did I hurt you?" She lifted her hand, eyes lifting to his with concern in their depths. They weren't gray, he realized, but almost silver, with tiny flecks of green around the center. Eyes he could lose himself in.

Mine to protect. Mine to love. Just…mine. The possessive thought welled up from nowhere, taking him by surprise and stealing his breath away. Smiling, he shook his head. "Doubt you could. Not used to being touched is all."

"Oh, get out of here. I bet you have all the women hanging after you," she teased, slapping his arm. The blow didn't bother him one iota but her flirting floored him. Flirting. With him. Need surged quick and fast, diffusing through his bloodstream at light speed. He gaped at her for a moment before he got himself together.

"I wouldn't put it quite that way." He avoided her gaze.

Was he…blushing? Neri ducked down a little to catch his eye. "Hey, still with me?" she asked with a smile. He had beautiful eyes. They were dark, not brown but a faded black, like a pair of black jeans which had been washed until the color was going.

Forgetting she'd asked a question, Neri moved in closer. His scent struck her, the scent of a man, aftershave and shower gel over warm skin. She inhaled, filling her lungs. Entranced, she reached up and dragged the pads of her fingers down his cheek.

Knuckles sucked in a quick breath, his lips parting. Neri focused on them as her own parted in response. Beautiful eyes, kissable lips. Lips. Oh, hell yeah, *very* kissable lips. Would they be as hard as his skin? Or would they be soft and warm like human lips…like her lips?

Only one way to find out.

Neri reached up on tiptoe with one hand resting on a huge forearm for support. A soft touch on his jaw brought his head down to hers. His breath whispered against her mouth and sent a shiver running the length of her spine in response.

She brushed his lips with hers, the gentlest touch. His lips were warm and soft, just their touch against hers setting them to tingling. She moaned and pressed closer, needing more. Ever since the alleyway she'd been aware of him, been aware of the spark between them. The fact that he wasn't human didn't bother her in the slightest.

Oh please, let him feel it too, she begged silently as she slid her arms around his neck and angled her head for him, her lips parting in invitation.

Knuckles had changed his mind. She wasn't human; she was his own demon, sent to oversee his personal version of hell. A groan welled up from deep in his chest as she offered her lips to him, offered herself. There was no way she'd be able to fight off a determined gargoyle, and she had to know that. Then the truth hit him like a sledgehammer. She trusted him; despite the way he looked, she trusted him.

Not about to waste such a precious gift, Knuckles wrapped his arms around her, trying to be gentle. His legs parted as he leaned back against the counter to let her step between his thighs. One hand stole up her back and cupped the nape of her neck as the other settled gently in the cello curve of her hip. Wrapped around her he took his time, savoring the sensation as he brushed his lips over hers again, teasing them both with anticipation.

She didn't stiffen, or panic at his touch. Instead, soft hands crept over his shoulders, their touch burning as though the layer of fabric between their skin didn't exist. Her lips clung, his molded and caressed as he explored. And all the time half of him was waiting for her to panic and push him away. But it didn't happen. She came alive under his kiss, reacting so sweetly the savage ache in Knuckles' groin almost doubled him over with need and longing.

His tongue snaked out, flicking along the underside of her top lip to part them. She opened for him with a sigh and Knuckles knew he was lost. With a small moan of surprise and pleasure he deepened the kiss. His tongue slid into her mouth to explore, gently teasing her tongue to twine around his. It was a long, slow and sensual kiss which had her shivering and moaning in his arms.

The kiss got hotter, deeper, and he turned her around. They were no longer Knuckles and the waif he'd rescued from the alley, but just a man and a woman locked into a sensual spell as the world contracted down to the two of them.

He wanted more…needed to feel more…taste more. Pinning her in the corner where the counters met, he had the jacket off her shoulders and the ruins of her top dropping to the floor behind him before he realized what he'd done.

His large hand swept up her back, naked except for the band of her bra under her shoulder blades. Then she flinched, a soft sound of pain in her throat, and Knuckles realized what he was doing. What he'd been about to do…

"Fucking hell. Oh God… I'm sorry." He backed up, just now seeing the bruises across her hips and ribcage. Panicked, he stumbled in his haste to get away from her, put some distance between him and the sweet temptation of her curvy body and soft, fragrant skin. She'd trusted him to look after her, trusted him enough to let him kiss her and look at what he'd done.

"I'm so sorry." Frustration and shame filled him as he bolted for the French windows which led out into the night. He needed to get out of here fast, before he hurt her any more. The doors slammed shut behind him and he was gone, leaving Neri standing alone in the kitchen.

Chapter Four

Okay… Neri watched his retreating back in dumbfounded amazement. *What did I do to spark that one off?* She leaned back against the counter and ran a shaking hand through her mass of tumbled curls.

Then she saw the finger marks in the counter on either side of her hips. A perfect impression of his fingers in solid granite, like other people would leave in butter or dough. Her eyes as wide as saucers, she touched one. Her finger dipped into the depression.

The shiver chasing up her spine as she looked toward the closed door to the balcony wasn't anything to do with pleasure. It had more to do with her survival instincts telling her the man who had held her achingly gentle as he'd kissed her was dangerous.

Far more dangerous than Neil. Far more dangerous than Jason.

They could only kill her. She knew without asking that Knuckles wouldn't physically hurt her, gargoyle or not. No, something deep inside her told her he could be far more dangerous than that. She had a feeling Knuckles could destroy her heart and soul as well, if she let him close enough.

Pushing away from the counter Neri stood for a moment in the middle of the room. Indecision warred within her. Should she go after him? His tortured expression when he thought he'd hurt her had cut her to the quick. She brushed her hands over her hips where the dull ache of an old bruise told her what had set him off. She looked down. Fading bruises circled her hips and scattered artistically up her ribcage like an artist had gone to town on her body with browns and greens.

Jason's temper tantrum last week. The one, in fact, which had prompted her to try and leave him, for all the good it had done her. Why couldn't she have dated a normal guy who just deleted her number from his cell phone when she dumped him? No, she had to get the nut who decided she needed to die instead. And she would have, if Knuckles hadn't intervened…

She looked toward the closed door with purpose. If anything, she should at least let him know he hadn't hurt her. In fact, Neri couldn't remember the last time she'd been kissed like that, or held so gently or with such reverence. For a woman with minimal romantic experience, it was like showing a starving man bread. She wanted more, and soon.

Walking over to the door on silent feet, Neri paused just inside, her hand on the wooden frame. She couldn't see much in the darkness out on the balcony, just the shadows and a dark, hulking shape in the corner. A swish of movement near the floor caught her eye.

Whoa, was that a tail? Taking a deep breath for courage, she pushed the door open and stepped into the darkness.

Knuckles was aware the moment she stepped through the door. The balcony—which had seemed expansive before—was suddenly too cramped. In fact the world was too cramped when she looked at him with that look on her face, a combination of concern, vulnerability and need.

Everything gargoyle in him wanted to protect her, wrap her in his arms and comfort her. Everything male in him wanted to crush her to him and slake both the need he could see in her eyes and the need which raged unabated inside him, a need so great that only the scattered marks of violence across her pale flesh had stopped him.

His body wanted delicate and fragile. It wanted the haunting beauty standing in front of him, but his mind recognized the danger, the danger to her. His tail lashed the shadows as he shrank deeper within them and used the darkness to conceal his true, monstrous form.

"Go away, Neri. It's... I'm not safe." His voice was thick and guttural as he warned her off.

She screwed her eyes up, trying to see in the darkness. She was human. Humans saw about as well in the dark as a carrot-deficient rabbit; they were totally blind and defenseless. A huff left his massive chest, a slab of stone-like muscle far broader than the form she'd already seen. "Knuckles? Oh, honey, you didn't hurt me."

Her hand groped blindly in front of her as she took a step into the darkness. Knuckles retreated until his shoulders were against the wall. The irony of the situation wasn't lost on him. He'd faced down drunks high on mind-altering chemicals. He'd faced down violent Fae and hungry vampires, but it was a tiny human female who had him cowering in the corner.

"Sweetheart, these are old, almost gone." She swept a hand over her softly curved stomach. That was another thing he liked about her, his attention sidetracked for a moment. She had soft natural curves, not the angular curves of the half-starved perpetual dieter.

"Look at the color of them. You didn't cause them, Knuckles, I promise. You didn't hurt me at all. I don't think you would..."

Her voice wove a hypnotic spell around him, and he wavered in the darkness. She took another step forwards as if sensing his indecision. The air whispered over his hardened skin as her hand searched for him again.

"I could though." He coiled his legs under him and hopped up onto the ledge next to the balcony to put distance between them. He could feel himself wavering, the temptation whittling at his resolve. He could handle himself, handle his own desires, but when she was offering it on a plate...?

His claws dug into the stone and latched onto the steel bar buried within. She tracked the movement somehow, perhaps the air crossing her face, looking up to where his voice emanated from.

"You could. But you won't." Amusement crossed her expressive features. "Now this has to be a first. Usually it's the guy persuading the woman to have sex. Not the other way around."

Knuckles' control slipped; frustration and anger ripped through him in equal measures. How could she joke about this? Didn't she know the danger she was in? The growl slipped from his lips before he could stop it. To his satisfaction her eyes widened a little.

"You still don't get it, do you? I. Am. *Not*. Human," he repeated, as if talking to a child.

She shrugged, an elegant one-shouldered movement, one that made her breasts above the bra move in all sorts of interesting ways. Knuckles gritted his teeth and prayed for mercy.

"So? You're more human than most of the so-called humanity I've ever met."

Her flippant tone did it. She really *didn't* appreciate the danger she was in. With a growl of anger Knuckles dropped down from his ledge in front of her. She squeaked in fright as he loomed over her, the light from the room inside falling over him, falling over his true appearance at last.

Neri swallowed as the urge to step back filled her. She fought it down, looking up at him as awe and wonder filled her.

"You're...beautiful," she murmured. Her pale hand stole out of its own accord to touch his face. He moved like lightning, his large hand clamping around her wrist and stopping her from touching him.

Instead her eyes caressed the hard lines of his face. He was huge, far larger in this form and definitely not human. She'd never seen anything like it. Still humanoid, his skin held a gray tint and each of his fingers was topped with a razor sharp talon, the edge glittering in the light. He looked like a living, breathing statue, beautiful and terrible all at the same time. Totally inhuman.

"Take a good look, Neri." He hauled her up hard against him. Stumbling, she put a hand on his chest to catch her balance.

"Take a good look and tell me if you'd want this to fuck you." His words scalded her, burning through her veins and all the way down to her belly to start a fire. No, not a fire, a blaze. A moan escaped the back of her throat. "Because, make no mistake, if you stay I *will* fuck you."

The moment stretched between them, tighter and tighter, so filled with sexual tension Neri wanted to scream. When she didn't move or struggle to escape, Knuckles' other arm wrapped around her, trapping her, cutting off any chance of escape.

Not only that, something else slithered against her skin to wrap itself around one delicate ankle, something warm and hard, like his skin. She jumped in surprise and looked up into his eyes.

"We have tails," he reminded her, a twinkle in his washed-black-denim eyes. As she watched, his anger dissipated. She giggled as he waggled his eyebrows, gasped as the pressure around her ankle released and the warm tip of his tail stroked higher.

"It is possible...you and me, I mean? You're...uhm...kinda big?" Neri's hands stroked over the rock-like planes of his chest. His skin was warm, hot even, under the pads of her fingers and, oh, so responsive. She could see the goose bumps following her movements. On impulse she dropped her head and placed a kiss against his skin. He gasped sharply and his arms tightened around her. A large hand slid into the nape of her neck, using her hair to pull her head back gently.

She lifted widened eyes to his, a flush covering her cheeks and heat soaking her panties as the tip of his tail slid higher around her thigh. Oh God, she was getting turned on by the thought of sex with a...with a...

Neri couldn't complete the thought. The word she'd been thinking was "animal" but that wasn't right. He wasn't an animal. He was just...different. And no matter what form he wore, his eyes were the same. Eyes that watched her with immeasurable patience and kindness, tempered with a wicked heat that made her weak with hunger.

"Oh yeah, it's more than possible," he said and closed his eyes. Right in front of her he shrank, morphed back to the man she'd first seen with a speed that made her blink.

"Oh," she pouted playfully as his tail uncoiled from her leg and disappeared. "I liked the tail."

Knuckles chuckled, the rich sound filling the small balcony. "Maybe later," he promised, sliding his hand along the length of her hair, arranging it about her slender shoulders with obvious pleasure. "You're so...uhm... I don't want to hurt you."

Neri nodded, catching her lip between her teeth and nibbling. "So *are* we gonna...?"

He smiled. "Oh yeah, we're gonna...We're gonna all over the place. Many, many times," he said, sweeping her up into his arms again to step back through the doorway.

He strode through the door and into the apartment with a determined stride. Her arm wrapped around his shoulders and, when he looked at her, she cast him a smile from under the fall of her dark hair.

There was no hint of fear in her eyes, or the look he saw in those who wanted sex with him because they were paranormal groupies. Or worse, they liked pain and expected him to dish it out, assuming he was into that because of his appearance. There was just honesty and trust in her eyes.

His arms tightened convulsively around her, the possessiveness that was so much a part of his nature making itself known again. Quite why the fates had decided to grant him such a gift he didn't know but he didn't intend to let it slip through his fingers.

He strode straight through into the bedroom, kicking the door shut behind him with his heel. Neri grinned. "Not a guy to mess about with small talk, I take it?"

Knuckles shrugged, letting go of her legs so she could slide down his body. Every soft hollow and curve pressed against him in a delicious feast of sensation. People assumed, because a gargoyle's skin was harder than other species', that they didn't feel as much. They were wrong. Knuckles could feel everything; his skin was as sensitive as any other guy's and just as responsive.

He breathed in a lungful of her scent, the musky scent of an aroused woman overlaid with her perfume and the smell of a floral shampoo. Impossibly, his cock hardened even further.

"Why bother talking?" He bent his head to trail a line of kisses across the delicate skin of her shoulder. His lips caressed the silken skin, moving across until he reached the strap of her bra. One large finger hooked under and slid it down her arm just ahead of his lips. "I can think of far more interesting things to do."

Oh hell, he's good. Neri's knees weakened as the words rumbled against her skin and at the implication, but she forced herself to stay on her feet. She even managed a comeback. "Really? That's good. I can't wait to see what a man of your talents considers more 'interesting'."

Her hands slid over his shoulders, reveling in the expanse of skin and hard muscle. What she was coming out with was total crap—pure waffle. It didn't matter though. The talking was window dressing to physical action, stretching the sexual awareness between them tauter than a bowstring.

"Anticipation…" he told her, smoothing the other strap off her shoulder as his lips continued their maddening journey across her skin. Neri shivered as the butterflies in her stomach started an all-out riot. He'd been so eager to get her into a room with a bed but now he was acting like he had all night. All night to kiss every inch of her skin, those warm lips that wandered now up her throat wandering other places… She moaned as her clit ached at the thought.

"Yeah, just like that, baby… I can smell your need." He chuckled, the sound dirty and knowing. His fingers brushed across her back and her bra was gone. He swept the sides of her ribcage, his thumbs brushing the sensitive curve of her breasts. Her nipples stiffened as though begging for attention. Biting her lip, she looked up at him.

His eyes were dark and hot, the expression on his face tight, as if he was only holding onto control by a thread. A thrill shot through her, and she pushed her shoulders back to display her body to better advantage. She wanted him to like what he was seeing. She wanted him out of control, to want her more than anything in the world.

Jason had always been in control, always smooth, always aware. She knew now he'd never loved her. If she was honest she'd known that from the beginning, once she'd stopped being flattered someone like him would be interested in someone like her.

Jason had only ever seen her as a possession, a status symbol. You couldn't love a possession, you owned a possession, and Neri wasn't interested in being owned. She wanted to be loved. She wanted her partner to want *her,* her as a person, not as a thing.

"Fuck, you're gorgeous," he rumbled, reverence and desire in his eyes. He pulled her closer again, one hand fanning out over her back and holding her easily as he bent her over. His other hand cupped her breast, a gentle caress which offered her nipple up to his lips. Neri gasped as he pulled it into the warm cavern of his mouth and suckled.

A line of fire raced between her nipples and her aching pussy as he paid attention to first one, then the other. She writhed in his embrace, her hands clutching his upper arms, unable to stay still. His touch was addictive. She needed…no, she *craved* more.

Her soft moans made him chuckle, made him harder. He used his tongue to lave the tight bud under his lips just to see her gasp and shudder again. She was so responsive his slightest touch made her gasp in pleasure and arch against him.

He knew he wasn't a Casanova, but every second with Neri in his arms made him feel like some sort of sex god. His male pride bloomed as he picked her up. Instinctively she clung to him, as though she couldn't bear to be parted even for the spilt second it took him to crawl onto the bed with her.

Knuckles laid her down gently, stretching out at her side with his weight on his forearm as he leaned over her. "You're beautiful," he murmured again as he kissed her. This time he didn't hold back. He wanted all of her, everything she had to give. He kissed her like he wanted to crawl inside her and never leave.

Beneath him Neri moaned, the sound lost into his mouth as she opened up for him. His lips nibbled and caressed, his tongue teasing hers as his hands smoothed down her body. Without breaking the kiss he hooked a thumb into the lace of her panties and pulled them down her legs.

"Better," he whispered against her lips. He pulled away to look deep into her eyes as his hand trailed back up her leg. It smoothed along her calf, flirted with the sensitive skin behind her knee and slid across the front. She bit her lip, pulling the plump flesh between her teeth as he trailed his fingers up her inner thigh. Locked in his gaze she parted her legs on his unspoken command, anticipation coursing through her.

He smiled as he reached the juncture of her thighs. Neri's breathing caught then held as he parted the folds of her sex and slid a finger between them. He found her clit in a slow sweep, smiling as her hips jerked and her breath left her in a rush.

"Like that, do you?" His question was a soft whisper of sound against her throat as he leaned down. He kissed along the soft skin as his finger circled and stroked her clit, driving her arousal higher.

"Uh-huh" was all she could manage as her hips bucked against his hand. Somehow he knew exactly where and how to touch her to send her up in flames. "Yeah, th–that's nice."

The world had contracted to just the two of them on the bed and then even further, to just his voice and the press of his fingers against her needy flesh.

"Hmm, just nice, eh? How about this?" As he spoke, the wonderful pressure of his finger against her clit disappeared. Neri pursed her lips into a pout of disappointment, but then her breath was stolen as he slid his finger deep inside her.

"*Fucking hell…* You're so wet…and tight." A second finger joined the first. Neri almost came right away as he twisted them gently inside her, stretching her and preparing her body for penetration by his.

The room filled with soft gasps and moans, every response encouraging him onwards. A fine trembling started in her limbs as the heat in her belly increased, and her body clenched hard around his invading digits with her impending orgasm. Each stroke of his thumb over her clit and thrust of his fingers inside her pushed her higher and higher, nearer the edge.

She bit her lip as she reached for his hand, her slender fingers trying to loop around his thick wrist. "I can't take much more. Please…"

"Let it go, baby." He kissed her again, his lips clinging as he swept his thumb over her needy body. Neri shivered, the temptation to do as he said and let it all wash over her, let him take care of it for her, filling her. She shook her head, a flush covering her cheeks.

"No, please, I want you inside me when I come."

His answering smile in the half-light was immediate, and Neri knew she'd given the right answer. "Well, if that's what the lady wants, who am I to argue?"

He shifted position, raising his body above her to rest his weight on his hands. His broad shoulders blocked out her view of the rest of the world. It didn't matter, because her world now *was* him. A knee nudged her legs wider as he settled between them, and then he was there, a dip of his hips and the swollen head of his cock pressed against the slick entrance to her body.

Neri gasped, feeling the delicate flesh start to part and stretch around him. Then she frowned. "You had pants on!"

"I did, now I don't. Paranormal, remember? We're full of surprises." Knuckles chuckled as he pushed forward with his hips and stole Neri's next breath. She closed her eyes, all her attention concentrated on their bodies and where they joined. He was big… No, big wasn't the word. He was *huge.*

"Breathe, baby." His voice was soft by her ear as he kissed along her neck. "It'll feel better soon, I promise."

She managed a nod, biting her lip. She hoped that was true because at the moment it felt like he was damn well splitting her in two. Taking a deep breath, she tried to relax as he pushed deeper in a slow, relentless movement—a slick slide that stretched her in ways she'd never dreamed of. They both gasped when he bottomed out, filling her to the hilt. He whispered sweet nothings in her ear, and his hands smoothed over her body—gentle, reassuring touches which were full of concern.

"How's that?"

Something in his voice told her he'd already asked once, and she hadn't answered. He held himself so still it had to be hurting him.

Like I've been impaled on a bloody iron bar? She opened her eyes and smiled at him. The fleeting pain had worn off, leaving just an incredible feeling of fullness and a growing need to move. So she did, rocking her hips just a little. Pleasure hit her like a juggernaut, her moan mingling with his as her movement stroked intimate nerve endings and sent them into meltdown.

"Fuck, yeah, that's good." The cords stood out in his neck and shoulders. She could feel the tension in his body as he fought against moving. She knew him well enough even in this short space to know he was trying not to hurt her. Tenderness flooded her heart. He might look like a thug but she'd never had such a considerate lover. Jason had only ever been interested in his own pleasure, hers had been incidental.

"You gonna spend all night talking or fuck me like you promised?" she teased.

His grin was quick, a flash of white teeth in the gloom of the bedroom, and he mock-growled. "You want fucking? Like, proper fucking?"

It was a rhetorical question. In the next moment he started to move. Bracing his hands on either side of her head he pulled out of her and slid back in until his balls slapped against her ass. Neri's eyes rolled back in her head as he pressed and stroked nerve endings in her channel that had never been touched before. Her own excitement made things easier, coating his cock as he slid in and out.

"Oh, God. Yeah, proper fucking."

She didn't get a chance to catch her breath after that. He slid an arm under her neck, holding her still as his hips drove against hers. He drove into her again, filling her over and over until she was moaning his name in mindless pleasure. She'd never been taken with such thoroughness, and yet he was still gentle with her.

His movements were powerful, yes, but Neri knew all about the difference between power and cruelty. Once you'd experienced the one, you never mistook it for the other again.

His grunts joined her moans in the silence of the room, and through her pleasure-filled delirium, she felt his movements change. She kissed along his clenched jaw and wrapped her knees higher around his hips.

She was so close it was unreal, the tension in her own body at fever pitch. Every hard thrust he hammered home pushed her toward that precipice. Desperately she held on, wanting to wait for him.

"Please…now. I want to feel you come inside me," she begged, her lips clinging to his.

Her soft words were the last straw for Knuckles. He'd tried hard to hold out, but her body was like a silken vise around his cock. He could already feel the ripples of her impending orgasm, and it was driving him out of his mind. He grunted, the shackles he'd imposed on himself falling away.

Driven by need, he slid an arm under her hips to drag her closer. She gasped in pleasure but Knuckles barely heard her; his own release was so close he could hear it roaring in his ears. With gasps that bordered on grunts he loosed his control and drove into her, seeking his release in her warm and willing body.

Writhing in his arms, Neri cried out, his name on her lips as she came. Knuckles' eyes crossed as her body clenched hard around him, milking his already fit to burst cock. His heart pounded. He slammed into her again but it was game over. Muttering a curse, he stiffened as his release hit him with the force of a small truck, his cock pulsing as he came deep within her.

Chapter Five

Neri slept peacefully. Knuckles couldn't take his eyes off her. Curled up on his chest, she had her head on his shoulder, which couldn't be comfortable. However, she seemed to prefer using him as a bed instead of the one they lay on.

He smiled. His arm wrapped around her and he used a gentle finger to push a wayward curl away from her face. Closing his eyes, he savored the feeling of her in his arms. Behind him the light creeping around the curtains told him dawn would be here soon. He dropped a kiss on her dark hair, putting off the moment when he would have to leave her to sleep on her own. Like most of his kind he was at the mercy of the sun. As soon as it rose he would be forced into his true form and frozen into stone until darkness fell.

Neri sighed and wriggled closer. Her arm draped over his chest. She reminded him of the old cat Mac had adopted when he'd lived here, a creature which appeared to be able to get comfortable over any surface. Knuckles smiled. She reminded him of a cat, all sharp movements and catlike stretches to go with the exotic, slanted eyes. He wouldn't have been surprised to hear her purr.

Opening his eyes he watched as the glow behind the curtain grew brighter. He sighed and gently disengaged Neri's hold. His time had run out. With reluctance he slid from the bed and looked down at her, trying to imprint her image on his memory. She was beautiful. Like an angel from heaven, a beautiful sleeping angel he'd been fortunate enough to touch for a short while.

Trying not to harbor the hope that she would still be here when he woke up, Knuckles turned and walked out of the bedroom.

* * *

The day passed slowly. Knuckles, encased in stone by the sunlight, was only aware of it in a passing sense. "Sun slavery" his kind called it, and it affected them all. Well, almost all. There were tales, more myths in Knuckles' opinion, that some gargoyles were free.

The key? As in the best fairy tales…true love. Knuckles snorted in amusement whenever anyone mentioned it. He believed in reality, the here and now, things he could touch and feel. The idea that love could break the hold of the sun was madness. He might as well try the "sun-block" the backstreet wizards hawked. That didn't work either, except as vermin control for naive vamps.

The sun began to set and on the ledge next to the balcony Knuckles started to stir. Stone cracked and moved. Knuckles' eyes opened as the sun sank past the horizon. With a patience born of years of practice he waited for his limbs to ease up and lose their leadenness. The heavy claws on his feet dug into the ledge, punching through the concrete to latch onto the steel bars within as he stretched his wings and welcomed the night.

Filling his lungs with the crisp air, Knuckles rolled his shoulders and hopped off the ledge. By the time he'd dropped to the balcony floor his feet, and the rest of him, were human, or as human as he got anyway.

He was already pushing the balcony door open when the first stirring of unease hit him. Something was wrong. Something was very wrong. The feeling crept into his bones and washed over him like a malignant whisper. Eyes narrowing, he stepped through the door and into the small apartment.

The place had been ransacked. It was a mess.

Not the usual "bachelor pad" kind of mess. This was the full on "you've been done over by a gang of thieves" look. Every drawer and cupboard in the place had been opened, and the contents strewn all over the place.

Knuckles ignored the mess, treading it underfoot as he walked through the main area. Alarm coiled in his chest and wrapped around his heart, tapping out a warning beat as he got further into the apartment. There was something wrong; the burglary was too obvious. It was like the perpetrators had a copy of the cop's tick sheet; forced entry—check, electronic items missing—check… Knuckles strode through into the bedroom.

As soon as he looked at the bed, the bed he'd shared with Neri, all his instincts went into overdrive. It was rumpled, the covers half off, and the pillows were strewn around the room. *Okay, calm down. This could be innocent; she could have left before these yahoos arrived. She's fine.*

Then he saw one of her shoes peeking out from under the duvet, and his bellow of rage shook the building's foundations.

* * *

"It's that bastard Carrick. I *told* you he'd screw up sooner or later," Jaren snarled as he paced the small office like a caged tiger.

Knuckles, squeezed into the chair in front of the desk, felt like joining him, only willpower keeping his ass in the chair. That and an appreciation of just how much building work cost these days. The club was old and solidly built but it still wasn't up to dealing with an out-of-control gargoyle. There wasn't much that *was* up to dealing with a gargoyle on a rampage, not even a maximum security cell.

Knuckles' huge frame was taut with rage as he waited. It was a rage so complete the air around him all but crackled with it. The potential for his change coiled just under his skin, warning anyone with the right instincts that he was about to lose it big time. A rage so intense it put Jaren's spitting anger—and Knuckles had never seen the normally cool, calm and collected incubus so mad—on par with a childhood temper tantrum.

"And you're sure she couldn't have left early and made her own way home while you slept?" Daelas, who sat on the other side of the desk, asked. His voice was calm, his tone considering, the opposite of the irritation in his twin's pacing.

Knuckles bit down a snarl as frustration bubbled up and threatened to choke him. Daelas wasn't questioning his word; it was just, like Knuckles, he was having trouble believing someone had broken in with the gargoyle outside the room and Jaren downstairs.

The snarl deep in his chest escaped, rumbling around the room like the heavy bass did in the club. Carrick was an arrogant bastard. First he'd set his bully boy on an innocent woman, and now he'd staged a kidnapping on Knuckles' territory. Not things the big gargoyle took lightly. They were the sort of things he was happy to rip arms and legs off over...

A small hand landed on his shoulder and squeezed in reassurance. Knuckles started. He hadn't heard anyone move behind him, which was unusual with his hearing. He looked up into the kind eyes of Sage—Daelas and Jaren's mate. She held his gaze for a moment and a sense of peace settled over him, before she turned to the two incubi.

"She left her shoes." She nodded to the strappy sandals—exhibit A—which sat on the desk in front of Daelas. "Believe me, no woman forgets her shoes. Not with how much those babies would've cost anyway."

"It's that fuckup Carrick, I tell you," Jaren snapped from the doorway, obviously pissed off with the debate now. "When I find him I'm gonna rip his arms and legs off."

"Get in line." Knuckles' deep voice filled the room. "You can have what's left."

Daelas sighed. " *Children!* We have to find him first!"

Knuckles picked up one of the sandals; it was tiny in his hand. "Won't be a problem," he said as he touched the soft satin. He just wanted to touch something of hers and feel a sense of connection.

Despite the seriousness of the situation nothing kept Jaren in a bad mood for long. "Shoulda told me you had a fetish, man. I'd have put you in lost property with the Cinderella box."

Knuckles just growled in response and extended his middle finger, a silent but effective method of communication. The tall incubus didn't take offense, just grinned and retreated to the French doors leading onto the balcony, leaning against the doorjamb with his customary, effortless grace.

Knuckles turned his attention to the shoe. Closing his eyes he concentrated, taking himself back to last night, back to having Neri in his arms…her scent as he nuzzled her neck. Instantly it all came back to him, as though she were there right in front of him.

It was a scent imprinted on his memory. He'd know it anywhere, unique and perfect like the woman herself. He breathed deeply, savoring the memories: the smell and texture of her skin, the soft sounds of pleasure she made and the silken heat of her body as it wrapped around his cock like a tight fist.

"Down, boy," Jaren teased, his chuckle dirty and knowing. Knuckles' eyes flicked open and he treated Jaren to a nasty glare. Bloody incubi and their senses. What with these two and the siren down on the floor, a guy couldn't even think about getting a hard-on without someone teasing him about it.

"I can track her… Neri. I can track Neri."

Knuckles flicked a glance around the small group, then looked back at Daelas and Jaren. He was going after her regardless. However, he did feel a sense of obligation to his employers…although the staff at Moonlight & Magic were more of a family than anything he'd had before. They'd taken him in and given him a job. They'd given him a place to belong, a place to guard. To a gargoyle that was as good a commitment as getting married and raising two point four kids in a house with a white picket fence.

Daelas read the unspoken question and nodded. "Jaren, go with him. Take Tiny as well. We'll hold the fort here… I shouldn't think you'd have any trouble with Carrick's goons, ugly bastards the lot of them, but human. All the same, you have a problem, call for backup. Understand?"

Knuckles levered himself out of his chair, a smile pulling across his features. "We won't need backup."

* * *

Shrouded in darkness on a downtown rooftop, the three men from Moonlight & Magic watched the closed and shuttered warehouse they'd tracked Neri to. "Men" was a loose description; all three were undeniably male, but only Tiny could hold any true claim to humanity.

"Yeah, she's in there, all right. Trail goes cold here." Knuckles' voice was lower and rougher when in his true form.

Jaren lounged against the maintenance hatch, arms folded over his broad chest. Dressed head to toe in black and with a grim look on his usually smiling face he cut a dangerous-looking figure.

Knuckles was used to seeing him at the club, in all out charm mode, so it was weird to be reminded that the brothers were demons. They might not be on the nastier end of the demon scale like the torac or the azeash, but even an incubus could kick ass when the situation called for it.

Tiny, though, was less nonchalant. Where Jaren seemed unaffected by the situation and the fact they were about to charge in to the rescue, Tiny's heavily muscled frame radiated tension. Dark eyes intent, he studied the building opposite.

"One entrance and exit," he stated, standing fluidly. Like the rest of the staff at Moonlight & Magic, when in the club Tiny made an effort to walk and talk human but out here he didn't bother. His movements held the sort of fluidity and grace which hinted that the usual humanoid skeletal structure was optional for him. Not for the first time Knuckles wondered exactly what the non-human part of Tiny was.

"I don't like this. I smell a trap."

Jaren laughed. "From Carrick? Give me a break. The guy thinks he's a player, but he couldn't organize a drinking contest in a brewery. And even if he did manage to set something up, he's human. His goons are human. They wouldn't know what to do with a paranormal if one bit him on the ass."

"He got into the club and snatched the girl, didn't he?" Tiny's comment wasn't challenging or antagonistic, but it drove the point home.

Jaren winced. "Yeah, sheer fluke. We concentrated so much on wards and crap, defenses against paranormals, that we didn't guard against humans. We didn't think we'd have a problem there. Everyone *knows* what we are. But Daelas is working on alarms today to stop this happening again."

Knuckles shifted impatiently, frustration mounting in his chest. The heavy claws on his feet rasped across the concrete of the rooftop. "We bustin' this joint or are we gonna stand around talking all night?" he demanded, the need to find Neri forming a deep knot in the center of his body.

"Yeah, enough talk. Take us up then, big guy. Drop Tiny on the other roof. See if you can find another way in. Doesn't hurt to have a backup plan."

Knuckles unfurled his wings and spread them out with a small sigh. It felt good to stretch and feel the night breezes against the sensitive membranes. He flexed his wings and beat the air, the powerful muscles in his shoulders bunching and releasing.

Tensing his legs under him, he used the powerful muscles in his thighs and calves and sprang into the air. He easily caught the updraft from the street below and let it fill his wings. The next instant his claws were full of cloth as he grabbed his companions and dropped off the edge of the roof.

Chapter Six

"Wakey, wakey, sleeping beauty."

The soft, teasing voice broke through the darkness surrounding her. Despite the amused, almost loving tone, one that would have had most women smiling and snuggling down deeper into the covers, Neri stiffened in wariness. An automatic reaction to a voice she recognized.

Jason's voice, and she didn't trust that fake loving tone as far as she could throw it or him. Come to think of it, she'd *like* to throw Jason...under a bus for preference. How the hell had she gotten here? The last thing she remembered was Knuckles' apartment...

Unfortunately, even though common sense told her to fake unconsciousness until she knew what was going on, the small movement of her body had already given her away.

"She's awake. Time to get on with the show, I think."

Neri opened her eyes and groaned as a stabbing pain assaulted her. Her head hurt like hell and nausea rose in her throat as she tried to focus.

"Hmm, I think Carlos may have hit you a little hard there." Jason stood over her, smiling. As always he was dressed sharply, but there was something about him, something different. Neri frowned as she tried to work out what.

"Would explain the headache then," she replied in a flat tone, as though being hit by one of his bully boys was an everyday occurrence. She gave up on studying him, instead tried lifting her hands to her head. Then Jason and any difference in his personal style, real or imagined, ceased to be important.

She was tied up tighter than a bloody hog roast.

Fear flooded through her as she yanked on the cords around her wrists. "Jason, what the fuck is going on?"

He looked down at her, enjoying her discomfiture, his blue eyes alight with amusement and the charm that covered the darker aspects of his personality.

"I do apologize for the crude restraints, but I can't have you running off in the middle of what promises to be a highly entertaining party." He knelt down next to her and grinned, a grin which contained sharper teeth than she remembered, especially around the canine region.

"Shit..." She exploded into movement and tried to wriggle away, wishing she could scurry back as far as possible. Her eyes fixed on him as fear crawled up her spine to hammer on the back of her skull. "You're a vampire!"

He preened. "I have been elevated to that status now, yes. It's been a long time coming, but my potential has been recognized. I just have one small task to carry out, a task which you, my dear, are going to help me with."

That was so not happening. She wouldn't help Jason if he were the last man on Earth.

"Over my dead body," Neri told him, resignation threading through her fear. Knuckles turning up to rescue her would be the answer to her prayers, but miracles didn't happen to people like her. She'd always had to fight tooth and nail for any break she got, and if things could screw up, they did. She was going to die whatever way she looked at it, but she'd be damned if she was going to help Jason in any way, shape or form.

His smile chilled her. Another difference she'd been trying to put her finger on hit her. His eyes were different. Behind the amused blue there was something else, something hungry.

"That's not going to be a problem—" he started, but the rest of his sentence was cut off by a horrendous crash somewhere out of sight. His head snapped up and he smiled, a slow, terrible smile that had Neri's heart flipping over in her chest. She knew without asking that things were about to get a whole lot worse.

"Seems our guests have arrived, Carlos. Show them in, won't you?"

Her back still to the wall, Neri looked around and took in where she was for the first time. The mattress she sat on was in the corner of some kind of warehouse, one complete with containers across the opposite wall. However, none of this held her attention.

No, that privilege was reserved for Jason and his gang of merry men. She frowned. They'd cleared a space at this end of the building and had set up some sort of stage area. As she watched, two men were setting up spotlights on the edges of the space, all pointing inwards.

"Planning a little song and dance, Jason?" she asked to cover her confusion. What kind of guy kidnapped you for a show? "I didn't know you were into the arts. I hope you can dance better than you can sing. I've heard you in the shower, remember?"

She had a bad feeling about this, one reinforced when her former lover turned and gave her a smile that lifted the hairs on the back of her neck.

"Oh, I'm not going to be performing. You, Neri my dear, are going to be one of the star attractions."

Uh-oh. Neri scrambled to her feet, using her bound hands to grab whatever purchase she could on the wall behind her.

"Not a chance, Jason. I'm done doing anything for you. You handed me over to Neil to fucking die, remember?" she spat, fighting through her fear as a door somewhere in the building crashed open. At the same time, somewhere in the opposite direction another snarl sounded, one of fury. Jason lifted an eyebrow.

"Interesting, they brought a demon. Never mind. It just makes this far more fun. And don't swear at me, my dear, I don't like it," he chastised as, in the next breath, his cold hand closed around her throat.

Neri gasped and stiffened as his sharp, claw-like nails scraped against her throat. She hadn't seen him move. That was the thing about vampires—what made them so dangerous—they could move faster than the human eye could register. Stuff like that was all over the new "Keep safe after dark" leaflets they handed out at women's self-defense classes. Hell, at any self-defense classes. Vamps were equal opportunity when it came to opening veins: male, female, adult or child. Some of them didn't care as long as the red stuff flowed. The days of pepper spray and a personal alarm in your purse being all you needed were long gone. Now it was all holy water and personal protection spells from a spell warden. If you could afford them, amulets worked well, but good amulets were hellishly expensive.

"Show time," Jason announced, his breath fanning over Neri's face. It stank of old blood and death. She gagged, trying to turn her face away.

The door behind them crashed open. It was less the door opening and more the door disintegrating in the frame, as something hard hit it from the other side. The dust settled, revealing that something hard. A massive figure—an unmistakable figure—stood framed by the ruins of the door.

Knuckles.

Neri's breath caught as he walked from the shadows. No, not walked. He stalked. She hadn't seen him fully in the light on the small balcony at his apartment, but she was seeing him now.

Jason misread her gasp. "Yeah, disgusting, isn't he?"

Neri ignored him; she only had eyes for Knuckles. He was magnificent. Tall, well over seven feet, he had the body of a... Well, she'd say a Greek god but that would be clichéd. Heavily muscled and defined, he could have given any superstar a run for their money in the sheer sex appeal market. Okay, so his ankles were odd and the feet...definitely not human. Nothing human had claws that clicked and scraped the concrete as he walked. The differences didn't stop there. The wings folded along his back—hooked tops visible over his massive shoulders—and the tail lashing around his legs gave the non-human game away as well.

"No, he's beautiful," she murmured. Her eyes ate him up as he stopped in the middle of the space, dominating it, and looking around at the meager forces Jason had managed to marshal. Contempt filled his eyes.

"This all you could manage, Carrick? A couple of pathetic demon traps and a bunch of badass wannabes?" His voice was low, a rumble which hit Neri low in her ears, rasping against her eardrum like a heavy bass beat in a club.

Despite the situation, heat filled her, shooting through her bloodstream and settling in her center. Christ, what was it about the guy that just his voice could turn her on? Then she realized it wasn't his *normal* voice—or his more human voice anyway. It was the deep rumble of his natural voice.

She looked around realizing Knuckles was right. A grin stole over her face. The odds were not stacked in Jason's favor. She didn't know much about gargoyles, they were one of the more mysterious of the Night Races, but even she could see Knuckles was built to fight.

Heavy claws topped each finger on his hands and on each of his toes. Compact muscle covered every plane of his body and he moved...oh, the way he moved. Neri could feel herself getting wet just looking at him. More than being built that way, he knew how to fight. It was obvious in the way he carried himself, the way his eyes tracked his opponents. She had no doubt he was aware of every person in the room.

Even as she thought it, she knew something was off, something was wrong. She knew Jason and despite the new transformation to the "evil undead," he was still the same person underneath it all. Right about now he should be blustering, doing the whole macho routine to convince Knuckles, the other men in the room, and himself that he really was the badass he pretended to be.

Yet he was calm, his body relaxed where he held her pinned against him. Then he nodded and the room plunged into darkness for a second before a spotlight snapped on, trained on Knuckles. She blinked at the sudden change in lighting, still not sure what was going on. Two of Jason's bully boys stepped into the ring of bright light, sledgehammers in their hands.

"You know the thing about gargoyles, don't you, my dear?" Jason asked, his voice smug. "Get them in the sunlight, or under high intensity sunlamps in this case, and they're just stone to be broken up and reclaimed."

They were going to kill him.

Neri's heart stopped in her chest. No, this couldn't be happening. Surely a man—she refused to think of him as a creature—as strong as Knuckles couldn't be defeated by something as simple as a few sun lamps and a couple of hammers? Life couldn't be *that* unfair, could it?

A low growl split the air, drawing her attention, and she looked straight into Knuckles' eyes. Apology filled them as his body started to freeze into place, the sun lamps rendering his limbs to stone and a dull gray tint spreading up over his body. As she watched, he turned into a statue.

The guys with the hammers moved into place, swinging the implements of Knuckles' death high up over their shoulders.

"You shouldn't have left me, Neri; no one *ever* leaves me," Jason whispered as his grip on her neck tightened. A tear broke away, leaving a wet trail down her cheek as Jason tilted her head. "Now the last thing he'll see is me ripping your throat out."

Inside Neri, deep inside, something cracked. There was no more fear of her own imminent demise, which some might have found odd, but she'd always known she would die young. Orphaned and shunted through the social services system, she'd ended up living by her wits on the streets. It was only a matter of time before she ended up a statistic on some homicide sheet somewhere. It broke her heart to bring Knuckles down with her. All he'd done was offer her kindness. He didn't deserve to be involved in Jason's sick games.

"I love you," she mouthed as the gray stone creeping over his body reached his neck, wanting the last thing he saw to be love shining in her eyes.

Because—unbelievably—she loved him. She'd gone from being someone who didn't believe in love to falling in love at first sight. The irony wasn't lost on her, and she closed her eyes as she felt Jason's tongue rasp along the skin of her throat. She didn't want Knuckles to watch the life drain out of her eyes.

"I'm sorry," she whispered, somehow managing to force the words out past the huge knot which had taken up residence in her throat. She didn't know whether he would hear her but she had to say the words.

Jason's teeth pressed into her skin and she whimpered, terror filling her at last. This was going to hurt. A lot. Knowing Jason he would string out her agony as long as possible just for the fun of it.

A tremendous crack, like gunfire, sounded. Neri's eyes snapped open to stare at the ceiling as Jason lifted his head. "What the fuck?"

Another crack, and then another. What were they doing, using shotguns on Knuckles as well? Weren't the sledgehammers enough? Jason's grip relaxed. Instantly her eyes went to the bully boys with the hammers, but they hadn't moved.

They were frozen into place, matching looks of surprise on their faces. Neri followed their gazes to Knuckles, expecting to see him frozen into immobility. He was and he wasn't. The "stone" covered him from head to toe except for his eyes. His eyes stared back at her—no, at *Jason,* and the hatred in them made her shiver.

Crrrr—acckk.

The sound went off again, sending a spider web of cracks over Knuckles' stone-bound body. As she watched, the stone on his left arm crumbled and fell away, leaving the limb free.

"Now, on the whole, sun lamps... I gotta give it to ya, man, that's sneaky." A new voice broke into the conversation, and a tall, blond man stepped from the shadows. Neri held her breath. She'd seen him at the club earlier. He'd seemed to be one of the bosses, handsome, charming...and totally suicidal. He didn't seem to be the sort who was handy with his fists at all. He was glib-tongued, but one lucky blow was going to spread that classic nose all over his face.

He didn't seem concerned by the predicament he was in, casting a nonchalant glance toward Knuckles, who was flexing all the muscles in his body and cracking the stone holding him prisoner like a thin layer of plaster.

"Wha... That's not possible," Jason argued. "Hey, you two, grab him," he ordered, motioning at the sledgehammer-carrying minions.

"Oh, sorry. They aren't going to be much good to you now. They're mentally replaying every sick and twisted little fantasy they've ever had but as the victim. You know the saying; do unto others as you would wish?" He grinned. "You bet they're wishing they'd paid attention to it now."

Neri could feel the anger vibrating through Jason's body as his plan fell apart. "So who the fuck are you? And do you know who I am?"

Blondie smiled. "Oh, I know who you are. Jason Carrick, the dumb shit idiotic enough to take a gargoyle's mate."

"Mate? You mean you fucked him?" Jason demanded, shaking Neri so hard her eyeballs rattled in her skull. "You sick whore! He's an animal. They all are."

She chuckled, the sound emerging as little more than a squeak thanks to the cruel grip he had on her throat. She turned her head and looked him in the eye, a sense of power filling her.

"Yeah, I did. And you know what? It was *good,* Jason, better than anything I've ever had. Now kill me if you're going to, or fuck off before Knuckles gets out, because he's going to rip you limb from limb, wannabe vampire or not."

It felt good, damn good, to be taking control. It was probably the last thing she would do since Jason had a hair-trigger temper and would likely tear her throat out in the next three seconds, but even so, it was liberating. She smiled, reading the confusion in Jason's eyes.

Crack...craaaa-cck...

"Tick-tock, tick-tock," Blondie said behind her. "Run, Carrick. See if you can outrun a feral gargoyle. I hear they're like greyhounds when their women are threatened. And you know the best bit about 'em?"

"Vampire bites do fuck all." Knuckles' gravelly voice filled the silence, making the vampire jump.

Everything happened too fast for Neri to take it all in then. Something hit them at speed, throwing her to one side as Jason was wrenched off her. The next second, Blondie from the club steadied her and set her back on her feet. As soon as he touched her, a sense of calm wrapped around her. The effect was so marked she realized it; there was no way she'd calm down this quickly on her own. No, right about now she'd be going into hysterics, or should be anyway.

She looked up, right into one of the most handsome faces she'd ever seen, as he undid her wrists. It was the sort of face which should have graced a catwalk, or pouted from the pages of a glossy magazine. But even though she'd have taken a second or third look at that magazine in the past, she felt nothing, no pull of attraction, nothing.

"Not human either?"

"Nope, not remotely. Incubus." He grinned, a flash of white teeth in a charming smile.

"Ahh…" She didn't get to say anything else. The short conversation was broken up by the sounds of violence behind them. Jason screamed. It had to be Jason; there was no way Knuckles would have managed such a high pitch with his voice. A scream was followed by wet tearing sounds she didn't want to think about. Then everything went silent. She looked up at the tall man next to her, who was looking into the shadows.

"Err, is that it?" she asked, confused by his nonchalant stance beside her. "What about them?" she nodded toward the two men with the hammers, both locked into place like a bad waxworks display. "Are they okay?"

"If they are, they soon won't be," her companion replied with a grim smile. "And I'm a lover not a fighter. Besides, Knuckles seems to have everything under control."

"Under control? *Under control?* " Neri lost her temper, her voice rising in anger. It seemed her little outburst at Jason had opened the floodgates, and there was no going back now. No more Ms. Mousey for Neri. No, from now on she was going for the throat.

"What part of Knuckles about to be smashed apart with sledgehammers counts as *under control?* They nearly killed him," she ranted as she tried to hold onto her temper and failed. Her fingers itched to wrap around his throat and throttle him for being so blasé about the danger her man had been in. The feeling was so strong she actually started to lift her hands.

He stepped back before she could touch him. "Why would he need me when you're here to release him from sun slavery? And I'd appreciate it if you didn't touch me. Not with the mood Knuckles is in. I kinda like my limbs where they are."

Neri dropped her hands and frowned. "Me release him? What are you talking about? I thought you'd cast a spell or something to break all the stone off him."

Blondie gave her such a look of surprise and disgust a chuckle was startled out of Neri. "A spell? Have I got 'Warden' tattooed across my damn forehead?"

"Warden?"

"Ugh…a wizard? We call them wardens—" he explained, pausing mid-sentence as his gaze slid behind her. He went very, very still. Inhumanly still. If Neri had to describe it, she would have said this guy was the one who turned to stone in the day, not Knuckles. Then she became aware of the silence behind them.

The screams had stopped. All that was left was silence and the feeling of being watched, the feeling of being watched intently.

"Okay, I'm going to back up very slowly now." Blondie's voice held a hint of nerves. "Whatever you do, don't run. Gargoyles like to chase."

"Huh? What do you mean 'chase'?" Neri asked, starting to turn in the direction he was looking.

A pair of eyes flashed in the darkness. Dangerous looking eyes which were trained directly on her.

Chapter Seven

Neri swallowed. "Knuckles?"

Her voice emerged as little more than a whisper. There was nothing human in that silver gaze as his eyes caught the light, a reminder that he was a night predator.

"Don't panic. You'll be fine." Blondie's voice reassured her from the other side of the room. "You're probably the safest person in here right now. He won't harm you."

Neri flicked a glance over her shoulder. "You sure? I don't think he even knows who—" She stopped speaking as the air beside her moved and a prickle up the back of her spine warned her someone was nearby.

Shit, he was right next to her.

Neri squeaked in surprise and maybe a little fright as Knuckles loomed over her. How the hell had he moved so fast?

"Oh, he knows who you are, all right. Do me a favor and keep him occupied, would you? They can be violent when they're like that, and as I said before, I like my arms and legs where they are."

Neri locked her knees as she looked up at Knuckles to prevent landing in a pathetic little heap on the floor. She'd seen him in his natural form before but never like this. Before, she'd always been able to see the man in his eyes before, but now she could only see the feral gaze of the creature inside.

She took a tiny step backwards, an action which drew a grumble of warning from Knuckles' massive chest. "Great, so we just let him rip my arms and legs off instead. Sorry, handsome, but your plan sucks. Big time," she quipped, swallowing a "meep" as Knuckles lifted a hand to her hair, expecting to see blood and gore on his hands, but they were clean. How, she didn't know, but she was grateful for small mercies.

He wound the strands around, letting them slide through his fingers with every evidence of pleasure. Then he pulled her closer, yanking her into his arms so he could bury his nose in the tumbled mass of her hair.

"Mine."

Blondie's chuckle was dirty and knowing. "He's more likely to tear your clothes off and screw you on the floor. So if you can slow him down a little that would be great. Last thing I want is to see Ugly there butt nekkid. I'd have to bleach my eyeballs."

"Oh." The penny dropped for Neri with a resounding crash, like a truckload of cymbals had been dropped in a library. "Ohhh..."

The grip of her hands splayed out over his bulging biceps, changed and became less of a grasp for balance and more of a caress. He tilted his head and looked at her questioningly, as though unable to work out the change in her.

She stroked his hard skin. She'd been fascinated as soon as she realized he had more than one form. Did that make her some sort of shape shifter pervert? She'd liked the tail; that was for sure. As though thinking about it summoned it into existence, something warm wrapped around her ankle, looping and holding fast.

"Hey there, big guy. It's Neri. Remember me?" She smoothed a hand over his cheek and talked for the sake of it, saying anything she could think of to bring him back. His hand spread over her back in answer as he tipped her backwards. His lips nuzzled her neck, and the warm, wet rasp of his tongue against the skin there made her jump and melt as liquid heat flooded her body.

Oh, hell yes, she was definitely a pervert. Here he was struggling with the darker side of his nature, and all she could think of was how good his tongue would feel over her clit or plunging into her pussy.

"Hmmm..." The rumble of interest made Neri blush as he slid a hand down her spine to her ass. He cupped it and hauled her hips hard against his. Her eyes widened at the bulging hardness pressing into her belly. Christ, he was huge. Well, she knew that, but like this he was even bigger. There was no way all that would fit inside her.

She bit her lip, desire and fear warring inside her. He could obviously smell her excitement, but she didn't want it to be like this, with him not knowing who she was. It wasn't right.

He locked eyes with her again and the feral interest gave way to something else. As she watched, the feral light faded, and a more human intelligence leeched into his eyes. Dropping his head, he buried his face in the curve of her shoulder. A huge shudder racked him as he changed back to the human form she was used to, a full body shudder which covered every inch of his skin like he stood on a vibrating plate.

Concern filled Neri, banishing her arousal to the corners of her mind. "Knuckles, you okay, sweetheart?" *Please let him be okay, he has to be okay. Please let him recognize me,* she prayed and held her breath. Relief hit her hard as familiar washed-black-denim eyes met hers. Knuckles smiled.

"I'm okay now." His arms tightened around her possessively. "I thought I'd lost you. That he...was going to kill you, and I couldn't do anything to stop him..." He shuddered, darkness entering his eyes again.

She nodded, emotion coursing through her as she smoothed her hands over his massive shoulders, trying to comfort him. "I'm so, so sorry to put you through all this." Her cheeks burned with embarrassment.

His arms tightened around her and he slid a finger under her chin to make her look up. "You didn't drag me in. As I recall, I destroyed half a wall to get in here to you," he pointed out with a nod toward the ruined doorway, which was when Neri realized they were alone. Blondie and the waxworks had pulled a disappearing act.

Alone. With a hot man...errr, gargoyle. Neri's smile turned naughty as she pressed closer. They said that people who'd been in danger of their lives felt the need to indulge in pleasure—eating, drinking, having sex—to reassure themselves they were alive. It was a theory Neri intended to test thoroughly at the first opportunity.

"So..." She paused to run a finger down the middle of his broad chest. "When are we going to get to the ripping clothes off part?"

Knuckles gave her a confused look. "Huh?"

"The guy that was here before. Blond guy? Looked like a model or something—"

"Jaren," Knuckles supplied.

"Yeah, Jaren." Neri waved her hand dismissively. She wasn't interested in much at the moment beyond the man who was holding her like she was the most precious thing in the world. "He said you were dangerous. And something about having to bleach his eyes if he saw you naked."

She giggled as he stole a kiss, their lips clinging for a breathtaking moment. Hell, the guy could kiss.

"I am dangerous. To everyone but you," he growled, but the threatening sound was ruined by the sappy grin on his lips as he took her hand and placed it over his heart. "You saved us, sweetheart. If not for you, I'd be raw materials for someone's rockery right now."

Neri blinked. "Sun slavery? I thought Jaren was kidding when he said that. I thought you guys had a plan."

The gargoyle shook his head, smoothing her hair back from her face. His touch was gentle, almost reverent. "No, love, we didn't. Well, we did, but when we hit this place the plan went belly up. Jaren and Tiny got stuck in demon traps. They knew we were coming. I bulled on ahead because I needed to get to you."

"Jason planned this whole thing? That conniving son of a bitch!"

"But...*but*," Knuckles shushed her with a finger. "They didn't count on one thing. You love me." His grin widened as he said it, pride radiating from him like the rays from the sun.

Neri lifted an eyebrow. "That right, handsome? Awful sure of yourself there, aren't you?"

"Yup. I love you too."

The simple words took Neri's breath away. She was learning there was no subterfuge with Knuckles. It was one of the things she loved about him. When he said something, she didn't have to search for the hidden meaning.

"My question still stands about the clothes thing," she said, changing tactics. "Jaren said something very interesting about screwing me on the floor."

Knuckles hauled her up against his hard body. His lips descended over hers and claimed them in a demanding kiss. When he lifted his head long moments later Neri tried to catch her breath and her scattered thoughts.

"Jaren is not screwing you on *any* floor," he mock-growled, love shining in his eyes. "But *I'm* going to take you home and screw you all afternoon."

* * *

It didn't take them long to reach Knuckles' apartment. The broad wings Neri had thought were just for show made short work of the distance. She liked the wings—there wasn't much about Knuckles she didn't like—but the actual flying part she wasn't so enamored of.

As soon as they'd taken off, the ground dropping away in a stomach-churning lurch, Neri had squeaked, buried her face into his neck and refused to open her eyes for the rest of the journey.

Only when the heavy *whumph-whumph-whumph* of his wings stopped did she finally risk a look. A sigh of relief escaped her when all that met her eyes were the innocuous-looking French doors into Knuckles' living room.

"Wait. Shouldn't you tell someone we're back?" she asked as he shouldered the door open, obviously impatient to get inside. A shiver of anticipation filled her at what would happen when he did get her inside.

"They already know we are." He shrugged as he walked straight through the main room with her still in his arms. He headed for the bedroom, kicking the door shut with a flick of his heel, hard enough to rattle it in the frame.

"They already know? How?" Neri frowned as he dropped her onto the bed, ignoring the fact she bounced a little on the firm mattress in favor of looking up at him.

Standing at the bottom of the bed, he was a sight to behold. He hadn't changed back to his human form. Neri got the feeling he was more comfortable in this one. He stood there letting her look her fill.

And she did, her eyes drinking in every inch of him greedily. Tall and broad-shouldered even before you factored in the wings, his heavily muscled body gave Neri chills just looking at it.

"Jedi mind trick," he snorted in amusement. Then his dark eyes fixed on her and his expression turned serious as he noted the way she was looking at him. His head lifted, pride in every line of his body.

"You like what you see?"

Neri came to her knees on the bed. Her clothes were shredded beyond repair. Pushing her hair back from her face, she eyed him with hunger. Already her body was alive, a familiar ache settling low in her pelvis. It didn't matter to her that he stood there with wings, a tail and freaky feet. To her he was just Knuckles, and she loved and needed him, preferably sooner rather than later.

"Oh yes," she breathed and crooked a finger to beckon him toward her. He smiled, his teeth flashing white as he stepped closer to the bed. As he did, his claws clicked on the floor and Neri realized why the place wasn't carpeted. It wasn't the uber-modern, minimalist look she'd originally taken it for. It was just practical when your feet came equipped with claws a couple of inches long.

He moved toward her, his body filled with a lethal grace she found fascinating and as sexy as hell. Her heart rate doubled but she stood her ground as he stalked toward the bed.

A thrill going through her, she arched her back and posed for him. A sexy pose designed to show off her body to best advantage. Teasing. Tantalizing. Tempting him into the bed with her for the good hard sex she'd been promised.

His hands hit the foot of the bed, and he started to crawl across the satin-covered expanse. Neri giggled and backed away, bouncing against the pillows at the top of the bed, making him chase her.

A low growl of warning rumbled in the center of his chest as his eyes latched on to her. It was a look she'd seen many times when cats were stalking their prey. Even his tail twitched the same, the tiny rattlesnake type movement right at the end, just the tip snaking back and forth, back and forth.

An odd look filled his eyes, something between intense longing and shame, and he stopped halfway across the bed. Neri frowned in confusion, already starting to hold her hand out to him, her mouth opening to ask what was wrong.

He ignored it, dropping his head to take a deep breath, and his skin started to shimmer like the heat over a pavement on a hot day and shift across his bones.

"No!"

The shame in his eyes made sense now. He didn't think she wanted him in his real form, and as soon as things got serious he was dropping back to his human form. She bit her lip. He was crazy if he thought what he looked like mattered to her. Jason had been the archetypal blue-eyed boy, and what a piece of shit he'd turned out to be. She didn't care what Knuckles looked like; she didn't want him to feel ashamed, not with her. Not ever.

Inspiration hit her in a flash. Gargoyles like to chase. Blondie—sorry, Jaren—had warned her about that back in the warehouse, and she'd already seen Knuckles' interest sharpen when she'd evaded him a little on the bed. But did "like to chase" mean she was likely to get her arms and legs ripped off when he caught her, or would the end result be entirely more pleasurable?

He's more likely to tear your clothes off and screw you on the floor...

Summoning all her courage, Neri took a chance this wasn't going to end up in blood and tears and made a break for it. Scrambling off the bed, she ignored the growl of warning and dodged the grab he made for her.

She hit the door at speed, bursting through it and into the main room beyond. She had no idea where she was going, and honestly, there wasn't anywhere she could escape to. Escape wasn't the point though. Unlike her frantic dash only the night before, she wasn't trying to get away; she was trying to make him chase her.

Her bid for "freedom" lasted three steps through the door. With a roar Knuckles whirled and chased after her. The sharp retort of wood cracking echoed around the room, and Neri made the mistake of glancing over her shoulder to see how far behind her he was.

He was right behind her.

She squeaked, an odd sound somewhere between a squeal and a breathless giggle, and tried to twist away to avoid him.

It was too late. Hard hands clamped down on her shoulders, whirling her around with a speed that made her head spin. She didn't get time to gasp as she was yanked up against a hard body—a hard, very aroused, male body.

"Never run," he told her, his breath a hot whisper against her ear. "Never run from me unless you want chasing."

Neri groaned as he thrust his hips against her, the hard length of his cock pressing into her belly. Pulling back, he looked down at her. The look on his face made her breath catch in her throat and her heart hammer against her ribs so fast she thought it was going to burst free.

"And when you've caught me?"

His lips quirked in amusement as he looped her hands around his neck. "First I'm going to bring you to the edge, make you beg me to take you. Then you get fucked, good and proper."

Neri hid her triumph as she stroked soft fingertips down the line of his cheekbone, fascinated by his hard, male beauty. She was still amazed by his different forms. In this one he was huge but apart from the wings and the tail, not forgetting the freaky feet, everything else was pretty human, just bigger. Waaaay bigger...

"You promise?" She pressed closer, fitting her soft curves against the hard, angular planes of his bigger form. Her body clenched tight, everything feminine in her reacting to the promise of the hard cock pressed against her belly. She wanted him, wanted to feel that hard length—eye watering though it might be—sliding into her: stretching her, filling her, possessing her completely and making her his.

His nostrils flared at her words as his eyes blazed with sudden, ferocious heat. "Babe, you're gonna get all of me," he promised darkly, his voice a husky growl which reached deep inside her, stroking the fires of her already rampant arousal to fever pitch. His hand burrowed into her hair, using it to pull her head back gently. "Every single inch."

He trailed nipping kisses down the exposed length of her throat. She whimpered as liquid heat slid from between her thighs. His hand swept down her curves and molded her body against his, stroking down further over her hip and lower. Hooking long fingers behind her knee, he drew it up and over his hip, his big hand caressing her thigh.

Neri caught her lip between her teeth as the movement opened up her body, cool air washing against the dampened crotch of her panties. The position was erotic, her body open to his exploration should he just move his hand a little. His fingers slid under the thin sides of her thong, and the garment gave in a silken whisper, cut by his talons. The scrap of satin slid down her legs to the floor.

She started in surprise as something slid back up, coiling against her calf and flirting with the back of her knee before it wrapped around her thigh. Something warm and thick. "Is that your...?"

"Tail," he murmured against her throat, leaving a playful nip there as he let her lift her head. His eyes were filled with amusement. "I did say all of me."

It moved again, the tip stroking higher and sliding against the soft folds between her legs. Neri jumped again, feeling her eyes widening as it fluttered against her. Knuckles bent his head and claimed her lips in a searing kiss. His free hand slid under the shirt to cup her breast.

The tip of his tail, as dexterous as his fingers, parted her folds and stroked along the heated flesh. She moaned, the sound lost in his mouth as she writhed against him.

He chuckled. The sound was little more than a vibration in his big chest as he ran his thumb over one puckered nipple. At the same time he flicked the tip of his tail over her needy clit.

Neri gasped, her knees turning to jelly as the aching heat between her thighs became an inferno. It was all she could manage to cling to him and return his kisses as his hands and his tail working between her thighs conspired to drive her mad.

His tail flicked and stroked, circled and flicked again, endlessly, relentlessly. She couldn't stand it. Her hips rocked to get every last drop of sensation. It wasn't enough; every time she needed more and faster, he moved away until she calmed down a little. If calm was any way to describe the state she was in at the moment.

She needed more. Her pussy ached to be filled, to be plunged into over and over by the thick staff of his erection pressing into her stomach like an iron bar. She broke the kiss and leaned her forehead against him, panting.

"Knuckles, please!" She didn't care that she was begging, something she'd promised herself years ago she'd never do. She needed him right now, and if begging got her what she needed then that was fine by her.

She slid a hand down between them, boldly cupping him through his pants. Idly, she wondered how he got pants to fit—what with the tail and all—but recalled what he'd said about his talents before other more pressing matters took her attention. Like how to separate him from said pants so she could have her wicked way with him. She'd never felt such intense desire in her life.

Her soft words and her touch shattered the last little bit of control Knuckles had. He'd tried so hard to be civilized about this, even though his instincts were all screaming at him to drop her to the floor and bury himself in her warmth. But her whispered plea and the scent of her need on the air were too much, and his baser instincts broke free.

His gaze swept the room. There was no way he was going to be able to wait even the short distance through into the bedroom. He needed inside her and now, if not ten seconds ago.

His lips twisting in a grin, he pulled his tail from her heated sex and backed her up toward the kitchen counter. A single sweep of his arm removed its contents and scattered them over the floor with a crash.

"Turn around and bend over," he ordered, watching her through narrowed eyes. He was so wound with tension his body was shaking as she did as he told her, giving him a sultry look over her shoulder as she leaned over the counter.

"What? Like this?" she asked and wiggled her hips, drawing his attention to the luscious curves of her ass.

"Tease," he growled as he stepped up behind her. He couldn't wait another minute, another second. Not with her bent over the counter like that and the delicious pink lips of her sex peeking out from under the hem of his shirt. He had to have her. Now.

A talon down the back of the shirt dealt with that issue, and he kicked her feet wider apart. He wanted her totally open for him. A moment's concentration was all it took to rid himself of the few clothes he was wearing. His cock leapt free, eager, and he grasped it in one large hand. He ran the swollen head against her folds, eliciting a moan, before he pressed it against the slick entrance to her body.

Oh God, he *was* huge. Neri bit down hard on her lip as he pushed inside her, feeling the delicate tissues of her body give and slowly envelop his rigid cock.

"God, you're so hot and tight…feels so good," he groaned, leaning over her on the counter with his hands braced either side of her shoulders.

Her thoughts scattered as he slid as far into her as he could, adding a little roll of his hips. A small moan escaped her throat as she arched her back and thrust her ass back against him. She'd died and gone to heaven. He stretched and filled her in ways no man had before and she loved it. Fire filled every cell with the need to move, to push back against him and demand everything he could give her.

"Fuck!" His claws dug into the granite of the counter as he entered her another half inch, his male growl of need as he pulled back urging Neri on. This might have started with him being the aggressor, and she might be pinned under him, but that didn't mean she didn't have her own power.

She closed her eyes and pushed back again, meeting him thrust for thrust; her pussy clenched tight around his hard cock. Shivers rolled through that velvet sheath, transmitted from him to her as their rhythm got harder, faster. Both of them were reaching for something ethereal and wonderful hovering just out of reach, something they couldn't attain apart but together—it was perfection.

"Fuck it! I can't hold out," Knuckles groaned, his thighs spread for balance and his hips pounding against hers, each thrust driving them both closer.

"Then don't, you big lump," Neri gasped back, pushing up from the counter and bracing herself on her locked arms. The change in position made his cock press inside her in all sorts of new and interesting ways. Liquid heat flooded her channel and his cock in an almost scalding wave. "Just let go and fuck me."

His growl echoed around the small kitchen. Had it only been last night he'd brought her here dressed in his jacket and the remnants of her clothing? Knuckles snaked his arm around her body crosswise, pulling her upright with her back flush against his broad chest.

She whimpered in his arms. The tension in her body was so tight it was a wonder she didn't snap with it. Her head dropped back to his shoulder, and she rested back against him. He thrust into her again and again, impaling her on his rigid cock.

"Please..." she pleaded, twisting to kiss his neck again, her hands on his restraining arm.

Knuckles wrapped himself tightly around her, one leg pressing hers forward as he fitted himself to her body, the smooth slide of his cock in her pussy almost furious now. He answered her unspoken plea by wrapping his tail around her too, the tip snaking between her thighs and sliding against the hard nub of her clit. It stroked as he continued to drive into her.

Neri shivered at the first touch, cried his name on the second, and on the third she shattered, coming apart in his arms. His bellow of release followed as his cock pulsed and jerked, pumping white-hot seed into the depths of her body.

And, unnoticed by the lovers, the sun broke over the horizon, pouring through the small kitchen window as the gargoyle and his love were locked together in the afterglow of their lovemaking.

Epilogue

In this world it is possible for two souls to connect so deeply, in a love so profound, that it transcends death itself. The love between Knuckles and Neri was one such love, reaching beyond the grave.

Their souls were always destined to be together, to complete each other, and so, many years beyond our story when Neri has left this mortal coil, the gargoyle guards the grave of his love, locked in stone as he waits for her to be born again.

Waiting for the day they can be together: Forever.

The End

Deception & Desire

Chapter One

"Yeah? You and whose army, bloodsucker? Now piss off before I get irritated and decide to introduce you to a few friends of mine… They're a bit boring when it comes to conversation, but they really get the *point* across," Tiny snarled at the vampire facing him down. He flicked the side of his jacket open to reveal two short and businesslike stakes nestled along his ribcage, right under the Glock in the shoulder holster.

They weren't the rough hewn, chair-leg type stakes of the amateur vampire slayer either. These were iron-banded custom beauties, made to Tiny's precise specifications. When it came to weaponry, the demon believed in multiple redundancies so the wooden shaft dealt with the vamps, the iron bands put a crimp in the day of any Fae he had to sort out, and anything still standing with six inches of banded wood stabbed through their ribcage…well, that's what the Glock was for. To say Tiny was loaded for bear was an understatement. He was loaded for anything that breathed.

He needed to be. Working as a doorman at the city's premier paranormal nightclub, Tiny and the other guys on the security team saw most things in the course of a night. They'd had a dragon in last week. Well, a were-drake to be precise—one of the Keller brothers—and even the bosses, Jaren and Daelas, had come down onto the floor to make sure Mr. Keller got everything he wanted. No one wanted a pissed off dragon, not even Tiny, who was one of the tougher of the paranormals on the staff, barring the head doorman Knuckles.

Dragons, though, were the exception rather than the rule. Normally the club got small fry, like the vampire glaring at Tiny because his pathetic attempt at a Jedi mind-trick had failed.

"Try it on someone with human blood, pal," Tiny advised with a small smile that was nowhere near pleasant. "But not on my watch. Now piss off."

"Fucking vampires…should be put down," the woman next to Tiny muttered as the vamp gave up to slink back into the shadows. He paused to cast a baleful glare over his shoulder at Tiny, who smiled and waved.

A long-suffering sigh sounded beside him. "Will you *please* stop pissing them off? You know it causes problems at chucking-out time."

The demon chuckled and slid a glance sideways at his partner. Misty was a walking, talking frat boy's wet dream. She was Amazonian tall, with pale ivory skin that made a man's mouth water, and masses of midnight hair which fell to curl lovingly about a waist small enough for Tiny to wrap his hands around.

Add a stacked rack and full lips which gave any red-blooded male ideas about them running over his naked body and you had a woman capable of stopping men dead in their tracks at a hundred paces.

This was a useful skill on the front door of Moonlight & Magic, where the humans sometimes got a little out of hand, like the group of young males approaching them, an edge in their laughter that said this was not the first stop of the evening.

"Yeah, yeah…whatever. You like a little rough and tumble just as much as I do, doll. Don't try and deny it," he threw back. He nodded towards the group approaching the door. "You're up. Work your magic, girl."

Tiny stood back, his hands clasped loosely in front of him with the fingers of one wrapped around the wrist of the other as Misty swung into action. Dressed in the black slacks, shirt and jacket of the door staff, an outfit not known for its sex appeal, she still managed to garner the attention of every man in the vicinity as she made her way down the steps by the main doors.

How she did it, Tiny didn't know. She didn't sashay or roll her hips as she walked. In the heavy boots she marched more than walked, but it was all done with a sensual grace so unstudied it had to be natural.

However, that wasn't the appeal. What drew men to her wasn't her stunning looks, but the sense of danger clinging to her like a second skin as though to touch her would be to glimpse heaven, just for a moment, before the reaper moved in for the kill.

A rather accurate statement, Tiny mused, acknowledging wryly he'd had to resist temptation himself a few times. Resist he did because, unlike the young mortals ogling her with "God, I'd like a piece of that ass" looks, Tiny knew what Misty was. Brave he might be—indeed, he'd been called suicidal in some circles—but even he wasn't going to start messing about with a Valkyrie.

In her case, *la petite mort* might be too permanent for comfort.

"Now, now, lads, gonna need you to calm down a little before we let you in…"

After another glance to make sure she had the situation under control, Tiny looked away, eyes scanning the queue waiting to get in and the passersby in the street. A cold night, it seemed all the colder for a demon-born like Tiny. Shuddering, he hunched into the turned-up collar of his thick jacket. His gaze swept the road. A rush of jealousy—sharp and immediate—rose as the vampires circled like sharks waiting for a meal. If any of them wore a coat, it was for effect rather than any need for warmth. They didn't feel the cold.

"Bastards," he muttered under his breath and wondered if he could crawl inside his jacket completely. Tiny hated being cold with a passion. But then, for any creature born and bred in the warmth of one of the seven hells, cold was pure torture. The fog put a layer of moisture in the air that coated everything, the dampness penetrating deep into Tiny's bones. He was never going to be warm again—no doubt a punishment for running away from his duties.

Shivering again, he muttered another curse about the weather as a bunch of vamps having a little tete-a-tete on the corner opposite caught his attention. He ignored his discomfort as the little group whispering between themselves didn't break up as he'd expected. Tiny flicked a glance at Misty, who had calmed down the group she had approached. The line moved quickly now.

Feeling his gaze on her, she lifted her head, silent communication passing between the partners for a second before Tiny turned his attention back to the vamps. Misty would keep an eye on the line and call in backup if needed, whilst he dealt with the circling predators intent on picking off the weakest of the human herd.

He didn't move for a moment, just leaned against the wall, his eyes sharp and alert. Vamps were predictable creatures most of the time, but occasionally one would get a kick in their gallop and try to make a play for someone in the queue, a decision which ended with them having a little chat in a side alley with Tiny or one of his colleagues. There was a running book on how high they could get vamp blood and snot on the brickwork.

However vamps weren't normally pack animals and they didn't hunt together. This little group seemed to have missed that particular memo. Tiny's eyes narrowed as two of the group sauntered across the road and engaged a trio of young women in conversation. Human women, of course; they wouldn't bother with any of the paranormals in the line.

The third was slower to approach, piling on the vampire "glamour" as he did. The vampires moved in a slick routine, separating the women, who were easy marks. They herded the last girl toward an alley, the arm of her new "friend" wrapped around her shoulders. The tall demon sighed. Vampire charm was hypnotic and she was getting it full force, her head back against the vamp's shoulder as he gazed deep into her eyes.

"Great, just what I need tonight. A fucking synchronized vampire feeding squad." Pushing off from the wall, he rolled his shoulders, cracking his neck as he readied himself for action. There was going to be blood and snot on the walls again. Perhaps with three vamps to play with he'd beat Knuckles' record...

His lips compressed as yet another vamp moved to follow the others into the alley. What was this, an all you can eat until the meal drops dead buffet? He turned, angling his walk to intercept the new player as his heavy boots crunched over the road. Then he got a good look at the newcomer and his step faltered.

She was gorgeous. She was a vampire, but she was gorgeous.

Tiny's eyes widened in surprise as his brain tried to reconcile the two words in one sentence, even as his body reacted. She was average height...the perfect height to wrap into his arms, slide his hand into her hair and tilt her lips up...

Tiny snapped out of his reverie, his eyes narrowing as he clamped down on the reaction of his body to a fine piece of female ass and forced himself to study her.

She didn't seem the "type" to be a vampire was the first thing to hit him after the immediate "I want" reaction. Vampires, especially the ones who hovered around Moonlight & Magic, played up to the stereotype: pale skin, dark hair, dark clothing... Goths with attitude, or Lestat knock-offs.

This one could have been the poster-girl for the wholesome, all-American, girl next door type. Not blonde, but in the light cast by the street lights, he could see her hair wasn't the midnight black most vamps preferred, either. Instead, it contained a waterfall of autumn colors.

She had a tan, as well—not at all the norm for a vamp. When even a small dose of direct UV turned you into crispy critter, tanning was a high risk option. Fake tan, unless his instincts were fooling him.

Were they? Was she something other than a vampire?

For the first time in a couple of hundred years Tiny found himself holding back. He'd always been a player, watching his back and ready for action of any sort—although in the demon courts the more pleasurable kind always came with a price—but this was the first time he'd doubted his instincts.

Face set, he watched the vamp chick head into the alleyway after the couple and tried to ignore the seductive sway of her hips. He noticed anyway; his body had completely different ideas about the matter, his cock already at half mast in his pants. *Damn vampires, messing with a guy's head.* He glared at a couple of humans who cut in front of him, then walked into the alley.

Whatever Tiny had expected from tonight, it wasn't for the problem to be solved before it became a problem. As he entered the alley, he expected to find the vampires fang-deep in the girl's throat—or other appendage of choice. He expected to have to deal with them in short order whilst trying not to get the human killed. His hand was already reaching for one of the stakes along his ribcage when the woman's cool voice drifted on the night air to him.

"Okay, honey-bun, we can do this the easy way or the hard way... No, now that was just unpleasant, wasn't it? No need for language like that at all, especially in front of a lady... Oh really? How about we don't and say we did..."

Tiny had barely a second to react as the human was thrust into his arms with a "Here, hold this," before all hell broke loose.

To say she was annoyed didn't begin to do justice to the emotions running high through her slender frame as Cassia watched the three musketeers do their "divide and conquer" routine yet again. "You guys never learn, do you?" she muttered as the vampires moved into action, each charming smile digging their graves deeper. New town, new threads...and looked like they'd been here a while, long enough to get themselves established.

No matter. It was too long. If the agency hadn't called her off in the last place... God, what had the town been called? She shrugged as the name eluded her memory. Second tumbleweed on the left and straight on until morning type of town, total Hicksville... If the agency hadn't called her off the trail to go join the hunt for a rogue angel, she'd have had these three under lock and key a month ago.

She automatically checked the chains hooked onto the loops of her belt. A buzz of power vibrated against her fingers as they brushed the restraints. The chains were intricately woven Fae-steel, enhanced with magic to make them far more powerful.

Fae-steel could hold almost any paranormal out there, essential for a woman with a delicate build like Cassia's. Yeah sure, she was a vampire, but contrary to human belief, vampires weren't the biggest badasses walking the dark. Some of the creatures Cassia dealt with in the course of her job were far nastier, so she needed every edge possible.

Cass was a bounty hunter, one specializing in paranormals. Bounty hunting was a dangerous game at the best of times, even if you dealt strictly with humans. When you didn't, you needed serious kick-ass weaponry...or a death wish.

A third vampire emerged from the shadows, engaging the lone female—the mark—in conversation. Cass felt the blast of charm as he dazzled his victim and started to draw her towards an alleyway. The two other vampires followed.

"Thank you, handsome. Dead end alley. That makes my job easier," Cassia muttered, and pushed off the wall. Her heels clicked against the tarmac as she followed, single-minded on her objective despite the tantalizing scents in the air. Human blood, contained within skin and veins but so close to the surface, called to her. She ignored the rumble in her stomach. Work first, then a snack. She could get lucky later and find someone in the club who wasn't opposed to supplying both her needs; blood and sex.

Her long strides ate up the tarmac as she crossed the road, hugging the leather biker jacket close about her slender form. Her shiver was automatic and almost authentic. Cass didn't feel the cold. It was an act, and one she was good at.

Some vampires couldn't fake human. It was all in the details. Most lost the ability once they'd been "dead" a while. A couple of decades later, vampires forget things like breathing and that humans couldn't go statue-still for an hour as they thought about something.

Cass, though, had been playing human far longer than she'd been one. It helped that she was a turned vampire. Some born-kyn never worked it out, never really understood the minute differences in human and vampire behavior.

Then there were the ones who knew the differences and knew the rules—there were a fair set of those when you were turned: *Don't harm when you feed. Be considerate to your donor. Clean the skin up and don't leave a mark,* Cass listed as she turned the corner into the alleyway. Some people knew the rules and broke them anyway.

Like the three musketeers here.

She paused a step inside the alley, her eyes narrowing as she took in the scene. Just as she'd suspected, Charmer, her least favorite of this oily little trio, had his fangs gum-deep in the girl's neck. His arm was locked around her in a no-nonsense hold, snaking under one arm and crosswise across her body to the other shoulder, and one of his hands forced her head over to one side so he could feed. The others watched from the shadows.

Even from her position at the entrance to the alley Cass could see the girl's face paling, her hands scratching at her captor's arm. The muscles of the vamp's throat worked as he swallowed, his eyes half closed in bliss. A deep sigh escaped Cassia as she flicked her jacket open. "Okay, honey-bun, we can do this the easy way or the hard way."

The vampire lifted his head, lips stained with blood. "Fuck off and get your own food." He bared his fangs before biting the girl again, a savage strike that made the girl's body jerk like a puppet. The other two moved to his side.

Cass didn't let her worry for the human show on her face or in her voice. "Now that was just unpleasant. No need for language like that, especially in front of a lady."

She made her move, her hand reaching past the short stakes holstered at her hip and going straight for the warded chain. The bounty on these three was high so she didn't want to dust the guy. A girl had expenses. The streaks in her hair alone cost a fortune and the specialized vampire tanning booths? She might as well re-mortgage her condo.

The vamp chuckled, his eyes raking her slender figure, and he disengaged his fangs for a moment. "Hold your horses, sweetheart, plenty enough for everyone. If you're good, I'll do you while you feed… You look like you need to get laid, help calm you down a bit."

"Oh, really? How about we don't and say we did…" Cassia glided across the ground between her and the vamp, the movement taking less than a heartbeat.

"Wha…" Her quarry blinked in surprise. It was obvious he hadn't expected Cass to move so fast, nor the Fae-steel in her hand. Cass suppressed the small smile on her lips. They thought she was a newbie, a baby vamp barely out of her grave.

She didn't blame them. The human-like coloring, the tan and the streaks in her hair were all designed to give that impression. Surprise was one of her best weapons—no paranormal expected a near-human to be hunting them.

Stepping back, he thrust the girl at her. Cass took it in stride, sidestepping to catch the human with her free arm. She sensed rather than saw someone enter the alley behind her. The aura, the buzz against her skin was of power, but it didn't have the sharp, zippy feel of another vamp. Taking a chance she spun the girl under her arm and pushed her that way. "Here, hold this."

The girl taken care of, Cass's attention snapped back to the vamp. He backpedaled, eyes frantic as they moved between her face and the length of chain in her hand. Cass flicked her wrist, snapping the chain out like a whip.

"You…you…" he stammered, reaching the back of the dead-end alley and looking around for an escape, desperation on his face. Cass had seen it all before. A previously docile paranormal could go skitz at the mere sight of a Fae-steel chain, like the dryad she'd brought in the other week.

She'd had a very pleasant conversation with her about the money she owed to certain people, and she'd been very co-operative—right up to the point where Cass had pulled out the warded chains. Then she'd gone bat-shit on her. It was like the sight of the Fae-steel had brought it all home.

"You expected someone else? Maybe the Easter Bunny? Kinky… Sorry, guys, role-play costs you extra." The chatter rolled off her tongue easily as she stalked them. Cass was far older than she appeared, and she'd been tracking and bringing marks in since before this guy had been born, in either of his incarnations.

Charmer's gaze latched onto Cass as she stood blocking their path, a lazy flick of her wrist snapping the chain in her hand every so often. All she had to do was get the chain on him and the wards would do the rest. It didn't matter where; just one closed loop of chain would be enough, then the enchantments would lock and seal the loop into place.

"Bitch," he snarled and made a break for it. He feinted right but darted to the left instead quick as a snake. Cass was ready for him. Another snap of her wrist and the chain whipped out lasso-like. Catching him around his wrist, the Fae-steel went from fluid to a solid manacle in a heartbeat.

"That's Ms. Bitch to you." She yanked on the chain, hauling him to her in a quick movement that belied her appearance as a newbie vamp. New vampires only had such strength just after they were turned, then the high of the conversion drained off and it took years to build up again.

Ignored his struggles, Cass snagged the other two, and reached for the charms set into the chains. A practiced flick of her thumb triggered each of them. She smiled and waved as the magic expanded out from the warded beads and enveloped her captives in glowing orbs reminiscent of a sci-fi transporter.

Beam me up, Scotty. The orbs shrank back to nothing, taking the chains and the vamps with them. They would reappear in holding cells back at base, ready for processing, and in three days' time, her money would appear in her account. Minimal fuss and no paperwork. "God, I love my job." She turned to thank her impromptu helper and stopped dead in her tracks.

Still holding the girl she'd thrust into his arms was the hottest looking guy she'd ever seen. Well over six feet, he had a build yummy enough to make her mouth water and the face of a dark angel. Her eyes skipped over him, from the top of his shaven head—a look she'd never considered hot before—picked up the silver ring in his brow and flicked down to check out the package before she looked back at his face.

Everything female in her went tight, a yearning she'd never felt before drawing her to him as her vampire side went cold. He was her ideal man. Just one problem…

No way was she fucking a demon.

Chapter Two

She was amazing, more than amazing. Tiny's heart still raced from watching the no-nonsense way she'd dealt with the vamp. He had a healthy respect for a woman who could take charge of a situation. In Hell women were as capable as men. They had to be. A person had to look out for number one down there, end of story. However, of all the things she could have been, a bounty hunter hadn't even crossed his mind. He eyed the delicate chains hanging from her belt with trepidation.

Warded Fae-steel with a hunter's mark, they were the kind of thing even he'd be hard pressed to get out of. Well, he could, but that would require a shit-load more power than the low-level, part demon he appeared to be should have. Using that much juice would ripple across the witching, alerting every warden and demon in the area, not to mention cluing the other staff at the club into the fact he wasn't who he said he was.

Hell, the amount of power he'd have to use to break those chains would burn an image of his face into the witching for all to see. Like the paranormal version of "Tiny wuz here." He smiled to himself. Perhaps he should drop his trousers and leave an imprint of his ass instead, flick the bird to the universe.

"Something's amused you at least. Glad I could provide the night's entertainment, but hadn't you best check on sleeping beauty? She isn't looking so hot."

Her voice pulled Tiny out of his reverie and he blinked. As the words penetrated the thick fog clouding his brain, he looked quickly at the girl in his arms—the unconscious girl in his arms. "Fuck."

"Short and succinct." The female vamp's lips curled into a smile as Tiny tried to find a pulse. He swore when he couldn't locate one. His fingers were too big for delicate work like this.

"Don't worry. I'm picking up a heartbeat, and her heart isn't laboring, so he didn't take too much blood. You might want to get her checked out at the local emergency room to be on the safe side though. Humans can be weird when shock sets in."

Tiny breathed a sigh of relief as he found a pulse, confirming the vamp's words. The last thing he needed was a death on his watch, particularly a vampire kill. His boss Knuckles would go insane. If there was anything Knuckles hated, it was vampires. Tiny couldn't blame him. The guy had nearly lost his wife to a bloodsucker, so it was understandable.

Then the tone in her voice struck him, the caring, concerned note threading through the honeyed timbre. He looked up to find her closer and stiffened at the buzz of power emanating from her. The wrongness he always felt in the presence of a vampire brushed against his skin. Unlike before, though, this didn't feel too bad. Just different, like the zip of electricity in the air before a storm, but not the sick to the stomach feeling he normally got.

Focus, he told himself as his cock twitched. Getting a hard-on with an unconscious girl in his arms was just crass, even if she wasn't the object of interest. It wouldn't make any difference; the guys—and Misty—on the door crew would still give him shit over it.

His brows snapped together into a frown, and he took his frustration out on the only available target. "What do you care? Or do you get attached? Sort of like keeping a pet pig to fatten up for Christmas?"

The tension in the alley mounted as he stared into deep, chocolate brown eyes. Flecks of gold danced in their depths and the tiny lines in the corners—she must have gotten those before she was turned, he mused absently—indicated she smiled a lot. Not at him though. For him her eyes were cold, and her anger swirled around her like a cloak. "I don't play with my food. I'm strictly a takeout sort of girl." Head held high, she stalked out of the alley.

The image of her autumnal curls bouncing across her shoulders, her straight back and the siren's curve of her ass—oh, God, what an ass—stayed with Tiny all evening. The girl was quickly seen to, checked out behind the top bar by Jac, a siren with healer training, then bundled off to the nearest emergency room to comply with human regulations the club had to abide by to keep their license.

It was one of the ways humanity tried to put a leash on the Night Races; the only way they could. Force wouldn't work, and there was the saying the pen was mightier than the sword. If that was the case then bureaucracy was a Challenger tank.

Tiny stood behind the main desk for a while and watched the stragglers wander in. There were always a few who decided late in the evening that a night in Moonlight & Magic was what the doctor ordered. This meant someone had to be on the door to make sure nothing…undesirable snuck in under the radar.

On a normal night Tiny didn't mind. It was indoors and out of the cold, always a bonus as far as the demon was concerned. Tonight though, he was edgy and fractious, and he didn't know why.

A sigh escaped him as he admitted the lie. That vamp chick had messed up his karma today, what with her attitude, mouth-watering figure and not sitting nicely in the little box he'd mentally put her in.

Vamps needed to stay the bad guy, not start beating up other—admittedly asshole—vampires and being someone he could get to like. They were the enemy. Demons and vampires didn't get on. Ever. There was an enmity between the two races that had been running so long no one questioned it anymore.

He didn't need to get soft and start seeing vamps as people. That way led to madness and somebody getting killed, something his conscience wouldn't allow. Especially if it was him. No, vamps were the bad guys and he couldn't let his guard slip because of a pretty face, or a hot body. *Bloody women, trouble whatever their species,* Tiny grumbled to himself and pushed off from the heater. Perhaps a patrol outside would help settle him down...

The doors next to him burst open and Misty piled through. "Tiny!" Relief flashed stark across her face. "We need you on the floor. Knuckles is on the warpath. We got a vamp inside somewhere."

A vampire. In the club.

"Crap! How the fuck did she get in..." It had to be her. He didn't know any other vampire who had the ability to get past the door controls. Certainly none he'd seen recently could, but this one... She walked and talked human, too human. Most people, even paranormals, would have taken her to be mortal.

He flicked a glance at Janie, the girl on the desk. "Ring up and get someone on the door," he ordered and followed Misty back into the club.

"She?" Misty asked, as they made their way through the crowded club to the top bar where head bouncer Knuckles was pacing. Tiny took one look at him and grimaced. Knuckles was furious, the Gargoyle's rage all but setting the air around him ablaze.

"Yeah, caught a vamp hunter dealing with a bloodsucker in an alley earlier." His voice low, he guided her around a group of clubbers, his hand settling in the small of her back in a protective gesture. As she flicked her hair over her shoulder, she looked up into his face, a wry smile of amusement on her face.

Tiny winced. Of all the women in the club, Misty was one of the few who didn't need protection. From anything. "Sorry, force of habit. My mother did try and instill some manners in me."

"Not a problem..." Her tone was dismissive. "Tell me about the vamp. She took out another vampire? I thought only their warrior caste were allowed to do that."

Tiny's shoulder lifted in a small shrug. "Didn't see the huge-ass tats those guys normally have so guess not. I'm no expert on vamps. Listen..." He glanced at Knuckles wearing a groove in the floor behind the top bar. "Head the big guy off for me, would you? I want to catch this chick and get her out of here. She might be a vamp, but she did us a favor by taking out that bloodsucker, and I'd rather not explain why we had to clean a hunter's blood off the walls."

Surprise flickered in Misty's eyes. Hunters were one of the few "police" forces in the paranormal world, and very much creatures of urban myth. Most people went all their lives without seeing one, but everyone knew someone who'd had dealings with one. They seemed to be everywhere and nowhere all at the same time.

"Yeah, sure," she sighed. "Make it snappy though, because he'll see through me in about three minutes flat, okay?"

One of the few men in the place tall enough, Tiny dropped a kiss on the Valkyrie's temple. "Misty, you're a star, love you to bits."

"Yeah, yeah whatever..." She flicked her fingers in dismissal, but he could see the pleasure in her eyes as he turned to disappear into the crowd.

They were a couple, had to be. Cassia watched the little interchange between the demon bouncer she'd seen earlier and a woman, also one of the security team, from the other side of the club.

Not just a woman though. Cass recognized a Valkyrie when she saw one. Which meant tall, dark and demony was spoken for and, interesting as he might be, Cass was not pissing about with a Valkyrie's property. Her lifespan may have been extended until she was virtually immortal, but unlike a true immortal, Cass was still allergic to having her head ripped off.

Doomed is the kyn who ever fell under the lying demon's spell...

The old chant running through her mind, Cass sipped her drink, secure in the darkness of her booth. A minor aversion charm dangled from the bracelet around her wrist, the soft lavender light telling her it was active and keeping the cattle away as she watched the goings-on. She didn't want to be bothered, and the way she was dressed—knee-high black boots, mid-thigh black leather skirt and a black leather top under her fitted black leather jacket—would gather too much attention.

The outfit wasn't intended to be alluring. The boots were sensible heels, not stilettos. The skirt was slightly flared in case she had to run, and the jacket only there to conceal she was packing heat.

"Maybe someone threw a lust spell in the water or something," she mused, studying the bar with interest as yet another guy paused for a second to look at her. She ignored him, watching the bar staff to see if she could spot any charms or spells being slipped into the drinks. A girl never knew her luck; she might be able to pick up more than the bounty on the three vamps if she could uncover an establishment like this breaking the law.

Snagging one of the cards off the table, she checked the name... Moonlight & Magic. She'd heard of this place. Something about a club for paranormals run by paranormals, but mainstream rather than the usual seedy dives warded six ways to Sunday to keep the humans out. No, this place actively encouraged humans, allowed them to see the Night Races up close and personal...

Everything but vampires. Cassia's memory kicked in and provided the little detail which had been tugging at the back of her mind, trying like hell to get her attention. This place didn't allow vampires in any way, shape or form. Cass swallowed, feeling a chill go up her spine. Not only that, they were reputed to enforce their rules with violence.

"Crap." Tipping her head back, Cass drained the last of her drink and shivered as the whiskey burned all the way down. There was something about a good whiskey she couldn't give up, even though she couldn't get drunk anymore, which was a pain in the ass—some days she'd kill to be able to get completely plastered and forget her woes for a night. She'd even welcome the bloody hangover afterwards. Vampires didn't get drunk on human alcohol, and even though she could get the same effect drinking Fae blood, Cass didn't think trying to cadge a meal in here would go down well.

No, discretion was the better part of valor, Cass told herself as she slid off her seat and stood. Her hands automatically smoothed down the back of the skirt to make sure she wasn't flashing her panties. The aversion charm was good, but not that good.

Out of nowhere a hand clamped on her wrist and twisted that same charm. A silent *pop* pressed against Cassia's skin, telling her it had just gone dormant. "Hey!" She started to turn but her movement was cut off, and she was hauled back into a hard, male body instead.

"If you want to keep your pretty little head attached to your body, I suggest you shut up and do exactly as you're told."

It was him. Cass didn't need to turn around and see his face; his voice was instantly recognizable. Everything female in her woke up and took notice. A shiver ran down her spine and blood raced to her cheeks as her pussy clenched in anticipation. Her body was getting itself ready for his, and all he'd done was growl a warning in her ear. Jeez, what the fuck was wrong with her?

Cass gritted her teeth. She didn't know much about demons other than the "kyn good, demon bad" thing, but she sure hoped they didn't have the same keen sense of smell as vampires did. Otherwise he would be able to smell her interest, and that would be embarrassing.

No such luck. A very male sound of surprise and appreciation rumbled through the big chest behind her, and a chuckle sounded in her ear. "Baiting the tiger there, doll, or should I say baiting the demon… And believe me, you don't want to do either."

She didn't, she really didn't. Vamps and demons didn't mix. No way, no how. Cass knew that, but her body wasn't getting the message and clenched tight with yearning. Instinct told her he would be an excellent lover. Something about him said he knew how to please a woman. Cass tilted her head back against his shoulder to look up, her eyes heavy-lidded and sultry. "Perhaps I do…"

Heat flared in his eyes for a second. Heat and something else, something dark and dangerous, which made the fluttering in Cass's stomach a hundred times worse. He dragged a breath into his lungs, his eyes riveting to her lips as he bent his head. He was going to kiss her. A fierce ache descended and took over, making her body pliant as she lifted her lips…

"Shit." The expletive was short and sharp as the pair were shoved from behind. Instantly, Cass was wrapped in a strong hold as her "protector's" free hand shot out to brace him against the wall, shielding her with his larger body. "Fucking idiot, watch where you're going," he snarled at the group who had almost knocked them sprawling into the shadowed booth.

"Oh hey, sorry, man, didn't see you there," one shot back, his tone flippant until he turned and caught sight of Tiny. He paled and turned tail to disappear into the crowd.

"Young. Human. *Male*," she commented. "So, handsome, where were we?" She turned in his arms to look up at him, an inviting expression on her face.

His eyes, an azure blue like a tempestuous sea waiting for a storm to break, met hers. "You were playing with fire, as I recall." He eased closer to her to get out of the way of another group of club-goers, but stayed there instead of moving back again. The heat of his body burned through her clothes, warming her skin. It was like basking in front of a hot fire, and all Cass wanted to do was wrap herself around him like a cat.

Were all demons like this, this warm and intriguing?

They weren't though, she knew that. On a normal day she couldn't stand to be in the same room as a demon. Their very presence, their aura, set her hackles to rising and she couldn't get comfortable until she put some distance between her and them. But this one was different. The normal unpleasant buzz was more of a pleasant whisper across her skin, like a teasing caress.

"I'd like to play with something else..." she trailed off suggestively and ran her hand up his chest. Solid muscles met her fingers as she pushed his jacket open to explore. Hell, the guy was built like a brick shed.

Hard fingers closed around hers, like a striking snake, and stopped her explorations. "You would, would you?"

Her gaze shot upwards. A muscle in his jaw pulsed and the expression in his eyes...a battle royal raged there; lust and need warring with something else, something she couldn't identify.

He scanned the club. "We need to move." His tone was uncompromising.

Cass shivered again, a dark thrill slithering along her spine and pooling in her loins. Oh, she had no doubt he didn't intend to turn her on, but there was just something about a man who took charge that, to her disgust, turned her on...turned her on big time.

He hurried her ahead of him, hand firm in the small of her back as he propelled her towards the nearest exit. At the last minute a huge figure loomed in Cass's peripheral vision. Her demon friend swore under his breath and yanked her into one of the alcoves along the walls, spinning her around to haul her close. She had barely a second's warning before his lips crashed down onto hers, claiming hers in the hottest kiss she could recall.

Her lips were soft and oh-so-sweet. A rumble sounded in Tiny's chest as he pressed her back against the wall in the darkened alcove and took what he wanted, what he'd been wanting since he'd seen her in the alley kicking ass.

God, she tasted good, her lips softer than silk under his. A siren's temptation that enticed him, called out to him, even though he knew this was wrong. He shouldn't be kissing her, touching her... Hell, he should be hustling her out of the club before Knuckles got a look at her and even then, if the gargoyle knew what he'd done, he'd rip Tiny a new one. He should stop. Tiny knew he should stop. He would stop. Just one more kiss and he'd...

She wriggled to get closer, and the sexy little moan in the back of her throat blew the last of Tiny's control. Grabbing a handful of her autumn-colored hair, he pulled her head back to bare her throat—a submissive position for a vampire and a vulnerable one. She stiffened, but the wariness in her body melted as he leaned in to blaze a trail of hot kisses down the delicate skin.

Tiny's response was near frenzy. A deep need drove him so he forgot where he was, who he was with and the danger they were still in. He couldn't get enough of her, moving back up to claim her lips again. His tongue swept out and brushed her lower lip to request entry. As soon as she granted it, he deepened the kiss ruthlessly, seeking—no, demanding—a response. One she gave easily as her tongue flirted with the thrusts of his, teasing and tormenting him.

Tiny growled a warning in the back of his throat. The hand in her hair tightened to hold her still as the other slid around her waist to press her hips against his. He was hard, rock hard. All he could think about was pulling up that little skirt she was wearing, shoving her panties aside, and burying himself balls deep in her softness.

"Hey, man, get a freaking room!"

Chapter Three

The rebuke snapped them both back to reality. Tiny tore his lips from hers. Christ, he'd been ready to free his cock and take her right there, up against the wall of the club. Heat chased over his body as he realized just how dangerous the situation was. Any moment now someone could catch them and realize his companion was a vampire. Then all kinds of shit would hit the fan. Vampires did not venture into Moonlight & Magic—not if they wanted to live.

"We need to get out of here. Come on," he told her roughly, scanning all the exits. All but one, the one to the offices, were covered. Misty he could see over the other side of the club with Knuckles, the huge gargoyle's figure easily picked out.

They were running out of time. It wouldn't take Knuckles long to pick up the trail, even with the Valkyrie distracting him, and Tiny needed to get his companion out of here before he did.

His hand still in the hair at the nape of her neck, Tiny urged her across the crowded club, turning her around his body in a move as complicated as a dance routine as another of the security team passed them, also on the lookout for the vampire.

"All right?" the guy mouthed, his voice lost in the heavy music. Tiny jerked his thumb towards the toilets, indicating he was heading there to check. Relief filled him as the other bouncer nodded and carried on the way he was going. They might actually make it.

They reached the dubious sanctuary of the corridor. The music dropped to a dull roar as the door swung shut behind them. Rather than carry on down towards the toilets, Tiny hung a sharp left and bundled his companion through the door there. Half hidden by the opening of the first, it was cloaked by a similar aversion spell to the one she wore around her wrist, albeit a larger, more powerful one embedded in the doorframe. Pushing her ahead of him, he threw the lock with a quick gesture and leaned back with a sigh.

"What the fuck? Was there a particular need to assault me and haul me in here in such a highhanded manner?"

Her voice broke through his little reverie and Tiny sighed. Why was he doing this? She was a vampire; he was a demon. A demon about to get his ass kicked and lose his job if anyone found out he had her in here.

Lifting his head he fixed her with a direct look. "I risk my ass to save yours and I'm the fucking bad guy? You need to get your priorities straight, lady."

Cassia stood in the middle of the small office with an angry demon and wondered why she wasn't worried. On a normal day, this kind of situation would have her reaching for any available weaponry and looking for the nearest escape route. But it didn't because she wasn't worried. Hopping mad, yes...and still shaken up from that hotter-than-all-hell kiss.

"My... I need to get my priorities straight?" she spluttered, going from blazing mad to furious in the blink of an eye. Of all the fucking cheek! First the place discriminated against an entire species. Then they had the balls to make her feel like the criminal here? She half threw her purse on the scarred desk and advanced on him. "You listen to me, buddy. If you lot weren't so fucking anal about vampires in the first place... If you all climbed down off your high horses for a second, we wouldn't be having this problem."

Each word took her one step closer to him until she was mere inches away, glaring up into his face. For some reason his good looks irritated her all the more. Frustration and fury boiled over, and she substituted jabbing him in the chest with every word instead of her earlier steps. "You do realize I could sue for species harassment?"

He stood, looking down at her, one eyebrow raised a little, which made the silver ring through it catch the light. "Harassment?" His voice was deep and rough as hunger flooded his eyes, taking Cass's breath away. In an instant, the mood in the room changed from tense to erotic, from highly charged to supernova. He laughed, a harsh sound of amusement. "Sweetheart, that was nowhere near harassment..."

His hand quickly closed on her wrist, and he twisted her around into a lock with her arms crossed over her body. Cass squeaked; he was faster than anything she'd ever seen. Hell, she'd never seen anyone move like that. His lips found the skin of her neck as she struggled, and trailed gentle kisses along her throat as his thumbs stroked the insides of her captured wrists.

"How's this for harassment, hmm?" His voice was a low rumble just below her ear. A hot, sweet ache joined the sudden panic flaring in her core and moved outward.

She didn't speak—she couldn't. Despite the domineering hold, the soft brush of his lips back and forward over her throat was hypnotic. Wariness drained away, leaving pure need. She tilted her head to the side a little to give him better access, and his lips found the sweet spot behind her ear. Oh, yes, she needed this...

"You like that." Not a question, but a statement. His lips curved against her skin at her response. Then her hands were free and his moved over her, one sliding up to close around a breast. He located her nipple through the thin fabric and pinched lightly, rolling it between his fingers before pulling.

Each soft pinch and pull shot straight through her to where her clit throbbed in response. She shifted her weight, moving her feet further apart, and lifted her arms. Her hand slid to the nape of his neck, holding him to her as she turned her head to seek his lips.

Her moan lost in his mouth, he parted her lips and took what he wanted. His fingers on her nipples kept her off balance as he explored her, plundering the softness of her mouth, and then, just when Cass was ready to beg, he upped the ante.

His hand covered her soft belly and pulled her back hard to grind his hips against hers. Heat swept through Cassia again when his cock pressed against her ass, fitting into the valley between her cheeks. God, he was huge…surely he wasn't that big? It must be some trick of sensation. Then he rotated his hips and she almost passed out. Yeah, he was that big. Nerves and excitement filled her. She wanted—no—she needed his cock inside her. Right now…in fact, the quicker the better.

"More," she whispered against his lips, thrusting her ass back and trying to hurry things along. There was only so much teasing a girl could take before a guy had to make good on the promise.

His hand slid lower. He hauled her skirt up as he ran his hand up the inside of her thigh. Anticipation filled her as his finger danced along the lace edge of her thong. Then it was gone, the delicate ties snapping as he pulled it from her in one quick movement.

"Hmm, shaved…very nice." He took his time running his fingers along her smooth folds. "Kinky little thing, aren't you?"

Cass opened her mouth to answer but all she could manage was a strangled moan as he parted her folds and found her clit. He circled it once, a very male sound of appreciation in his throat as she whimpered, then his fingers dipped lower to her already soaked pussy.

"Very kinky, and very wet." He spread the wetness he found there, rubbing it over her clit in small, maddening circles which wound the tension in her body tighter and tighter.

"Very, very wet. You're into this, aren't you?" His voice wove an erotic spell around her as his clever fingers worked against her clit. "And in a minute, I'm going to be in you. You like that idea, huh? A good hard fuck bent over that desk?"

Cass shivered. Oh yeah, she liked...in fact, it couldn't happen quick enough for her. "Yeah, when you quit chattering and actually get on with it. Sheesh, and I thought women were bad for talking."

A chuckle rumbled through his chest pressed against her back as sharp teeth nipped her ear playfully. "Didn't your mother ever teach you patience is a virtue?"

He tweaked her nipple through the satin and lace again, sending a thrill through her body to her aching clit. A pout of frustration formed on her lips as he moved his hand. She was already missing the sensation. She opened her mouth to complain just as he pushed her forwards. In one smooth movement, he pulled the remaining warded chains from her belt—she always carried more than she needed on a job, just in case—and spun her around.

Before Cassia could react, the chain snapped and locked about her wrists, binding them together. "Hey! What the fuck do you think you're playing at? Let me go!"

Twisting her wrists, she tried to get free of the Fae-steel. Even as she struggled, she knew it wasn't going to help. It would take something a lot bigger and meaner than her to break the enchantment on the chain, so all she succeeded in doing was rubbing herself raw on the steel.

She looked at him and tried to stay calm. If he'd wanted to hurt her, then he wouldn't have helped her get out of the main area of the club. *Yeah...you think? So what's he done other than brought you somewhere out of the public eye? He's not helped you get out of the place completely, has he? And now you're stuck in warded chains, in a club which doesn't allow vampires, with a demon who looks like he intends to eat you for breakfast...*

Cassia swallowed nervously and plastered a "Well?" look on her face. *Never let them see your fear.* You did and you were a goner, pure and simple. His answer was a quick jerk on the chain. Cass fell against him, her bound hands landing in the middle of his chest as she tried to balance herself.

"Well, it strikes me that I have a vampire who's been trespassing here." As he spoke, he reached up and looped the end of her chain over one of the exposed pipes running along the ceiling of the office. He pulled, drawing the end of the chain down.

"You bastard! Let me go!" Cass struggled madly as her wrists were drawn upward. She was kyn but even so, her strength was no match for his.

"Just let me get out of these, and I'll make you wish you'd never been born," she promised, fury in her eyes.

He laughed, locking the chain off around the pipe. "Sorry, doll, been there, done that, got the T-shirt to prove it. Besides, there are procedures when we catch a trespasser. I have to search you and your belongings for weapons, contraband...you know."

Grinning over his shoulder he opened her purse and rifled through it until he found her ID. "Cassia Leyland. Nice name."

Cass went pale as he looked in the bag, knowing what was inside. She wasn't bothered about him finding weapons because she was still wearing them for all the good they had done her. She'd fought and brought in demons before, but she'd never seen anyone...anything...move as quickly as he did.

"Oh, now this is interesting." He pulled something small and pink from the depths of the bag and she went scarlet. It was her special little "friend," a rampant rabbit mini vibrator with a finger loop to help direct those vibrations exactly where needed. "Very interesting indeed."

He abandoned the purse, and leaned back against the desk, sitting on the edge as he fiddled with the controls of the vibrator, displaying all the enthusiasm of a child with a new toy. The dial clicked and a soft buzzing filled the room.

Cass leaned her head back, closed her eyes and prayed for strength. When she looked up, she was still irritated. Why had she thought he was sexy? Right about now she'd much rather slap him upside the ear than get down and dirty with him. Okay...maybe that was a lie.

"You know, it's rude to go through a lady's things."

He experimented with the settings, the little rabbit going from slow and sexy right the way up to va-va-voom, Cass's favorite setting, and her cheeks got hotter. "I know, but why not? Especially when I find such interesting things?" He looked up. His eyes swirled with dark heat, a heat laced with naughtiness, and her breath caught. All of a sudden, being tied up in a room with a demon didn't seem so bad after all...

"You know, I think it might be faulty." He shook it, holding it up to his ear and listening for a rattle. It buzzed back at him. "Yeah, it's sounding a little odd to me. I think it needs testing. Just to be on the safe side, of course. Can't let you go about with a faulty electrical item. You might hurt yourself."

Cass shrugged, attitude locked into place and hiding the fact her knees had gone weak at the suggestion in his tone. "Whatever floats your boat, sweetheart. Just let me out of here before you start getting happy, would you?"

He pushed away from the desk, his expression intent. "Oh no, I'm not using it on myself. That wouldn't be any fun now, would it?"

Cass lost the ability to speak as he sauntered over to her. Most of the female population would kill to be able to move so gracefully, yet there was nothing feminine in his manner. Everything about him screamed virility and masculinity. He paused a mere hair's-breadth away from her, looking down.

Their eyes locked and Cass knew he could see what he was doing to her, knew that her insides were quaking, and her clit throbbed at the promise she read in his eyes.

"I think this would be far more fun to use on you," he breathed, bending his head to kiss her again.

Bite his lip, do something...don't give in... Cassia's thought process trailed off as his lips whispered over hers. Touching, teasing, tasting. The gentlest touches, almost innocent in their own way, if not for the fact he'd turned the clit stimulator right up to full and began to trail it up between her thighs.

Anticipation rolled through her as the buzzing plastic got higher and higher. Her pussy clenched in need, wanting it there now and damn the consequences. The flush still riding her cheeks, Cass parted her thighs, silently inviting his touch and that of the pink plastic rabbit in his hand.

He moved in closer, reached down without breaking the kiss and pulled one of her legs up over his hip. Cass whimpered into his mouth as the change in position exposed her pussy to the cooler air. God, if he didn't do something soon she was going to fucking explode.

Cass's world shrank to tracking the rabbit's movement across her skin and the feel of Tiny's lips on hers. She was so turned on that the instant the vibrator touched her clit she knew she was going to come.

She didn't. Tiny made the rabbit's ears circle then brush over her clit. Cass moaned, her eyes closing as Tiny kissed down her throat again. Her hips bucked against the movement of his hand as he ran the vibrator over her clit again, seeking every last drop of sensation.

"Oh yeah, you're a kinky little thing, all right," his voice, velvet temptation over steel, murmured in her ear. "You know what I'm going to do? I'm going to make you come with this, listen to you scream. Then I'm going to fuck you and make you scream all over again."

"You sure you're that good?" Cass asked as he circled again. The tempo of the vibrator changed. Not a constant vibe now, but bursts of vibration building up and up until there was a longer, sustained section of them—the va-va-voom setting, the one Cass could never last long on. Already she could feel the familiar tension low down in her body as her clit throbbed in response to the rabbit's speed.

"Oh, you're going to find out soon enough." He used his free hand to hook a couple fingers into the front of her shirt and pulled down, popping all the buttons as he went. Her breasts, encased in a purple satin and lace demi-bra, spilled out.

"Packing dangerous weaponry here, I see." Without warning, he leaned down and took one of her nipples into his mouth and suckled it through the lace.

"Ohmigod." The exclamation was torn from her as he sucked hard while at the same time he thrust two fingers deep into her pussy. Quite how he managed it still holding the vibrator against her clit, Cass didn't know and she didn't care. All she cared about was that he carried on doing it.

"That's it, sweetie, come for me. I want to feel you come. I want you all wet and ready for me."

She shuddered at his words, grabbing the chain and holding on for dear life. Her hips pushed against his fingers and the vibrator as heat raced through her veins and licked across her skin.

Then it was all too much. A ragged moan escaped her lips as her body clenched tight and her hips shuddered in an erratic rhythm against his hand as her climax hit her hard, washing her away in a tidal wave of hot pleasure.

Breathy moans and soft cries filled the room; noises Cass belatedly realized were from her own throat as he kept up the pressure, the rabbit's ears still tickling her hypersensitive clit. She whimpered and tried to shift away. "Too much..." she muttered and sighed in relief as he pulled away from her.

Her relief was short-lived. "You feel fantastic." His voice was hoarse and filled with need as he slid his fingers into her pussy again, a pussy slick from her climax. Even though she'd just come, the pressure of his fingers as they curled back to seek her G-spot made her catch her breath again, a frisson of excitement arcing through her like a bolt of lightning.

Cass's eyes opened wide. She couldn't be ready again already, surely? Normally using that setting wiped her out, but here she was needing more. Something she had no problems with vocalizing. "More," she demanded, moving against him insistently.

"You want more? Then you're going to have to beg," he whispered by her ear, and turned her again in the chains. This time, when his cock pressed against her ass, Cass moaned out loud and thrust back, wriggling her hips in temptation.

His chuckle filled the small room and he kicked her feet further apart. "Tease, that's not begging." His large hand smoothed up under her skirt and over her ass, cupping and massaging the cheek. His fingers dipped down to stroke her needy flesh again. "Perhaps I should leave you to think about it then..."

"No! You can't!" Her voice held all her panic and frustration. "You bastard, don't you dare leave me here like this! Do something!"

Tiny's lips quirked at her imperious demand, and he was glad she couldn't see him. It was hard to act the badass when he was grinning broad enough to split his face. "Beg."

He held his response ruthlessly in check, circling her clit again to savor the helpless little sounds she made. Sounds that made him want to drop his pants, free his cock and thrust hard into her willing body. He knew she would be hot, wet and tight. A ride guaranteed to take a man to heaven and back.

He wasn't going to, though; not until she begged him, not until she gave him the surrender he craved. A shiver raked his body as she thrust her ass back and wriggled against him in blatant invitation.

"I want to hear the words. I want to hear you beg, sweetness." He nipped her ear, his tone hard and uncompromising. Inside, though, he was begging. Christ, she had to give in sooner or later, or he was going to lose it. "Beg and I'll give you what we both need."

She moaned, the sound tortured, and Tiny knew he had her. "Yes! Yes, please!"

"Please what?"

"Oh, for heaven's sake—fuck me! I want you to fuck me!"

His groan mingled with hers as he yanked the zipper of his pants down. Within seconds he was free, and he kicked her feet even wider. Dipping his knees, he pressed the broad head of his erection against her slick entrance.

Their groans mingled in the small room as he gradually and insistently entered her body. It was like sliding into warm silk. "Gods, you feel good." His voice was hoarse and strained as he fought to keep control when all his body wanted to do was drive into the ambrosia offered to it and revel in excess. Slow and sure was the order of the day though and he wanted this to be as good for her as for him, even if it killed him. She was tight and wet, as he'd known she would be. The combination nearly blew him away as he slid in her as far as he could go and stilled.

Oh. My. God.

Cass's nostrils flared as he paused, his cock stretching her pussy almost to the point of pain. She was glad he'd stopped. It gave her body time to adjust, to get used to him. It was time she desperately needed. She'd had many lovers over the years and some as big...well, almost. None had treated her with the quiet care of the demon behind her.

His hands soothed her, one sliding down her arm. The other slid south over the slight mound of her stomach to seek her clit again. He played with it, soft strokes followed by teasing circles until her initial discomfort had worn off.

An insistent restlessness filled her, centered in her groin. She needed to move. The need kept growing until she couldn't resist. Twisting the chain around her wrists, she used it to anchor herself and then rolled her hips. Sensation exploded within her, the nerves along her feminine sheath going off like a fireworks display at the friction as he slid almost all the way out of her.

"Oh gods, yeah, baby, that feels so good." His voice was guttural and harsh. Cass could hear his need and desire. He thrust back into her. "So, so good."

Cass couldn't stop. Like the floodgates had been opened, she had to keep moving, pulling away from him and waiting as he held her hips still and slid back into her. A whimper sounded in the room, and it took her a moment to realize it had come from her. His slides became thrusts, then slams, and her whimper became moans as their hips met in a frenzied dance.

All semblance of civility lost, he took her in a hard and fast rhythm, encouraged every step of the way by her gasps, moans and half-articulated demands for more. His fingers danced against her clit in time with the movement of his hips. She stilled, her back arched and her body stiffened. The tension wound in her reached breaking point.

For one glorious moment she stood on the edge, gazing down into the abyss, and it was filled with a million shimmering lights. His hips continued to move, his cock ramming home again, and she cried out, shattering apart and falling into the light.

Chapter Four

It had been the best sex he'd had in years. No, probably the best sex he'd had in his life, even if he counted the hot redheaded succubus at his eighteenth birthday party. And she hadn't just been hot, she'd been scorching.

"Well, don't you have a face like a wet weekend? Careful, if the wind changes, you'll stick like that." A feminine voice broke through his daydream. Tiny jerked to attention to find Misty smiling at him and holding out a mug of coffee.

He took it with a wary look in his eye. Misty made coffee thick enough to double as industrial degreaser, and the stuff dissolved spoons on a regular basis. The caffeine content was so high, it was more liquid "no way are you sleeping for, oh, a week" than a hot beverage.

He took the mug anyway, and frowned as her words filtered through the sluggish mass of his brain. "Where do you come up with these sayings?" He took a sip and grimaced as the bitterness attacked his taste buds. "Christ, Misty! Would it kill you to put some sugar in here?"

"You're sweet enough. Besides, don't want your ass getting any bigger. Move over, you great lummox," she ordered, sitting down on the cold stone step next to him and wrapping her hands around her mug. Both of them had stopped smoking a year ago, but they still came out at their allocated breaks to get some fresh air. Or, in Tiny's case, to try and clear his head.

"Charming. Trash my ego, why don't you?" He shoved his nose in his mug again. This time the foul stuff didn't taste quite as bad, probably because it had stripped most of the skin off his tongue with the first sip.

"So where did you disappear to last night?"

Tiny did everything right. He didn't freeze, didn't go silent, just sipped casually from his mug and slid a glance sideways at her. She wasn't looking at him, looked out over the empty street instead, but he knew she was onto him. "Had a little run-in with a patron; had to do a search and packed her off with a warning," he said, his tone noncommittal and bored.

"That some kind of demon-speak for you two did the nasty?"

Tiny sighed. It was going to be a long morning. "You should wash your mouth out with soap, young lady," he admonished, knowing full well Misty was older than him. Although she appeared to be in her mid-twenties, there was something old about her eyes...like the vamp chick last night. No, not the "vamp chick." Cassia Leyland, it said on the ID card nestled in his pocket.

"You did!" Misty crowed as she punched the air. "You screwed some chick in the office. I knew it!" Her gaze cut sideways to him, her expression shrewd. "You must have been going some to track down and get rid of the vampire and pick up a bit...of..."

She stopped, a strange expression crossing her face for a second, a combination of shock warring with surprise and disgust, then, almost hidden, a reluctant interest. "Tiny, tell me you didn't screw the vamp in the security office?"

"Okay, I won't."

"Fucking hell, you did! You fucked the vampire. Are you stupid, or did your momma drop you on your head as a baby? Do you know what the bosses would've done if they'd caught you?"

A scowl settled on the demon's face as he contemplated what it would take to throttle a Valkyrie. "Yeah, well, they didn't," he grunted, his tone defensive. He'd known it was a bad idea, but damn, it had felt good at the time. Trouble was, he wanted more, a lot more, and soon.

He shoved his nose back in the mug again, hoping beyond hope to avoid more questions. But this was Misty, and like most women of his acquaintance, once she'd gotten her teeth into something, she didn't let go.

"So, you seeing her again?"

His shoulder moved in a shrug. "Dunno. Not exactly healthy, is it? Demon and the vampire. Gods know how many people would get bat-shit about it."

"Yeah, I never understood that. What is it with you guys, anyway?" Misty shifted on the stone step to try and get more comfortable. "I mean, to me there's not much difference between your aura and a vampire's apart from theirs are blood-red most of the time."

Tiny arched an eyebrow. "And mine?"

She turned to look at him, her eyes distant. Tiny knew without asking she was looking beyond the physical and into his soul. "Black. With...gold veins."

"Gold flecks? Yeah, right, next you'll be telling me I'm the lost prince of the demon court," he chuckled, his broad grin hiding his unease. Hide in plain sight, nowhere better.

"Oh yeah, they haven't found him yet, have they? What was his name? Sevren, or something?"

Seren. Seren Di Lakai Telosa. Son of Lakai, Prince of the Night and Shadows, Lord of the Seventh Gates. Tiny knew the name and titles by heart, because they were his names, and they'd been hammered into him from birth. "Yeah, something like that. Anyway, break's over. You coming?"

The day was a long one, too long for Tiny's liking. The small ID card he'd lifted from Cassia the night before was burning a hole in his pocket.

For the seventh time in the last hour he pulled the card free. She wasn't smiling at the camera, but her lips had a mysterious half smile some women did well, sort of like the Mona Lisa but way sexier. Tiny wasn't an art lover. He preferred his women live and lusty rather than rhapsodizing over some dead chick immortalized on canvas, but sometimes only a classical reference would do.

Cassia. A pretty name but was it real? Questions about her whirled about his brain, questions he hadn't gotten to ask last night. Once they'd finished, she'd demanded to be released and as soon as he had, she'd grabbed her stuff and disappeared out the door as though all the hounds of hell were after her.

The card stayed in his jacket pocket for the next couple of days. Days in which, try as he might, Tiny couldn't get the sexy vamp out of his thoughts. His dreams were haunted by images of her, and he woke up hard and aching, dreaming of plunging into her soft body only to realize he was dry humping his own damn sheets.

"Fuck it!" he gasped, dropping one of the drinks menu holders as he helped the bar staff set up for the evening.

"Hey, you all right, man?" the waiter asked in concern. Tiny kept his expression blank as he tried to remember the guy's name. Mark… Matt…something beginning with M anyway.

"Yeah, yeah, I'm fine. Laid funny on my arm last night, and my hand keeps going dead. It'll wear off in a minute." He shook his hand for emphasis, the skin across the palm stinging like mad, as the waiter picked up the menu and holder to place them on the table.

Tiny opened his hand to check. He must have been bitten. Either that or he'd touched something dodgy during clean-up this morning. There was always some joker leaving something lying around, and one man's pleasure was another man's poison.

No rash greeted his eyes as he opened his palm, but a series of pseudo-tribal marks decorated the skin. What the fuck? His breath left his lungs in a rush as he stared blankly. Closing his hand quickly he looked around, but no one was watching him.

Matt… Malcolm moved away along the line of tables without another glance in his direction. Like a lot of the staff he was human, so Tiny didn't have to worry much about being snuck up on. Carefully, he opened his palm again, hoping the marks would be gone.

No such luck. They were still there, as plain as if a tattooist had taken a needle to his skin. Not tattoos, he decided, pulling the skin this way and that. They didn't move like tattoos on the skin. Tiny had enough of those, although his demonic blood broke them down after a few weeks, and he kept having to go have them redone. So he knew how a tattoo reacted on the skin. No, these marks were under the skin somehow...

He sighed and closed his palm. He knew what they were. Vampire marks. Somehow Cassia had marked him. Tiny's expression set, his lips compressing into a thin, hard line. The question was...why?

"No, no, no. You've gotta be kidding me," Cassia wailed as she studied the palm of her hand and the symbols etched across the skin for all the world to see. Symbols which would tell another vampire she'd bonded with a mate.

She looked up and into her bathroom mirror, haunted brown eyes staring back at her. This wasn't happening, it couldn't be happening. She didn't need or want a mate. Especially not when...

"No!" The blood drained out of her reflection's face. There was only one way a vampire bonded with his or her mate—the combination of sex and blood. The only guy she'd had sex with recently had been the sexy as hell demon at Moonlight & Magic.

"Crap. This is not good." She couldn't be bonded to a demon. She shouldn't even have given him the bloody time of day, let alone gotten down and dirty with him.

Cass stared at the marks again, hoping they'd have already faded, or better yet, been a figment of her imagination. No such luck. They were still there, clear dark symbols against her pale flesh.

Her brow furrowed. How had she managed to bond to him? She'd made sure there hadn't been a blood exchange. Because, whilst there were a few things she could think of more unpleasant than being addicted to demon blood, they were the sort of things she never intended to try out—like getting her arms and legs ripped off by a were-dragon, or heading on into the dark plains to find a Medusa to irritate.

Somehow, though, even without the blood exchange, she had bonding marks all over her palm. How the hell... Was it even possible to bond with a demon? More importantly, how was she going to keep quiet about the fact she had?

Realizing she was still staring at herself in the mirror Cass dropped her gaze to the offending marks again. Perhaps she could just cut her hand off and have done with it? No, that would hurt like hell.

She'd once had to regrow the tip of a finger after an accident with a Keres demon and an industrial steel press. That had been bad enough. She could only imagine what regrowing the whole damn hand would feel like.

As soon as the idea occurred to her, though, it wouldn't let go. She had to get rid of these marks somehow, but cutting her hand off wasn't the only solution. Padding barefoot back into her bedroom she sat on the bed and pulled the lamp over so she could get a better look at the marks.

Ignoring the small quiver in the region of her heart, she studied her palm. Bonded mates were rare. Every vampire girl dreamed someday—if she was lucky—she would meet Mr. Perfect and wake one evening with these marks on her hand. Cass hadn't been born a vamp, but even she'd bought into the romantic dream of a bond-mate.

Using her fingertips she manipulated the skin of her palm under the light. The mark wasn't on the skin, more under the skin, like something had been inserted there. Her full lips compressed into a thin line.

Turning, she grabbed her purse from the other side of the bed and rifled through it. In the chaos that reigned supreme in the bottom, she located her knife. Pulling it free from the bag, she released the blade with a practiced flick of her finger and considered her palm again. This was going to hurt...

There was blood on the air. Tiny might not have been a vampire, but his senses were still acute enough to pick up the scent of new blood. Not surprising since vampires were a form of demon, just not one from this world.

Tiny didn't know the full story as to how they'd ended up in this world, and he didn't much care. It was a secret both races kept religiously. It was also the reason demons and vampires didn't get along; they were too alike.

Tiny checked the card in his hand again and looked up at the apartment building. It had taken him a while to track her down, but there weren't many people who could remain hidden from a demon of Tiny's power for long. What did surprise him was the fairly "normal" looking building. Didn't vampires need to sleep in their graves? Or was that another myth interfering with the facts?

The scent of blood got stronger, a sweet, almost tantalizing scent. Tiny's nose twitched. It smelt good, good enough to eat. His stomach rebelled at the same time his mind rejected the idea. He wasn't a bloodsucker, no way, no how. So no blood should smell that good.

He climbed out of the car, his tall frame unfolding from the seat and stretching as he eased muscles cramped from the long drive. Never having driven for so many hours straight, he was in agony, but driving had been the quickest way here, and he'd needed speed. He'd only managed twenty-four hours off work. It was the most he could swing at late notice without telling Jaren what he needed time off for. An explanation he couldn't give. Tiny couldn't see the vampire-hating incubus being understanding about his need to track down a vampire he couldn't get out of his head.

The tall demon snorted to himself. Yeah, Jaren was more likely to slap him in a straitjacket and cart him off to the paranormal equivalent to a mental ward. Probably slap him around a little en route for his sheer stupidity. Jaren was one demon who held the ancient enmity between vampire and demon close to his heart.

He heard her before he saw her, a feminine muttering emerging from the other side of the door as he approached the building. He smelled her before she came into view. The fragrance of a new wound hung on the air like an exotic fragrance. Tiny's brow furrowed. What was up with him? He'd never been this sensitive to fresh blood before.

The door opened and she was there, a frustrated expression on her heart-shaped face which disappeared when she saw him. Her eyes widened in recognition and anger. "You!"

"Me?" Tiny leaned one shoulder against the doorframe. By the gods, she was glorious when she was mad. Her eyes flashed with fire, her features came alive and even her hair crackled with energy.

"Yeah, you! You're the bloody problem!" she snapped, advancing on him and jabbing him in the chest. Tiny noticed two things at the same moment. One, her eyes were wet with what looked suspiciously like tears and two, her hand was bandaged.

He grabbed her wrist, careful not to put any pressure on the dressing over her palm. His eyes narrowed as he registered the placement. "What did you do?"

"Nothing."

Anger hit him broadside, washing over him as he twisted her palm upwards and stripped the dressing away with quick, efficient movements. She struggled, swearing at him, but Tiny ignored her as he revealed her palm. Or rather the mess she'd made.

She'd tried to carve the marks out of her palm. But she hadn't managed it. Blood oozed around the ragged edges criss-crossing her palm and in one section the skin was missing completely. Almost as if she thought by removing the skin she could remove the mark. It hadn't worked; the mark was still there in the flesh below. His lips compressed as he looked up at her, his gaze glittering and hard.

"Doesn't look like nothing to me. I was going to ask you what these were," he said, holding his own hand up, the palm decorated with similar markings.

"They're obviously not something good if you tried to do this. Fancy cluing me in any time soon?"

"Go screw yourself." She snatched her hand back, cradling it against her chest as she pulled a clean handkerchief from her pocket to use as a dressing. Worry threaded through his chest, winding around the anger. What were these marks and why had she tried to get rid of them in such a drastic manner?

"Tell me." His hands curled around her upper arms to drag her hard against him. Perhaps a little harder than he intended, but when the result was her breasts pressing again his chest in such a manner, he wasn't going to apologize.

She flicked her hair back over her shoulders and glared up at him in challenge. "Or what?"

Tiny dropped his head back, his eyes closed as he prayed for strength. This woman was going to be the death of him. "Never challenge a demon." His voice strained, he counted to ten, a hundred...hell, he might as well go for broke and make it a thousand.

"Why?"

He jerked his head up, the look in his eyes feral and dark. The fierce challenge in her eyes wavered for a moment, as though she was unsure. As well she might be. Demons weren't the most stable of creatures, and being in the arms of a pissed-off, sexually frustrated demon probably wasn't the best place in the world to be. Tiny smiled as he watched the realization enter her eyes.

He slid a large hand into her hair and cupped her nape. The bones of her neck seemed so delicate and fragile as his large fingers stroked them, applying pressure to tilt her lips up to his. "Because," he breathed through lips barely a hair's-breadth from hers, "we like it. It gets us...me...hot."

He took her lips, biting back a groan at the sensation. They were like cool silk beneath his. Luscious and full, they quivered for a moment under his sensual assault, but the softest brush of his tongue against her lower lip had her opening for him. Triumph washed through him like the incoming tide. Tiny murmured in pleasure, and drew her deeper into his embrace to deepen the kiss. It felt good—felt right—and to hell with anyone who said it was wrong.

When he lifted his head a moment later, they were both breathing raggedly. Need and something else, something softer Tiny didn't want to define, raged through his blood. It urged him to pull her outside into the darkness in the lee of the building, and slake the thirst which claimed him.

Their eyes locked in a long moment of shared, stunned realization. Tiny watched the darkness flare in her eyes, matching the darkness racing through his own body. She wanted this as much as he did.

"Your place? Or mine?" The question was more of a plea than he wanted to think about. Naked need and longing rang in his voice. He wanted her and he didn't care what he had to do to get her where he needed her, on her back under him.

She didn't answer. The seconds ticked by as she studied his eyes, her own going from one to the other as though looking for the answer to an unknown question. Finally she nodded, her lips pursed for a second before she smiled. "My place, on one condition."

"Which is?"

"This time, I'm in charge."

Chapter Five

Cass, what the hell are you doing? This is such a bad idea. The thoughts circled in Cassia's head as she turned to lead her demon lover back up to her apartment. How he'd found her, she didn't know, but as soon as she'd seen the marks on her palm she'd known he would come for her. Bonded mates couldn't stay away from each other for long. Not even, it seemed, when one of them wasn't a vampire but a demon instead.

His larger hand engulfed her uninjured one, and his thumb stroked over the delicate flesh on the inside of her wrist. The gentle movement sent sparks of awareness through her, all meeting to pool low down in her belly. Cass's footsteps sped up—the need to get somewhere with a comfortable and horizontal surface uppermost in her mind.

He must have felt the urgency in her grip. He matched her step for step as they turned the last corner on the stairs and her door came into view. She'd been lucky and managed to get the apartment closest to the stairwell. Made it easier with her coming and going at all times of night. She led him down the corridor to her door in silence, the sexual tension stretching between them like a third person in the narrow hall.

Without a word, she unlocked the door, swallowed her nerves and stood aside to let him in. This was a big thing for her; she didn't bring men here, back to her "lair," a laughable description of her tiny apartment.

Her calm expression as he walked past her hid a seething mass of nerves. The kiss downstairs had re-ignited the need which had been a constant ache since the night at the club. Not only re-igniting it but fanned it to the blaze racing through her veins, causing liquid heat to dampen her panties. It was a need which transcended even her drive to feed, an overriding desire for her mate which couldn't be denied.

Mentally she shied away from that fact in favor of watching him. Even standing still, he was the sexiest thing she'd ever seen. The last few days apart seemed to have increased his attractiveness, even though she knew that was baloney. Her grip tightened on the door handle, knuckles showing white as she fought the urge to do something stupid like march over and rip all his clothes off.

He had agreed she was in charge though, hadn't he? Her mouth went dry, and she closed the door behind her with a decisive click, cutting off his escape to the outside world.

"Bedroom. Now."

Tiny didn't need telling twice—not when she was ordering him about in such a sexy, take-no-prisoners voice. It made him think of leather-clad dominatrices and whips. Unbidden, an image of her in a leather corset leapt to mind. He bit back a moan of need as his cock, already half hard from their kiss downstairs, came to full attention.

A tiny jerk of her head clued him into the right direction for the bedroom, and he headed that way, barely seeing the neat apartment around him. All he cared about was getting them into a room with a bed so he could get them out of their clothes, slide his cock into her warm, willing body and ease the ache that had tormented him since she'd run out on him the other night.

Once inside the bedroom though, he slowed and started taking notice. This place was her sanctuary, and finding himself wanting to know everything about her, he drank in all the details. The room was neat with the small, personal touches that said this was a home rather than just a place for someone to lay their head.

The only clue to her true nature was the heavy shutters on the inside of the window, between the gauzy net and the curtains, which were open to the night air at the moment but in the day would protect her from the sun's harmful rays.

Tiny pot dragons in cute poses cavorted between the cosmetics and perfumes scattered across the top of the dresser. Tiny's lips quirked. He knew a few dragons, none of whom looked quite as innocent as that. It was cute though, a hunter who collected pot dragons. Didn't do much for her fearsome reputation, but the revelation of a softer side to the woman did things to him on levels he didn't want to think about.

His gaze moved on, flicking over the bed and the deep scarlet satin draped there. Arousal knotted hard in his stomach as he turned to her, eager to pull her into his arms and onto the bed with him. His hands itched to strip off the jeans and top she was wearing, revealing her luscious body to him again. Already he could feel the weight of her breasts in his hands as he molded and caressed them, his lips on the soft skin of her throat, before lifting one darkened nipple to his lips and —

"Strip."

Tiny jerked out of his erotic daydream at the command. He blinked in surprise. When she'd said she was in charge, he hadn't thought she meant it that way. Her expression, full lips drawn into a determined pout and her eyes hard on him, told him that oh yes, she'd meant it.

Excitement hit him in a dizzy surge, like a sugar rush after drinking too much soda, and he ditched his jacket and removed his T-shirt in the same move. His boots hit the carpeted floor with two dull thuds, the footwear quickly covered by his pants and boxers until he stood proudly naked in the middle of her bedroom.

Her eyes wandered over him, taking in the breadth of his shoulders and the hard planes of his chest. Tiny puffed up with male pride at the look of admiration in her eyes, unable to resist posing a little. He knew he looked good, a combination of genetics, species and trying to keep up with Knuckles in the gym. Since getting married, the guy had become obsessed with making sure he didn't get fat or anything else that could mean his wife lost interest in him. Why he bothered, Tiny didn't know; anyone with eyes in their head could see the woman was besotted.

Her eyes widened slightly and he knew she'd spotted the silver ring through his nipple. There were a few paranormal races who could withstand the burn of silver—the Fae, for example, were only susceptible to iron—but demons weren't one of them. The ring through his nipple burned every day, as did the one through his eyebrow. They were there on purpose. Pleasure mixed with pain, the hallmark of the demon courts, reminders of who and what he was.

A demon.

Currently a demon with the hardest erection he could ever remember, and a hot woman looking at him as though she'd like to eat him whole. His cock jerked, signaling its approval of the idea, blood pulsing and pooling in the engorged shaft. He resisted the urge to reach down and palm himself. He wanted only one set of hands on his body, and they weren't his own.

Her dark chocolate eyes slid from his face down to his rigid cock and back up again. A groan reverberated in Tiny's chest as her small pink tongue flicked out to wet her full lips.

"A man can only take so much teasing, honey," he told her hoarsely, but she was already moving towards him, a sway in her hips.

"Oh, I don't think so." Trailing a finger up from his waist, she placed her hand on his chest and fanned out her fingers. He bit back a gasp as her fingertip caught the ring, and a lance of pleasure-pain shot through him, from his nipple all the way down to his cock.

"In fact, I think..." She leaned down. Her mouth hovered just over his pierced nipple, and her warm breath whispered over his heated flesh. His body tensed in anticipation. Her lips were just millimeters away. All she had to do was open her mouth and he'd feel her soft tongue against him. "...you'll take everything I dish out."

Then she did what he was waiting for. Her tongue snaked out and circled his nipple in a lazy spiral before she sucked it into the warm cavern of her mouth and suckled.

"Fuck yeah, baby, do that more."

His hand latched into her dark hair, holding her to him as she lapped at his flat male nipples. She alternated from one side to the other, seemingly fascinated by his piercing. Her small nips and licks were heavenly, not that a demon like Tiny had any concept of heaven, but it felt damn good. Better than anything he'd felt before. Then she moved, pulling and teasing the ring with her tongue and teeth, leaving him cursing. God, he wanted her clever mouth working his cock.

She pulled away, smiling as she noticed his pout of disappointment, but he didn't stop her. For such a hulking, well-built guy—she had to face it, he was built along the same lines as the average linebacker—he had some expressions which reminded her of the small boy he'd once been.

"On the bed, lover-boy, and be quick about it," she ordered as she reached for the silk scarves over the chair at the side of the bed.

He was quick, easing his long frame onto her bed almost before she'd finished the sentence and watching her in the intent way he had, like a cat watching a mouse. Cass avoided his eyes and stole a glance down his body to the impressive erection lying rigid against his flat belly.

He was as well built down there as she remembered, or rather, as her body remembered since she hadn't actually seen him that night in the office. So she drank her fill now, biting her lip as she lashed his wrists to her bed. She wanted that cock inside her again. Liquid heat slid from between her thighs as she imagined straddling him and guiding that thick shaft to her wet pussy and slowly, oh so slowly, sinking down onto it. Then she'd ride him until they were both slick with sweat and sated with pleasure.

Hands trembling with need, she checked the knots against both his wrists. The scarves held his arms captive above his head. Silk could be slippery, and it had been a long time since she'd had someone tied to her bed. The last thing she wanted to do was hurt him and end up in whatever the demon version of the Emergency Room was. She had far more interesting things in mind.

"Comfortable?" She tweaked his pierced nipple, the eager thrust of his hips answer enough.

"I will be when you stop fucking about and sit on my cock."

Cass grinned and leaned down until her lips brushed his ear. "Patience is a virtue." With that she left the room.

What the hell? Where had she gone? She couldn't leave him high and dry like this, not when he was about ready to burst with need. Hell, all he needed was a minute with her hot little body wrapped around his cock like a velvet glove, and he'd be shooting his bolt faster than a bloody rifle.

"Cassia? Cassia! What the fuck are you doing? Naked guy on your bed feeling a complete twat…" he called out, the demand in his voice unmistakable. Craning his neck, he glared at the door she'd disappeared through, hearing the sounds of movement from beyond.

It wasn't the door they'd come through so she hadn't just led him down the garden path, tied him up and left. Although, if she left him here much longer he'd be expecting the guy with the hidden cameras to step out of a cupboard or something.

"Smile, Prince Seren, you're on *Candid Camera!*" Gods, wouldn't that screw the pooch completely? If he was caught out by something so stupid, it would be more than embarrassing. Worse, it would lead to his father finding out where he was. Going back to the demon court for another couple of centuries of boredom was definitely not on Tiny's to-do list.

He started to pull on the silk. Flimsy restraints, they weren't strong enough to make even a pretense of holding him. It was a sensual-erotic thing; they symbolized him giving up control to her.

"Cas—fucking hell!" Sensing movement in the doorway Tiny looked up halfway through his complaint and cut off with a curse. His mouth dropped open as he stared at the vision in the doorway. Gone were the black T-shirt and jeans he'd been fantasizing about peeling off her, and in their place she wore a black leather corset which nipped her tiny waist in and pushed her breasts up until they were in danger of spilling over the top with a pair of killer-heeled thigh-high boots.

A thousand erotic images hit him at once, and his cock swelled even further. Shit, once he got between her thighs, this wasn't going to take long at all.

"You like?" She sauntered towards him, a mysterious little female smile on her lips, and each step revealed a flash of her pale thighs and the scrap of satin masquerading as a thong which tied at the sides.

Ties she played with, running the silky ribbons through her fingers as she watched him. Tiny swallowed and nodded dumbly. In truth, he couldn't have framed a response even if he still had the power of speech.

"You want to see more?"

Another nod. Of course he wanted to see more. What did she think he was, some kind of monk?

The ties pulled taut, sliding from the bow centimeter by slow centimeter. All Tiny's attention was riveted on the thin scraps of ribbon. He'd never watched anything as intently in his life as he watched those little ribbon bows get smaller and smaller until they weren't there at all.

The satin fell away, revealing the bare mons at the apex of her thighs to his interested gaze. Blood surged through his body as his arousal deepened, tightening the skin of his cock and balls in a vise-like grip as she turned away, bending over and spreading her legs so he got a good look. The plump pink lips of her pussy glistened as she spread them a little, teasing him, and the scent of her arousal filled the air like fine perfume.

She wriggled her hips. "How about now? Seen enough yet?"

"Witch," he growled and strained against his silken bonds. All he wanted to do was grab her, place hands on either side of those wonderfully curvy hips and plunge his tongue as far as he could into her delicious pussy. "Come here." His voice was hoarse. "I want to taste you, run my tongue over your clit. Suck and nibble on it until you come screaming. I want to make you scream, let me make you scream," he begged.

Pretending to think, she "absently" slid a finger deep into her pussy. He lost the ability to breathe, watching as she worked her cunt with first one, then two fingers. "Well... I guess you've been a good boy and good boys deserve treats."

She pulled her fingers out with a wet *pop* and crawled onto the bed. Instead of straddling his face as Tiny expected she turned the other way and faced down his body.

Tiny closed his eyes and counted to ten as her pussy waved tantalizingly just inches from his face and her mouth hovered over his cock. Bloody hell, he'd just died and gone to heaven.

Cass held her breath as she sat astride him. Her whole body tightened in anticipation as his hot breath fanned over her exposed pussy. She'd been fantasizing about this since the night at the club, wanting to taste him and have him taste her in return.

He didn't disappoint. Before Cass could take another breath, his warm tongue explored, sweeping from her clit to the soaked entrance to her body and back again. Unerringly he located her clit, nibbled and sucked on it, not letting up as Cass shuddered and moaned above him.

Dipping her own head, she ran her tongue over him, wetting him from root to tip before sliding her lips around the swollen head. She sucked him in, feeling the surge of blood in his cock as she took him as deeply as she could, the tip pressing into the back of her throat. A groan against her clit was his only response, the sound more a vibration against her sensitized flesh. Cass gasped, her eyes threatening to roll back in her head.

Using her hands, lips and tongue, she worked his cock and relished every helpless jerk of his hips, each moan and muffled curse from between her thighs. The tension in her body wound tighter as he upped the ante, teasing her with quick sweeps against her clit then plunging deep into her body and fucking her with his tongue. He played her body with frightening ease until she was hanging on the very precipice, just one more move threatening to push her over and into her climax.

"Stop." Pulling away from him with a gasp, she rested her forehead against his hipbone. "I want you to be inside me when I come."

She felt rather than saw his smile, and a second later he laid a gentle kiss on her clit. "Okay, honey, you take what you need. You're in charge, remember?"

Cass lifted off him, unable to resist a last slow lick along his cock before she did. He tasted fantastic, far better than any other man she'd had, a message in itself. Her mate would be compatible in all ways. Even taste.

Impatient as the needs of her body made themselves known, Cass swung her leg over his hips and settled herself into his lap. His rigid shaft was trapped between them, settling into the cradle of her thighs. Biting her lower lip, she rocked, rubbed against him, and chuckled when his back arched in response. So she did it again, her eyes half closing in pleasure at the delicious friction.

"Are you going to screw me, or do I have to rip these scarves off, turn you over and fuck you from behind again?" he demanded, passion flaring bright in his eyes as he looked up at her as though she was the only thing that mattered in the world.

Cass shook her head. Her hair danced over her shoulders as she leaned forwards to brush her leather-covered breasts against his naked chest. "Oh no, lover-boy, this time is all mine," she whispered in his ear, "but next time you can take me any way and any how you want."

With that tantalizing promise she reached between them, positioned herself and slowly sank down onto his rigid cock...

Chapter Six

"Ugh, do you demons actually need to eat or..." Cass asked the next evening, her disgust at the prospect of eating apparent as she popped her head around the door whilst Tiny showered. Catching sight of him naked and soaped up, her expression changed. A sparkle of interest in her eyes had Tiny rising to half-mast automatically. "Naked man. If we weren't on a deadline here, I'd be tempted to join you."

Tiny grinned and opened his arms. "Plenty of room for two; give you a replay of last night," he offered her, his grin widening as her cheeks flushed pink. She'd been insatiable last night, but to be fair, so had he. After the first time on the bed, they'd done the round tour of the apartment—the bedroom, the bathroom, the shower, the lounge, the kitchen. They hadn't missed a room in the "christening."

"You are an evil man," she told him and disappeared from the doorway. Tiny chuckled out loud as the sounds of muttering filtered through the open door. Something about "damn teases of men who got a woman all worked up and then let her down."

He wrapped a towel around his lean waist as he walked through into the bedroom, and snagged her around the waist as she tried to bustle by him. "We can always leave a little later," he suggested, nuzzling the sensitive spot behind her ear.

She sighed in pleasure and stretched against him, catlike and lazy, but her voice filled with regret as she disengaged his hands and turned in his embrace. "I'd love to but..."

She wouldn't meet his eyes. Her gaze dropped down to his shoulder instead. At first he thought it was the usual female emotional kickback. Most women needed to be reassured after a night of mad, passionate sex. Needed to be reassured it meant more than two people fucking like bunnies.

Usually Tiny didn't have the patience for it. He tended to leave as soon as possible and avoid it all. Leaving wasn't an option with Cassia, though. Without the apparent intervention of his brain, he found his arms tightening around her and never-before-uttered words of comfort on his tongue.

Then he realized her attention was fixed on the pulse beating strongly in his neck. The flush he'd taken to be shyness—although why she should come off as shy after all they'd shared—was revealed to be hunger when she lifted worried eyes to his. Tiny didn't need any mystical abilities to read her mind. The worry that she'd disgust him was written all over her face. Without thinking, he tilted his head to the side and offered her his throat.

"Feed if you need to," he said in a quiet voice, something which shocked him. Where the impulse came from, he had no idea, but it was a no-brainer. She needed to feed so he would provide.

"No!" Cass recoiled, putting the distance of the bedroom between them. She sounded horrified, her eyes wide in her face as she stared at him. Even from this distance, he could see the trembling in her limbs and the stark longing in her eyes. "I—I'm sorry. I can't."

Frustration raced through him as she turned away to finish getting dressed, sitting down on the side of the bed to slide her feet into more sensible boots than she'd worn in bed last night. It was frustration laced with puzzlement as he pulled his own clothes on. Why had he offered to let her feed from him? In all his long life he'd never offered his throat, or his blood, to anyone. Apart from the fact nice demons didn't do that sort of thing there was the whole darker side of domination he'd never been comfortable exploring with anyone before.

But with Cassia it seemed natural, seemed right, to take care of her and her needs, all her needs. This was something else that was new, like his sensitivity to the smell of blood and the marks on their palms.

Pulling his jeans over his hips, he left them unbuttoned to look at the symbols etched on his palm again. They seemed deeper and more defined than they had last night. It was probably a trick of the light. Surely they couldn't be getting deeper?

Realization hit him hard and fast, like a full broadside from a galleon's cannons. He loved her. Somewhere between their night in the club and this morning, the sassy, awkward vampire with the killer figure had grown on him. He'd fallen for her, and when a demon fell, they really fell—hard and fast like an angel from the heavens.

He'd offered her his throat—his blood—for no other reason than she needed to feed. She hadn't coerced him; she hadn't used mental manipulation—she didn't think that was possible with Tiny—or even the physical force some vampires resorted to. He'd offered of his own accord, and Cass was still in shock an hour later when it came time to leave.

"Ready?" she asked, picking up her purse and going to check the belt on her jeans where her warded chains usually hung.

"Mind still on the job?" Tiny asked, a half smile on his lips as he caught her movement. "Remember, tonight you're all mine." The expression in his eyes was a sensuous promise of long nights spent in pleasure.

Cass swallowed as her heart fluttered madly again, distracting her for a moment from the hunger gnawing at her gut. "Yeah, old habits die hard."

Like not going in even though it was her day off. She couldn't remember the last time she'd had a day off. She'd had a bad run-in with a Keres demon a couple of years ago and been off her feet for a week or two healing up.

Wrapping strong arms around her, he pulled her into an embrace. Cass sighed and rested her head against his shoulder. She closed her eyes, relaxed, and let his touch soothe her, absorbing his quiet strength.

They were bonded. Finally Cass accepted the fact and gave into the tugging on her heart she'd been ignoring. Released, the denied bond settled into every fiber of her being. Echoing her own response, his heavily muscled chest expanded in a sigh of relief, but he didn't say anything, just carried on stroking her hair gently.

She had no idea how this was going to work but she didn't care. Somehow they would make it work, even if he was a demon.

A chill ran the length of her spine. She'd have to tell the city court she'd bonded. If she didn't give too many details and said her mate wasn't local then they wouldn't realize. Bonding was rare anyway and she'd never heard of anyone bonding with a demon. Ever.

In fact, if anyone had mentioned the idea even a week ago, she'd have laughed at them. Now though, with the bonding marks on his palm and him displaying all the possessiveness of a bonded male already...there was no other explanation for it.

Reluctantly, she eased away from him. A loud growl from her stomach signaled other needs and without a word the pair headed for the door.

"You gonna last until we reach my place or do we need to stop for...um, drive through?" Tiny asked as they emerged from the double doors at the front of the building and into the night. On instinct Cass took a deep breath, letting the cool air filter over her tongue, tasting it awash with scents. She could tell a group of humans had passed this way not long ago. Female, heavy on the perfume and hairspray. Girls' night out.

Cass's lips quirked in amusement as she searched for the right term to use. "Drive through would be perfect." Better than stalking the girls' night out group. Besides, Cass preferred male donors, which wasn't such a good idea with a newly bonded male in tow. Possessive would be the understatement of the year. Bonded males had been known to half kill another male for even looking at their mate. She dreaded to think what one would do seeing his woman sink fang into another guy's neck. "There's a blood bank just outside the city limits I can use."

A chuckle escaped her at his startled look. "Surprised? Oh, we're all organized around here. Hunters can have trouble getting time to feed, so rather than have us rush a feeding and potentially brutalize a donor, we can pick up blood pack —" She cut off mid-sentence as three figures materialized out of the darkness around them. "What the hell?"

The figures took on a more defined shape as she watched. Within seconds shadow became substance which turned into texture and color until three men stood in front of them. In business suits and clean cut, they reminded Cass of lawyers. Apart from the smell of fire and brimstone surrounding them, this impression was reinforced when one of them stepped forwards and offered a card.

"Good evening. I trust we're interrupting something," he said, smoothly offering Cass the card when Tiny waved it away. Curious, she took it. There was no logo, no fancy design someone with far too much education and a tendency to talk about complementary colors and "white space" had slaved over for hours. No, this card was plain and simple. Just three lines of text which read:

Josiah Jhinks & Sons
Legal Representatives
House of Telosa

"You're lawyers? Demon lawyers?"

The guy who'd given her the card inclined his head and offered a small professional smile. "I'm afraid so, Miss…"

"None of your business," Tiny broke in, an unmistakable edge of threat in his voice as he glared at the three men. "Your business is with me, not with her. You can let her go."

Cass gasped in surprise as he shoved her behind him with a rough hand. Rough she could do. In bed it was kinky. Being pushed about out of it wasn't. She opened her mouth to tell him she'd fight her own battles, but stopped as something tugged at her memory. She looked down at the card in her hand again.

Telosa.

There was something familiar about the name, something she should be remembering. Her brow furrowed as she rooted through her memory. A year or so ago, there had been something in the press about a missing prince, and there had been a picture. Cass blinked and looked up at Tiny. He didn't look the same. The gorgeous long hair had been shaved off and the ring through his brow was new but…

"You're the missing prince."

Tiny ran a hand over his head, his expression bleak. "Fuck, Cass, you shouldn't have said that."

The demon lawyer smiled. "If you would both please step this way."

"Why didn't you tell me you were a prince?" Cass whispered as they were marched down corridor after corridor, each more impressive than the last. Cass felt like she'd stepped into a history book. It was quite easy to forget they were in hell rather than a European palace other than the heat.

It was as hot as a sauna, and within seconds of stepping out of the magic circle they'd been brought through, Cass's thin shirt had cleaved to her back. It made her feel hot and grubby, especially as no one else seemed to be bothered.

A small muscle jumped in Tiny—no, Seren's jaw as they turned another corner. Cass rolled the name around in her mind a little. She'd have to get used to it. It was strange, knowing his real name after thinking of him as Tiny since she'd met him.

This corridor was different from the others. Not a thoroughfare, it ended in double doors higher than three men, dwarfing the guards on either side. A tremor of fear crawled up Cassia's spine. Nothing good was going to happen on the other side of those doors.

"I was in hiding. Not much point being in hiding if you're going to tell everyone who you are, is there?"

"But —" She'd been going to say "we're bonded," but at that moment, the doors in front of them opened and cut off her response. A tall man—another demon—stepped through. Unlike Seren and the lawyers, who were at least doing half a job of concealing their true natures, this man made no effort to hide his demon heritage.

Skin the color of molten copper stretched over a heavily muscled frame. Blue eyes blazed in the middle of an impossibly handsome face complete with two small horns set on his forehead.

"Ah, Prince Seren, so good of you to join us." His tone was smarmy and condescending. Cass eyed him with distaste, deciding she wouldn't turn her back on this one any time soon. It would be full of knives if she did. She'd seen enough of his type in the vampire courts.

"Lord Zarek. The pleasure, as always, is all yours." Tiny's reply was dry and implacable, the subtle insult wrapped up in a polite smile, his dislike for the other demon clear.

Zarek beamed wider, as though winding people up was his favorite pastime, and transferred his attention to Cassia. "You brought your little pet.

Excellent. Things have been so dull around here. An execution will really liven things up."

"Huh? What? Execution?" Oh shit, that didn't sound good. "Tiny, what's he on about?" she demanded, as they were shunted none too gently into the hall after Zarek.

Tiny didn't answer, which worried Cass. He just reached for her hand, which worried her even more. Walking ahead of them, Zarek threw a smile over his shoulder. "Lover-boy didn't tell you? Tsk, tsk, Seren, that's naughty of you. It's illegal to bond a member of the royal family without the king's permission and to do so is —"

"Punishable by death."

The deep voice was unmistakable. Tiny's heart sank in his chest as he turned to face his father. As always, Lakai looked little older than Tiny did himself. In fact, the two men could have been brothers except for the fact Lakai sported two small horns. Quite understated for a demon but there, nonetheless, and truthfully, the man was as twisted as demons came. Lakai the Corrupt, they called him, Tiny's revered father.

"That's your dad?" The surprise in Cassia's voice matched the stunned look on her face as she stared at the lounging figure on the throne. Tiny nodded, lips compressing as he noticed her expression. She shouldn't be looking at any other man but him and definitely not his damn father! Not like that. Never like that.

She was his, end of story. Jealousy rose hard and fast, almost choking him before he got it under control. But it was too late; already Lakai's eyes had filled with interest as they swept over the slender vampire.

"Although, if you've brought a treat to share with the court, Seren, we might be persuaded to forgive you," he drawled lazily, propping his chin on one hand as he watched the two. "And she is very pretty; she'll be entertaining to watch as she services the lords. A vampire, though...we might have to de-fang her first—just to be on the safe side."

"Touch her and you're a dead demon," Tiny snarled before the words were fully out of his father's mouth. Beside him Cass paled, a small sound of fear escaping her which wrenched his heartstrings. He knew enough about vampires to know the threat of rape was nothing at all to the threat of de-fanging. She might survive rape, even here, but losing her fangs would be a death sentence.

"Ohhh, baby boy grew some balls." Lakai laughed, contempt for his son evident as he pushed off from the throne and sauntered down the dais steps. Tiny's lip started to curl, but with effort he kept it in check. All he wanted to do was rip his dad's arms off and tear his eyes out for looking at Cass that way, but here and now? It would be suicide.

"You'd better believe it. You and me, old man, in the ring." Tiny jerked his head towards the challenge ring set to one side of the throne room. Nearly every civilized race, paranormal race that was, operated on some sort of challenge culture and the demon courts were no different. Dried blood from the last fight still decorated the circle carved into the stone.

"Oh, no. Me and her in the ring, now that could be fun," Lakai countered, circling the two of them and snarling at Zarek when he didn't hop out of the way fast enough. That was the thing with the demon monarch. He was as changeable as the weather and just as foul at times. At the moment, he appeared to be amused so long as he was getting his own way. However, he was getting Cassia over Tiny's dead body, so his dad's good mood was going to disappear fast.

"Not a chance, Pops. Me or no one."

Lakai shrugged one shoulder, his movements filled with an elegance Tiny had always avoided emulating. In fact, he tried to be as different as possible from his father in all ways. Yeah, sexually he could be a twisted bastard, but he wasn't a patch on good old daddy here.

"You see, now I have a problem." The amusement which had colored the demon king's voice a moment ago was gone as he walked back around them, completing his circle and turning to look directly at them. The expression on his face was hard, his eyes unforgiving.

Without asking, Tiny knew they'd stopped dealing with Lakai the man and were now dealing with his Majesty, King Lakai Di Jeran Telosa, King of the Seven Hells.

"My word here is law, and your female has broken the law, made a fool of me. So tell me, can I allow that to go unpunished?

"No!" he answered his own question before Tiny could open his mouth, the reply short and barked, making not just Cassia but some of the assembled courtiers jump as well. "I bloody well cannot. If I did, then it would be anarchy. Everyone would think they could defy me. Hell would descend into the chaos it already balances on the edge of. So your female must be suitably punished. It is the law."

The two demons locked eyes, king and prince, father and son. Tiny knew he had to tread carefully. He couldn't lose this. Cassia's life was at stake. "No. No one touches her. She did not know the law."

"Ignorance of the law is not an excuse."

"She broke no law. She didn't want the bond."

"Makes no matter—she bonded you without permission. Or do you call me a liar, challenge my word?" Lakai's eyes glittered dangerously as he advanced on his son.

Tiny didn't bat an eyelid, staring his father down and realizing for the first time he was taller. Taller, heavier and younger, with two years working as a bouncer putting out the scum of the earth because when the shit hit the fan at Moonlight & Magic, it really hit the fan. He'd thrown out argumentative goblins, violent banshees and faced down more werewolves than he cared to think about. But it got better.

A smile curved Tiny's lips. Lakai wanted him alive, which was the only reason he was still standing after running out on his duty as he had. Which gave him an out, gave him leverage.

He shrugged nonchalantly. "So take her…"

Cass gasped, the sound full of hurt and fear as Lakai grinned in triumph and reached for her. His eyes, so like his son's, were already shining lewdly as he made no pretense of the fact he intended to strip her naked as soon as he got his hands on her.

Tiny's next words stopped him dead, cutting across the silence of the court like a whip. "But you do and I leave. I'll go so far away and hide so completely you'll never find me. Never drag me back to sit on that," he nodded towards the throne. He laughed, a short sharp sound of dry amusement.

"I'd even go as far as finding one of her people and getting them to turn me. How'd you like that, Dad? Your son, a bloodsucking leech. It's one for the history books, isn't it? Lakai the Corrupt wasn't even capable of siring a decent demon of a son. No, he managed to sire one who ran off to become a vampire."

All the blood drained out of Lakai's face as he stared at Tiny. "Don't be stupid. You can't. No demon can be made into a vampire."

Tiny held out his palm, displaying the marks there for all to see. "You sure about that, Dad? I'm already bonded to one. We've already shared blood. So who knows what's happening in my body right now? The conversion's probably started already." He bared his teeth, feeling at his canines as though checking if they'd lengthened. "What do you reckon? They feel a bit longer to me. I think I'd only need another bite to cross over."

The demon king's expression wavered as he looked from one to the other. Sensibly, Cass remained quiet. Hopefully she realized what he was trying to do. If not, when they got out of here, if they got out of here, Tiny had a lot of explaining to do. Probably whilst maintaining a crotch-protecting crouch.

"You wouldn't."

Tiny's voice was hard and unemotional. "Try me."

Chapter Seven

Oh God, I hope he knows what he's doing. Fear riveted Cass to the spot as Tiny faced down his father. Even through the terror, she noticed how alike the two men were. The Telosas were a very good-looking family.

"She didn't bond me, I bonded her. So your issue is with me, not Cassia..." He trailed off and looked at the challenge circle again, his meaning clear. Lakai's expression shifted, calculation showing stark on his face as he considered them both.

"Hmm, well... I see that as merely asserting your authority. You're my son, all right. Not many would stalk and lay claim to a vampire." Lakai grinned broadly and threw his arms open to hug his son. His lightning quick mood changes threatened to make Cass's head spin, but Tiny took it all in his stride and suffered the embrace. She did notice, though, he extricated himself as quickly as possible and took her hand. A rush of warmth hit her as his large hand surrounded hers, rough but protective at the same time.

"No! She's a vampire. She can't...you can't..." Forgotten behind them, Zarek's frustrated exclamation made Cass jump. The copper-skinned demon strode towards Lakai, his eyes beseeching. "Sire, she's a vampire bonded to your heir. Would you put a leech on the throne as queen?"

The room fell silent, deathly silent, as all eyes turned to Cassia. She swallowed in nerves. Now she knew what a goldfish felt like surrounded by a roomful of cats. This was bad, very bad. For a moment Lakai had seemed amused by the whole situation, proud of his son's audacity in bonding a vampire. But the instant Zarek uttered the word leech—an insult to any vamp—centuries of interspecies hostility had joined the party, filtering into the room like a heavy, cloying perfume. Cassia swallowed again. She felt sick.

Lakai's head snapped around, his eyes blazing as he glared at the demon lord. "Ready to be rid of me so soon, Zarek? Perhaps you have a little ambition for my throne there yourself?" His voice dropped dangerously low, a subtle threat in his tone recognized by everyone in the room. Even Zarek—especially Zarek—his skin paling as Cass watched. Even though she didn't like him, Cass knew how he felt. Challenging the king, even inadvertently, wasn't the smartest of moves.

"No, no, sire," he hastened to reassure his king. "I merely meant that no demon prince has mated outside the blood before. Demons have needs, needs no non-demon could possibly comprehend."

"Hmm…" Lakai returned to his throne, his tall figure slouching elegantly across the crudely carved seat. Unlike the fine craftsmanship of the rest of the room and the corridors beyond, the throne itself looked to be carved out of a rock. "For once, Zarek, you have a point." His eyes narrowed on Tiny and Cass again. What had Zarek meant by "needs?" Was there something else she didn't know about, something freaky he needed he hadn't told her?

Whatever it was, she knew she'd do it without hesitation if she could, and if she couldn't, she'd go to the ends of the earth to get it for him. That was the nature of the bond. Whether she'd picked him or not, he was the center of her world. She literally couldn't survive without him.

"Cass meets all my needs." Tiny's lip curled slightly as he answered Zarek, and the hard expression on his face promised retribution. "All of them. I don't need anyone else."

"Prove it."

The two quiet words hung in the air like a neon sign, flashing for all to see. Tiny sighed and turned towards her.

"What's happening?" she asked, looking about warily. She'd seen crowds act this way before. Right before said crowd turned into a lynch mob. Human lynch mobs, whilst not pleasant, could be dealt with. Cass didn't even want to see the demon version. She moved closer to Tiny as he ran his palms down her arms to take her hands in his. When she looked up his eyes were full of apology.

"I'm sorry, babe, but they want proof."

Cass frowned. "Proof of what?"

Tiny looked uncomfortable, savage flashes of color like banners on his cheeks. "Proof you can give me everything I need…" His voice trailed off, and he dragged her into his arms without warning. His lips sought her neck, brushing against the soft spot under her ear and making her knees buckle despite the danger they were in.

"Christ, Cass, you've got to have figured it out." Tiny groaned, burying his face into her neck. "I need…for you to be assertive."

"Is that it?" Cassia pulled back to look at him in surprise. He wanted her to boss him about? Her mind flashed back to when she'd tied him to the bed—his instant, eager reactions…the rock-hard cock…the need and longing in his eyes. She'd put it down to being the first time after the club, but now she thought about it, it had also been the only time she'd taken charge. Really taken charge and tied him to the bed.

"Well, no. You need…" His color deepened. "…you need to make me come. Prove you can dominate me. Each demon has a weakness; that's mine. Fuck it!" he swore. "You shouldn't have to do this!"

"Problem?" Zarek's voice broke in, all eagerness and gloating triumph.

Cass straightened her back and glared at the other demon. She could do this. She had to do this, or she could kiss goodbye to her mate. And if that happened, as a bonded vampire, the rest of her long, long life would be meaningless.

"And why would there be a problem?" Cass arched an eyebrow coolly at Zarek. It was easy to channel her inner bitch with the demon lord and his ilk. Tiny shifted slightly, as though to answer, and she snapped her attention back to him. Looking him over, she allowed heat to fill her eyes, the heat she felt every time she was near him, but schooled her expression to an impassive mask.

"Did I say you could speak?" she demanded, her voice a harsh whip. Maybe a little overboard but she needed to do something and fast to establish the mood she needed. "No. I'll tell you when I want you to use your mouth, and what to use it for."

Role play. It was just role play, Cass told herself. She could do role play. After all, she played the mean bitch every time she donned a hunter's chains. She could do this.

She wasn't prepared for the darkness in the demon prince's eyes, or the excitement and longing written across his tight expression. His nostrils flared as the look on his face begged her to carry on.

Christ, he really did get off on this. A thrill shot through Cass as she realized the power she held over this powerful man, one far more powerful than she'd realized at first. Of course, she'd known from the outset he was something special, but she'd thought it was just her feminine side reacting to him. She'd always had a thing for a strong man, a bit of a bad boy, and they didn't come badder than the way he looked with his shaven head, the piercings and the tattoos.

She circled him like a shark circling prey. How the hell did she do this? She'd never had to act the dominatrix in front of a crowd. In the privacy of her bedroom with her "clothes" on was one thing, but to do it in normal clothes with people around was going to be difficult. She closed her eyes for a second and reached deep inside herself, knowing she had no choice.

How could she make him come whilst still being dominant? The quickest way to make him come was to suck him off, but being on your knees with a cock in your mouth wasn't exactly the dominant position she needed.

"Strip," she ordered, her voice a cold, hard reflection of her normal tones. To most she would have sounded like the ice queen she meant to. Out of the corner of her eye she noticed more than one of the demons surrounding them flinch in response. Interesting, perhaps a need to be dominated was common amongst them. Despite her act, someone who knew her well would hear the underlying tension and worry in her tone.

Tiny was eager to comply. His jacket hit the floor a second later, followed by the T-shirt he all but tore from his torso. He flexed his shoulders, the sleek muscles rippling under his satin skin as his hands reached for his belt buckle. She let him. She stood with her hands on her hips arrogantly, and her mouth watered as she watched his strong fingers work the heavy buckle.

She knew how clever those fingers were and what they could do to her body, the pleasure they could bring. Arousal shot through her body. She wanted him, pure and simple. Embarrassment shot through her when she realized she didn't even care there were people in the room watching them. Somehow that added an illicit thrill, her panties dampening as he held her eyes, pulling the belt slowly free, the sexual tension between them mounting to unbearable levels.

The guy was a tease and he damn well knew it.

"That's enough. Hands on top of your head and spread 'em." Her voice was husky with need but wavered as the audience pressed forward a little, breaking the spell. How many people were in here watching them? The small crowd that had been in here when they arrived seemed to have doubled in size, as though word had gotten out something was going down in the throne room, and all the voyeurs had emerged out the woodwork.

"At me, babe, concentrate on me." His voice brought her eyes back to him. "Look at what you're doing to me."

Her gaze followed his downwards, past the sculptured planes of his chest and over his toned stomach. How the hell had she managed to catch the attention of a guy like this? Hell, with a presence like he had, he should be on the screen. He sucked a sharp breath in as her gaze travelled over him. Her attention was hijacked by the thin line of dark hair which trailed down the center of his stomach and disappeared under the waistband of his jeans. She ached to follow it with her lips and tongue, nuzzling down his toned stomach to push the denim aside until she could release the hard cock, pressing against the fabric.

"Stay still. Don't move. Understand?" Her voice threatened dire retribution as she slid to her knees. All else fell away as she reached for the snaps at his fly. Screw how it looked, she was in control here.

He nodded silently, jumping a little as her fingertips brushed his hard stomach. The muscles flexed in reaction as she snapped open each fastener one after the other. He went commando so the denim parted easily, his cock bursting free into her hands. Cass murmured appreciation in the back of her throat and licked her lips. There was something about giving head she liked, something about the feel of a rigid cock in her mouth or the pulse of blood so close calling out to her in an erotic siren's song. Whatever, it made her pussy clench hard with need and her fangs ache as they dropped into her mouth ready and waiting.

Holding his eyes she opened her mouth and licked slowly along the underside of his shaft.

He swore as she swirled her tongue about the swollen purplish head. Fingers closing around the base of his cock, she held him still as she explored, taking her time to enjoy him at her leisure. A wave of…something rose around them, something dark and heated, something new. Cass snapped her eyes open in surprise as it brushed against her skin, like the touch of a lover's fingers. What the hell?

She stilled in wariness, her tongue flicking out across him as she opened her senses. It was the same buzz she always felt about demons, but instead of feeling wrong, it felt familiar and comforting, like the pleasant tingle she always felt when she was around Tiny but stronger. The beat of his heart sounded in her ears, the rush of blood through his veins pulsing in the same rhythm. His magic, it had to be.

She relaxed and closed her eyes, a murmur of pleasure in the back of her throat as she slid her lips over him and finally took him deep inside her mouth.

"Oh fuck, yeah, baby, do that more."

She worked him with her lips and tongue, using all the knowledge she'd gathered the night before along with every dirty little trick she knew, some she'd not yet used on him. She'd been told she was good at this and by God she intended to prove it. Not to the demons pressing around them, but to her mate.

The crowd around them ceased to matter. All that mattered was the thick cock in her mouth and the man it belonged to. All that mattered was his pleasure and bringing him to the edge of his control, proving her own power over him.

She pulled back to tease him with soft licks and nibbles. His respiration shortened and became harsher, his heart pounding. She felt his movement before he dropped his hands, his fingers about to slide into her hair to hold her in place.

She moved her mouth off him, eliciting a moan of protest, and gave him a sharp slap on his thigh. "Did I tell you to move? Hands back on your head, and don't come until I say you can."

A shudder racked his heavy frame as he locked his fingers back over his shaven scalp. Curses escaped his lips as she leaned forward again and rewarded him with a quick flick of her tongue.

"Quiet," she ordered as she cupped his balls. "You know what I'm going to do with you?" she asked between quick licks and even quicker sucks. "I'm going to make you beg. Turn you on so much you can't think of anything but my mouth on you, my lips around you and my tongue across you."

He groaned again, his hips thrusting forwards to try and get more of his cock in her mouth. "Don't stop."

She smiled as he jerked in her hands, tension in every line of his body. He was close but not there yet. She wanted him closer.

She licked one more time, her tongue circling him before her head bobbed forwards and she took him deep again. This time they both moaned, locked in their own sensual world. Her hands smoothed over him and pumped his shaft in unison with her mouth on him. He resorted to reciting the seven times table, every cord in his body standing out as he fought off the climax fast approaching—the climax she'd told him he couldn't have until she said so.

His erection swelled in her mouth, beads of pre-cum warning her she didn't have much time. Biting back her own frustration, Cass pulled away and stood gracefully.

His eyes were closed, a muscle jumping in his jaw the only movement in his body as he fought for control. Well, apart from the throb of the big vein across the top of his thick erection. Cass licked her lips at the sight but turned and looked over her shoulder at Lakai.

"You wanted proof?" She spread her hand in a gesture towards the demon prince as motionless as a statue, a work of erotic art with his legs spread and his manhood jutting out proudly. "I give you dominance. Seren, do you want to come?" she asked softly.

All eyes focused on the still figure in the middle of the room. He opened his eyes slowly, their azure color a maelstrom of need. "Yes," he rasped, his body unnaturally still as beads of sweat broke out on his forehead.

"Now?" she pressed, hating herself when he was in so much need.

"Yes," he growled, his jaw clenching. "Damn it, let me come. I can't until you say...please, Cass," he begged, a real note of torture in his voice.

Cass felt awful and elated in the same moment. That he trusted her enough to let her bring him to this point in front of others brought tears to her eyes and a fresh wave of liquid heat between her thighs.

"Drop your arms, don't touch yourself." She stepped behind him and kissed his shoulder as she peeked over it at the demon king. Her hands snaked around Tiny's waist and grasped his straining cock. She pumped the satin shaft a couple of times, feeling the slick evidence of his excitement and need.

"Come. Come now."

He trembled and turned his head to claim her lips in a brief, torrid kiss. Then his hips thrust harder against her hand as his cock jerked and pulsed against her hold. His whole body went rigid and he tore his mouth from hers, a ragged cry escaping his lips as he came in her hand.

"Fucking hell, don't stop, Cass. Please don't stop," he begged as she continued to work his cock. Cum splattered up across his stomach, covering her hand, but she ignored it and concentrated on the strong throbbing between her fingers, intent on wringing every last bit of pleasure from his climax. When the last shudder washed through him he groaned and sagged against her.

Tenderly she cradled him in her arms, never more grateful for the strength granted by her vampire blood than at that moment, and raised her eyes to meet Lakai's. Was she imagining it or was there a new respect there?

"And that is all the show you perverts are getting," she announced. She stood Tiny back upright when she was sure he had his balance back and stepped around him. With a graceful movement, she scooped up his discarded shirt and handed it to him, standing in front of him whilst he cleaned himself up.

Lakai chuckled and addressed his son. "Feisty little thing, isn't she?"

"You have no idea." Tiny's lips quirked as he dropped the shirt unheeded to the ground and buttoned his jeans. If he was embarrassed about being brought off in front of a crowd he wasn't showing it. For some reason that excited Cass even more.

"And sorry," he added, as Lakai opened his mouth, a sly expression crossing his face. "I'm not sharing. She's all mine."

Lakai blew out a sigh, his breath stirring the long strands of hair about his face. "Can't blame a guy for trying. But tell me—is she worth your birthright?"

"Meaning?"

"Don't be dense, Seren. Zarek was right; you know the people will never accept a vampire as queen. So you need to make a choice, the vamp or the throne." The demon king sat back, his expression smug, as though he already knew what choice his son would make.

Cass caught her breath, not daring to look at Tiny. Misery closed her throat over. Put like that, he was going to choose the throne. Who would choose her as mate when it meant they would lose everything? And if he turned his back on her that was it. She was bonded to him; he might be able to walk away but she couldn't. She would never respond sexually to another man, only her mate.

A large hand curling about hers made her jump. She looked up into Tiny's eyes. Slowly a smile crept over his lips, one of promise and love. "Come on, sexy, we have some unfinished business—and this time you get to use those chains."

With that Prince Seren turned his back on his birthright and walked out of his father's throne room to be with the woman he loved.

The End

Pixies & Passion

Chapter One

"Not a cat in *hell's* chance."

Cy folded his heavily tattooed arms and looked around the office with a mulish glare. It was a small room anyway but crammed full of the *Moonlight & Magic* security staff, one of them nearly seven feet of Gargoyle, it seemed even smaller.

"C'mon Cy...you're our only hope," Myst pleaded, waggling the scrap of red satin on the end of her finger. Cy's eyebrow crawled further up his forehead. Myst's look was calculating as she held the article, a red satin thong, out to Tiny next to her. "Or I could always get the guys to pin you down whilst we put this on."

The demon recoiled, a look of disgust on his face. "I'm not going near *anything* that's going in the crack of his ass!"

Cy chuckled, "Good luck with that sweetheart. I don't think they're that interested. Why me anyway? I'm not even on the security team and I thought this gig was up to you."

Myst was still glaring at Tiny. "Yeah, it normally is. But with half this lot..." she jerked her thumb around the room. "...bloody loved up, Darius over there batting for the other team and the rest of us being of the female persuasion, we're looking at other options. Namely you."

Tiny and Knuckles looked sheepish at Myst's blunt statement but the whole club knew they were both newly mated. Tiny's wife, Cassia, was the first and only vampire allowed into the club. Well, the only vampire allowed both in and *out* of the club with her head still attached. Whereas Knuckle's mate Neri was just the sweetest human any of the staff had ever seen and to say the large gargoyle was besotted with her was an understatement.

"I see your point."

Cy put his stubborn face on. Myst thought she was a stubborn bitch but Cy was a pixie born and bred. The day-glo hair was gone, cut and dyed into a short black crop, but he still had the balls and the tattoo's to prove it, the latter stretching from his knuckles all the way up to his shoulders.

To most people they just looked like random swirls and marks but to another pixie they told Cy's life story. Who he was, who his parents had been, what battles he'd fought against which other clans and, if he'd ever been married, then they would have noted who to. Mostly tellingly of all though, the spot on his wrists where his clan name should be was blanked out. Tattooed over completely black so the name couldn't be read.

Cy folded his arms. "Still not doing it."

"Christmas day. Our place," Tiny offered, "Neri'd love to have more mouths to feed."

Cy groaned. That was just going for the throat. Cy didn't have a family. Not now. He used to have a family, but now his clan was gone. Wiped out. It's name erased from pixie memory forever thanks to the actions of one man. Thanks to one man he was homeless, condemned to wander and never find rest, never know the peace and comfort of family again. He was dishonoured. A man without a clan and, for a pixie warrior, that meant no other clan would accept him.

They were like sharks scenting blood. Tiny chipped in. "Cass makes fantastic mince pies, we could make a day of it. Shall we say eleven o'clock?"

Cy's eyes darted around the room. The temptation was overwhelming. A family Christmas...He thought back to his apartment. Little more than a single room with a bathroom on the side, kitchenette in the corner and his futon/bed in the other, it wasn't the most appealing of places. One reason he spent every waking hour he could at the club, either doing odd jobs or using the gym in the basement. And, over six foot of solid muscle anyway, he'd just put muscle *on* the muscle.

"Bastards," he muttered. They knew his weakness. They all knew his weakness. "Okay, what do I have to do?"

* * *

"Ladies and Gentlemen, welcome to Northfield Hospital's Christmas Auction. As you can see we have some delectable dates up for auction tonight, all of them very kindly provided by local businesses. All proceeds this year are going to the neo-natal unit..."

Teresa zoned the rest of the opening speech out as she rooted in her purse for her cellphone. Flicking it open she scanned for new messages and breathed a sigh of relief. No news was good news. It meant the babysitter was coping with her two monsters.

"...the owner of Mackenzie Plasma Products, Mr Mackenzie is offering to whisk the lucky lady who wins his date off on a luxury evening which will include dinner and dancing on his sumptuous yacht, the *Lady Jane*..."

"Oh my god...would you look at that!" Joanie, Teresa's co-worker and partner in crime, hooted as a man stepped out from the wings and started down the runway. Suave and sophisticated in a classic tuxedo he had the sort of dark good looks that wouldn't look out of place in a Bond movie.

"The name's Mac, Big Mac."

Joanie fell about giggling at her own joke as Mackenzie strutted his stuff on the catwalk. Teresa had to admit, he was good looking. But his brand of slick good looks left her cold. Too like Mario, her ex husband and the bane of her life. He'd been a charmer too and had had her convinced she was his one and only.

It wasn't until the car accident that had taken his life that she'd found out she was one of many. That the wedding vows Mario had taken he'd said so often he should have been word perfect, usually without the little matter of a divorce in between, and that a wife back in Italy ensured that neither she nor their two children were entitled to any of the De Luca fortune.

"You, are drunk. Already."

The bidding was fast and furious as Teresa shook her head at her friend's giggling. Joan couldn't hold her alcohol. Just one drink, especially the complimentary champagne on their table, and she was anyone's.

"Yup! And you should be too! To the good Mr. Mackenzie and his gorgeous ass!"

Joanie's catcall dropped right into a lull in the noise, her comment clearly heard throughout the room. Including the good Mr. Mackenzie himself who turned and winked right at her.

"Ohmigod, *ohmigod*, he heard me," Joanie squeaked and disappeared under the table as everyone in the room looked their way. Mortification burned across Teresa's cheeks as she thrust her hand under the tablecloth and tried to grab hold of Joan.

"Get your ass up here girl, everyone's looking at me," she hissed as her cheeks glowed neon. At least, if the lights in here went out, they'd still be able to see.

Joanie slapped her hands away, stopping her friend from hauling her back up to face all the people staring at them. People who were all grinning at Teresa, obviously thinking she'd been the one to make the ass comment.

"Girl, you are *so* dead when you come out from under there."

"Well, we know Mackenzie has one dead cert in the room," the auctioneer laughed and moved smoothly on. "Okay, next up is the listing from paranormal club *Moonlight & Magic*. Waiter Cy is a bad boy looking for the right woman to tame him, if only for one night...Christmas eve. So, for all the lovely ladies in the audience...here's one Christmas present you won't forget!"

The next figure to step out from the wings onto the catwalk stole Teresa's breath right out from her lungs. He was tall and stripped bare to the waist. All the better to see the tattoo's that covered his arms right down to the fingers hooked into the loops of jeans that rode low on his hips.

He stood in the middle of the stage for a moment, his attitude pure arrogance as he looked around the room. The lights had to be blinding him but still he looked, ice blue eyes sweeping across the crowded tables. A collective feminine sigh whispered around the room and even Teresa's traitorous body sat up and took notice. She didn't want it to, she was done with men. So done after Mario that if she'd found other women in the least attractive she'd have given up on men completely. But there was something about this guys defiant stance that sent a shiver down her spine.

His head turned and he looked straight at her. Teresa's breath caught as his blue eyes burned into hers. He couldn't possibly see her, could he? No, there was no way he could, not with all the lights trained on the catwalk. It was just a trick of the light.

"What's going on?" Joanie whispered, loudly, from under the table. More of a shout than a whisper really. Teresa didn't answer, struck dumb as Cy sauntered down the catwalk, his eyes still firmly on hers. The lights shimmered lovingly across perfect muscles, the six pack stomach flexing as he walked.

"Heeeeello...need info down here!"

Joan's hand emerged from under the table and waved at Teresa. Who totally ignored it as Cy reached the end of the catwalk. Instead of doing a little pose like the rest he ran a hand over his toned stomach and slid it down towards his groin. His eyes twinkled as his lips curved in a suggestive smile.

Teresa fanned herself with her program, her eyes not leaving the stage in front of her or the man stood on it. Had the temperature in here just jumped twenty degrees? They really needed to turn the air-conditioning up.

With a lazy flick of his fingers he popped the first, then the second button on his jeans...just enough to tell he wasn't wearing underwear. Then he blew a kiss at her.

Teresa's heart stopped. Joan's frantic waving by her side didn't register as Cy stalked back up the catwalk and disappeared.

"What happened? What did I miss?" Joanie demanded as she pulled herself from under the table on Teresa's arm.

"And congratulations to the lady in red on table five. One of our hostesses will be along shortly to collect your details for your date with our delectable waiter Cy."

Table five.

They were table five.

Suddenly the grins Teresa was getting from the other people seated around the table made sense. An awful feeling crept over her as she glanced down at her red top, then round the table at the other women's clothing.

"Shit, I think you just won me a date."

Chapter Two

Christmas eve. He couldn't believe he was on a blind bloody date on Christmas eve.

Cy pulled up outside the small suburban house and left the car engine running. Rooting in his jeans pocket he pulled out a scrap of paper and checked the name and address written on it. Ducking down he checked the number on the side of the house through the windscreen.

Yup, number seventeen. It was hard to spot half-hidden behind the illuminated snowman but it was definitely the right house.

Cy sat back in the drivers seat, his tattooed hand rested on the steering wheel, and let the engine idle as he looked at the place. Classic suburbia. Beige house, white picket fence, sensible sedan parked in the drive. No doubt owned by Mr. and Mrs. Average with two point four kids. Kids who'd be hyped up on the Christmas spirit already if the bright decorations in the garden and on the front of the house were any indication.

Cy sighed as he cut the engine and unfolded himself from the sleek sports car. It was his luxury, his little gift to himself and the only thing he bothered to spend money on. Why bother on anything else? His apartment he spent as little time in as possible and the club provided a uniform so he didn't need to bother with clothes. Okay, so maybe the sheer t-shirt was stretching 'clothing' a little bit. He flicked the central locking on and strode up the path towards the house. Better get this over with and thrill Mrs. Average who'd won a date with the bad boy he was supposed to be.

He knocked on the porch door, looking down and noticing the three sets of wellington boots set in a row just inside the screen to dry. A adult pair, female sized by the looks of them and two smaller pairs, one tiny pair in pink and a slightly larger pair with a cartoon hero emblazoned on the side.

Longing filled him. Family. Home. All the things he wanted but couldn't have.

*

"Crap, crap, crap. He can't be here already!"

Teresa raced around her tiny bedroom in search of her best strappy sandals, stubbed her toes in passing on the leg of the bed and erupted into more swearing. Joanie's voice reading a story in the next room grew louder, a subtle reminder to keep her voice down as little ears heard all and often repeated choice phrases at the most inopportune moments.

169

Teresa swallowed her cursing and dropped to her knees to search under the bed for her shoes. With a crow of triumph her fingers closed around the familiar straps and she pulled them from their hiding place.

"Okay, mommy's going now," she called out, hopping from one foot to the other as she crammed her feet into the shoes. They'd be killing her within the hour but she couldn't afford to get new ones, not with James needing new school shoes and Molly shooting up like a bean.

"You sure I look okay?" Teresa's face must have mirrored her concern because Joanie's eyebrow hiked upwards in an expression Teresa knew well.

"Honey, you look fantastic. Stop fiddling," she admonished as Teresa fussed with the neckline of the dress. Like her shoes it was a couple of years old, from before her ill-fated marriage, and she'd put on a couple of pounds since then. So it was a little more...snug around the bust than it used to be. Luckily it was a stretch velour so it was forgiving. Maybe...hopefully.

"You look like a princess mommy." Two sets of wide eyes regarded her above duvets in respective pink and blue and Teresa's heart melted.

"Thank you sweetie. You be good for auntie Joan, okay? And go to sleep or Santa won't come." She warned as she swept into the small bedroom and kissed two freshly scrubbed cheeks, collecting hugs which smelt of baby powder, toothpaste and sleepy child.

Joan smiled as she hesitated a moment, unwilling to leave her children even for a date with the hottest man she'd ever seen. Then the doorbell chimed again, somewhat impatiently, as though the man outside knew somehow he was being ignored in favour of two small children. Teresa didn't think that would impress him any. Not looking the way he did, he was probably puffed up on his own looks and not impressed with having to take a middle-aged mother out on a date.

"Go..." Joan mouthed and carried on reading from the book in her hands. It was a book of fairy tales, one Teresa knew by heart, but Joanie was ad-libbing. So far the princess had decided to rescue herself and was hacking her way out of a forest after facing a dragon. For some reason the story also included a rapier wielding hedgehog and a toad with the hiccups, all of which Joan was providing voices for.

Teresa shook her head with a smile as she slipped out the room and headed down the stairs. "All right, all right, I'm coming. Keep your hair on!" she called out as the chimes went again.

*

Keep his hair on. Cy ran his hand over his shorn locks. Most pixies wore their hair at least shoulder length to show off the bright colour. Like peacocks strutting their stuff to attract the ladies. Trouble was, day-glo hair tended to stick out like a sore thumb. No one had any trouble picking them out from a crowd and, with the reputation pixies had as trouble makers, it made them a target for most law enforcement officers. Not to mention warned the ladies, of any species, off.

Cy's natural hair colour was bright blue, the same shade at his eyes. Dyeing it every couple of weeks was a bitch but it stopped the questions about his species. Leaning against the door frame he waited for his date to get her act together and open it. At least she sounded nice.

Probably short, round and the wrong side of fifty, he thought to himself. The way his luck ran with women she'd be a twenty-pinter. Anyone caught him out with her they'd be calling him 'stumpy' for sure.

He closed his eyes for a second and slipped into the day-dream he'd been entertaining for a few days now. That his 'date' would be the mouth-watering little brunette he'd seen the night of the auction. As soon as he'd seen her he hadn't been able to take his eyes off her, spotting her easily despite the glare of all those lights in his face.

Who could blame him. Why would any guy in his right mind want to take his eyes off a woman like that? Just thinking about her heart-shaped face and those sinfully dark eyes was enough to have him at half mast again.

"Bollocks," he muttered and shoved his hand into his crotch to try and bate down his reaction. Great, the last thing he wanted was Mrs. Average to open the door and think he had a hard-on for her. Then the door swung open and Cy lost the power of speech.

Stood just the other side of the door was the brunette from the auction.

Cy's jaw hit the deck. He shook his head to clear it. Surely he was seeing things but no, it was her. The one he hadn't been able to get out of his head, the one who'd been giving him restless nights and wet dreams ever since. He'd tried to find her but she'd disappeared before he could make his way from backstage.

He'd been pissed off at the time, even more pissed off than he had been at the start of the evening. Pressured into the auction in the first place he'd refused to go the full monty and do the strip routine the guys had wanted. Red satin thong and all.

No way, no how. He wouldn't have put it past one of them to be taking photos from the back of the room and then they'd be plastered all over the walls in the staff room at work. Cy might be a little gullible at times, but he wasn't *that* stupid.

His irritation had grown deeper when no one at the table seemed to know who she was, giving him blank looks when he'd asked about the gorgeous brunette with the 'take me to bed' eyes and sinful lips.

Her lashes swept over her eyes as she looked down. Right to where his hand cupped his crotch. "Do you need to use the little boys room?" she asked coolly, a flash of amusement in her chocolate-sherry eyes. "I...ugh."

Shit. Cy snatched his hand away from his crotch as bright colour flared across his cheeks. He ignored it as his natural confidence surged back. His eyes dared her to keep looking and, if she did, to comment on the semi-erection starting to tent his jeans. Far from being embarrassed now he wanted her to notice it, wanted her to comment.

Her eyes widened, darted away, flicked back for a second, then settled on his face. Cy's lips quirked in amusement. If the sight of a semi like that got her flustered, he'd love to see what would happen if he whispered the wicked things he wanted to do to her in her ear. Starting with stripping that tight little dress from her luscious tits right here on the porch and suckling her nipples until she was moaning in pleasure.

"No, I'm fine, thank you. I believe we have a date this evening?"

Cy straightened up and flashed her his best smile. The one which normally had the ladies panting and ready to do anything he wanted. To his surprise, it had totally the opposite effect. Her lovely eyes shuttered over and she smiled a small, brittle smile.

"We do indeed. Let me just get my coat."

When she reappeared she was wrapped shoulders to mid-calf in a voluminous trench-coat Cy took an immediate dislike to. Not only was it hideous but it hid her wonderful figure. A figure Cy wanted to see more of...much more of. Preferably without that red dress, lovely was it was, on.

She'd be all satin skin over those glorious curves. Curves he intended to take his time exploring and finding all the spots that made her squirm in pleasure. The fun he'd have finding things out about her. Did she prefer her nipples licked or sucked? Would she be a moaner or a screamer as he made her come with his lips and tongue? Would she gasp as he filled her with his cock over and over again?

"My lady, if you'll allow me?"

Cy locked his thoughts away in a corner of his mind and offered her his arm, trying his best to be gallant. Not easy when she was looking at him as though he'd just crawled out from under a rock. *That* wasn't something he was used to. For a pixie Cy was considered good looking. Pretending to be human with dyed hair and the whole pixie/fae sexual edge going on, he was devastating. Something he accepted without question or vanity, but something he was more than happy to use to his advantage, especially with a woman like this.

For a moment he allowed a fantasy of what would have happened if she'd been a pixie to fill his mind. They'd have met at a clan gather—perhaps to celebrate a wedding or truce—and he'd have moved heaven and earth to possess her. Even to the point of starting a war so he could claim her as his own.

Might made right. The Pixie code. If you could take it and hold onto it, you could keep it. "Of course."

She placed a delicately boned hand on his arm. A shiver shot through Cy. The heat that had been banking up, fuelled by his thoughts, broke free of its constraints and flared into a full blown inferno at her touch.

The gasp which left his lips was as unexpected as it was unintentional. Play boy extraordinare Cy usually had better control than that. Even more surprising was her echoing intake of breath.

A buzz of awareness arched between them.

Cy turned his head and caught her eye. Again her eyes widened and, this time, anger filled them as she pulled her hand away.

"Let's get on with it, shall we?" she asked, breaking away from him to stride down the short path to his car.

What the fuck? She'd felt that too, he'd seen it in her eyes. Cy followed her like a puppy on a leash—all the while trying not to imagine what her ass looked like under all that material.

He failed. Miserably.

"Flashy. Guess you don't have a family."

The comment dripped acid. Cy frowned. Where had that come from? And the anger? Had he done something to upset her? Impossible, he'd only arrived a few minutes ago and even he couldn't piss off a woman that quick. Had he met her before and pissed her off somehow?

"No," he said, his voice clipped. "I don't have a family."
*

The drive to the restaurant was painfully silent. Cy kept stealing glances at his passenger. She sat in silence, no attempt to engage him in conversation. She just looked out of the window.

Cy's confusion grew. She was acting like she didn't want to be here. If she didn't then why the hell had she bid on the date with him?

His annoyance grew by the minute, swelling and filling him. Cy was a hot-head, always had been. He couldn't keep things bottled up for long and, sure enough, within minutes he cracked.

"Okay. Time out," Cy announced as he swung the sleek sports car out of the flow of traffic. He pulled up, yanked the handbrake on and looked at her. As he did he tried to school his expression to cool, calm and collected. So what if he thought she was the sexiest thing on the planet? If she wasn't into him, she wasn't into him.

"So do you want to carry on? Or should I turn the car around and take you home now?"

Finally she turned her head and the darkness in her eyes took his breath away. Then she shook her head and smiled. Well, she attempted a smile. Cy wasn't fooled. Someone, somewhere had hurt this woman and hurt her badly.

"Of course I want to carry on. Why else do you think I paid for the date?"

Chapter Three

Oh my god, he was gorgeous. More so than he had been the other night on stage, if that was possible. His hair was dark and cropped so close to the scalp it was hard to tell exactly what colour it was. Teresa curled her hands into her lap and fought the urge she'd been having since she'd first seen him at her door. The urge to reach out and run her hands over his head was overwhelming. An image of his dark head against the pale skin of her breast filled her mind. She could almost imagine the warmth of his mouth as his lips closed around her nipple. Teresa bit back a moan.

She'd always had a thing about guys with short, short hair. The ones with tattoos and attitude. Perhaps it was a self defence mechanism. She had fallen so easily for her charming liar of a 'husband' that she'd totally the other way. Whatever, there was just something about the bad boy image Cy exuded that just did it for her. Although there was no way she was ever admitting that to him, or anyone.

His hair was dark but his eyes were a bright electric blue. So blue she was sure they couldn't be natural. He had to be wearing contacts.

Teresa snuck another glance out of the corner of her eye. The car was low slung and powerful. He lounged with indolent grace behind the wheel, his movements masterful as he wove the car in and out of the traffic towards their destination.

His hands caressed the wheel as they made a sharp left turn into the car-park, the dark tattoos across the backs stark against his skin. Teresa shivered as a longing to have those hands stroking over her body filled her.

She fought it down. What on earth was wrong with her? Cy was just the type of guy she should avoid. Although he had the bad boy image she was sure it was a front. He was handsome and successful if the car was any indication. They'd said he was a waiter but she didn't believe that was what he really was.

Probably some rich kid living off daddy's money as he went through a rebellious phase. And as soon as he was out of it, laser surgery would take care of those tattoos and he'd be back into designer threads before you could blink. If he worked, and that was a big if, it would no doubt be in a luxury office somewhere as a suit. Maybe daddy owned a bank or something. Not the sort who'd be interested in a middle aged mother of two who was carrying a few extra pounds. No, he was the sort whose arm would be decorated with the latest upcoming stick insect starlet who was heavy on the breast implants and light on the brains.

Christ, if she didn't stop with the little glances from under her hair Cy was going to stop the damn car here and now, pull her into his lap and kiss her senseless. The quick looks were filled with an interest and speculation totally absent when he was looking at her. But when she thought he wasn't it was all there and more.

He swung the car between the rows in the car-park looking for a spot and refused to feel self conscious about parking the car himself. If she was looking for a place with valet parking then she really had the wrong guy. Finally he spotted one. Right at the back it was half hidden by the bushes surrounding the car park and shielded from the restaurant by a large SUV. A sly smile crossed his lips as he headed that way. Perfect.

Cy slid from the driver's seat with as much nonchalance as he could muster. Which wasn't much given what he was about to do. So what if she was married? Cy avoided thinking about her husband, if the man was weak willed enough to let her out on a date with him, then he deserved to lose her.

Might made right.

She'd bid on a date with a bad boy, so a bad boy was what she was going to get. In spades. Skirting around the trunk of the car he opened her door smoothly and extended a hand to help her out. Her feet emerged first, delicate and finely boned they were set off to perfection in the strappy sandals she wore.

Her toenails weren't painted the sort of dark colour Cy was used to. Instead they had a slight sheen and sparkle to them. The sort of nails that said she hadn't primped and preened for hours before she'd met him at the door.

It was different and Cy liked it. Right about now, although he'd never particularly had a foot fetish before, he could happily have kissed those delicate feet. En-route to other, more interesting areas of course.

Slender calves followed, then knees. The red velvet of her dress was hiked up and revealed curvy thighs that made Cy's mouth water. Sod the table he'd booked, all he wanted to do was lay her back on the hood, spread her legs and eat his fill of a far sexier dessert than any on the menu inside.

His date emerged from the car like a butterfly emerging from a chrysalis. She was petite, far shorter than him even in heels but Cy didn't care. He'd always had a thing for smaller women.

Smaller women with curves just like hers. None of the underfed rakes who threw themselves at him in the club, assuming every man found them irresistible. No, give him a woman with padding on her bones, a woman he wouldn't break if he got a little...rough in bed. Or against a wall. Or across a car hood.

*

Despite his dark and brooding bad boy image Cy turned out to be highly articulate and an excellent dinner partner. He also knew how to use the cutlery and didn't slurp his soup as some of the other diners appeared to assume given the looks they shot towards the couple's table. Teresa sighed. Some people just couldn't see past appearances.

"So..." she said after the waiter left their table with the dessert order. Nothing for Cy and, of course, Death by Chocolate for her. They seemed to be getting on so she felt comfortable asking a question which was a little more personal. "What are all the tattoos about? You have a fair few and they don't seem to be the normal 'love/hate' tattoo's you see. They're actually quite beautiful..."

She trailed off at his suddenly set look. From a charming conversationalist he suddenly clammed up and went quiet, his expression wary. He didn't answer as a small party walked past them towards a table at the back of the restaurant.

Realising her blunder she dabbed at her lips with her napkin. "I'm sorry, I didn't mean to pry."

He shook his head. "No, you're not prying. I...don't talk about them much." His voice was quiet and careful. Teresa frowned.

"Are you embarrassed about them, is that why? You know you can get tattoos removed these days? Laser surgery I think they use."

"No!" His reaction was as sharp as it was emphatic. The fingers of his left hand rubbed almost protectively over the knuckles of the other. "I'm not embarrassed about them at all..." He looked at her curiously. "You really don't realise do you?"

"Realise what?"

His lips quirked into a small smile that ignited the fire that had been simmering all night. She shivered and looked away, unable to hold his gaze. Within seconds though, she was looking back at him, as though the sight of him was magnetic.

"That I'm not human."

"You're not? Why, what are you then?"

Her look of surprise was so complete that, had it been any other subject they were discussing Cy would have laughed. But it wasn't any subject. It was him. What he was. Something he rarely discussed with anyone. Most of the people he kicked about with were paranormals, were part paranormal or had been around the scene long enough to realise what he was without asking.

Despite the clans trying to clean their acts up there was still a large amount of discrimination against Pixies. They were known as the thugs of the paranormal world. A reputation not entirely undeserved. Pixie clans or pixies in general, could be nasty as all hell.

He took a deep breath and looked at her. "I'm a Pixie. From upstate but my clan...let's just say I don't have much in the way of family anymore." Cy tried to keep his voice level but fell short of the mark. No matter how much he tried, the loneliness and bitterness he felt at his exile always crept into the words. Someone as sensitive as Teresa was bound to pick up on it.

"Oh. I'm sorry to hear that." She reached over and touched his hand gently, her dark eyes sincere. Then she smiled. "So, pixies? What...like on toa—"

Cy moved like lightening. His finger on her lips stopped her sentence instantly. "Please, no toadstool jokes. I'd have to spank you," he joked, his eyes warm. Teresa wasn't entirely sure whether he was joking or not but just the idea of being spanked sent a shiver through her. In fact, the idea of his hand anywhere on her sent fire racing through her veins.

"Careful," she threw back, growing more confident in the light teasing and flirting. It was a minor miracle in itself since Mario had done such a good job on trashing her self confidence. "I might enjoy it and then where would you be?"

"Oh, you'd enjoy it. So would I," he breathed, tracing the outline of her lips with a gentle finger. The blue of his eyes darkened to navy, the look in them hot enough to make Teresa blush. She dropped her gaze, looking down into her lap.

"I bet you say that to all the women," she laughed, shrugging the comment off. "But thank you. I'm sure you'd much rather be out with a pretty blonde thing rather than a middle-aged, plump mother of two."

"You think?" He arched his eyebrow, still watching her intently as he leaned forwards. "Sweetheart, if I told you what I would rather be doing...with you...you'd run for cover. Come on...let's get out of here."

Even though she hadn't had her dessert Teresa didn't argue. Mind you, she didn't have much of a choice since Cy rose to his feet and headed for the door leaving her to trail after him. He paused for a moment by the cashier's desk so she caught up with him for all of a second before he enveloped his fingers in hers and pulled her outside into the cool night air.

"You look fantastic." His murmured compliment as they reached the car took her as much by surprise but not as much as his next move. Still holding her hand he pulled her hard against him. One hand slid across the back of her hips to prevent her escaping. Teresa gasped as she felt the rampant hardness of his erection press into her. His other hand slid into the nape of her neck, his fingers winding around the silken strands of her hair as he tilted her face up to just the right angle for his kiss.

Her body stiffened as her hands slammed into the solid wall of his chest. Cy paused and looked down into her eyes. Anger and surprise flared there as they locked into a silent battle of wills. Would she let him kiss her? He hoped so, because he wanted to taste her lips more than he wanted to breathe right now.

"I'm going to kiss you," he warned, hearing the hitch in his own voice and marveling that one human woman could reduce him to such a mass of need. He leaned down, holding her eyes, until his lips were a bare whisper away from hers. She didn't move, frozen in place and her dark eyes on his. Dark eyes that smoldered not with anger any more, but need and longing.

Cy groaned. He couldn't resist her.

His lips brushed over hers as he tried to school himself to be gentle. She was human, not pixie. Not used to the demands of a full-blooded warrior as a woman of his race would be. So he would be gentle. Maybe. As much as he could.

Then disaster struck. Far from hardening under his as he'd expected, and pulling away at the first opportunity, her lips softened in silent invitation. Surprise running through his larger frame Cy flicked his tongue along her full lower lip.

She relaxed, her hands gentling on his chest as her lips parted. Just a fraction but it was enough. No way was he going to pass up even the smallest invitation from this woman.

Pressing her back against the side of the car Cy took control of the kiss. His hands drove into her hair, scattering pins as his tongue parted her lips and gained access to the sweet inner recesses of her mouth. It was heaven. Warm silk and just a touch of whiskey laced coffee.

Desire throbbing through him Cy lifted his head. "Whiskey?" She hadn't had an alcoholic drink over dinner and certainly not whiskey. "You needed Dutch courage before our date?"

She opened passion-darkened eyes and the look in them speared Cy. His nipples under the thin tee-shirt peaked and rubbed against the fabric, the silver rings through them growing colder by the minute. Pleasure arced through his body, his cock hardening another painful notch and rubbing against the inside of his jeans.

She nodded and laughed. The soft sound was melodious in the night air and Cy was entranced. It was a new feeling for the Pixie. Usually humans were entranced by him, not the other way around.

"Yeah, a little. I mean, come on. Me and someone like you?"

The nerves in her voice were enough to melt even the most hardened heart. His thumb stroked over her cheek in a gentle caress even as his lips curled into a sly smile. "You mean a bad boy like me?" he asked and leaned in to kiss her again.

This time he didn't bother with gentle. He crushed her lips under his and took what he wanted.

She didn't struggle, just opened up to him with a sexy little mewl in the back of her throat. He stroked his tongue along hers in an erotically charged dance, keeping her off balance as he gathered one of her legs up against his hip. His fingers hooked behind her knee for the lift then slid under the velvet.

She gasped at the bold touch but didn't stop him. His hand slid higher as he moved to nibble on her lower lip, then planted small kisses along her jaw. His sharp teeth nipped lightly at her earlobe as his fingertips smoothed over the rounded curve of her ass.

Oh my god, she wasn't wearing panties. Cy's arousal hit the stratosphere. So much for the 'touch me not' attitude, she'd come out expecting some action. He moaned against the soft skin of her throat and ground his hips against her. A red mist descended. All he could think about was busting his cock into her willing softness. He literally ached, shaking from head to foot as his fingers ventured further.

"Oh yeah baby, that's it," he murmured in encouragement as she whimpered and rocked her hips against his hand. Then, finally, he reached his goal and swept his fingers along her feminine folds. But, instead of the arousal slicked cleft he was expecting, his fingers touched hot, damp satin.

She was wearing a thong.

He should have been disappointed but, bizarrely, he wasn't. He was relieved she wasn't some bored and easy housewife looking for a cheap thrill. He pressed against the heated satin covering her clit and was rewarded with a shuddering whimper.

"Oh...yes, god yes."

Cy changed the pressure, rubbing in tiny circles over the sensitive flesh until she was gasping and moaning in his arms. Her hips rocked against his hand. A silent demand for more.

"Oh yeah, you like that, don't you baby?" he whispered against her ear then kissed behind it, seeking the spot there that made her squirm in pleasure. His free hand smoothed up her curves and cupped her breast.

"Fuck, you've got great tits. All I can think about is kissing them and sucking on your nipples..."

"Mhhhmmm," was her only response and the satin under Cy's fingers grew hotter and wetter as her arousal increased. She was so sensitive it was unreal. "Yes, please. The dress...stretches." The Pixie didn't need a second invitation. Within a heartbeat he hooked his fingers into the neckline of her dress and pulled it down. Fabric tore, ripped in his haste, but Cy didn't care. He was too busy staring at the glorious sight revealed to him to care about anything else.

The perfect mounds of her breasts rose above a delicate lace demi-bra designed to drive any red- blooded man wild. Cy's mouth went dry. He reached out a shaking hand to trail his fingertips along the satin edging of the cup.

She didn't say anything, didn't make a move to stop him. Instead her head dropped back, her eyes fluttering closed as she willingly gave herself up to his touch.

Yes! She was his. Cy snapped out of his trance and moved in for the kill. Anyone could walk past and break the mood. And he knew if that happened he'd never get her back into his position. Not easily anyway, certainly not offering him her half-naked breasts whilst he had his hand up her skirt. She'd be too embarrassed.

Whatever magic had her here now he didn't know and he didn't care. Might—or guile—made right.

"You're beautiful." His whisper was heartfelt as he bent his head to place a gentle kiss on the soft, creamy flesh of her cleavage. Christmas Eve and he had a willing woman in his arms. That had to be the best Christmas present in the world...well, bar being part of a family. *That* was the thing Cy wanted most in the world. To feel like he belonged again. This wasn't it but, for a little while, he could pretend.

It was the work of a second to slide his fingers into her bra and push the lace out of the way. A sigh whispered from his lungs as her nipple was released from captivity. Taut and puckered it was dusky against the pale skin of the rounded globe.

Cy licked his lips and leaned in. He swirled his tongue around the tight bud at the same moment he swept his fingers under the damp satin of her thong. She started in surprise at the dual assault. But Cy wasn't finished yet, not by a long shot. He drew her nipple into his mouth, rolling the sensitive bud against the back of his teeth, as his fingers stroked along the folds of her pussy.

He found her clit and smiled at the strangled whimper that escaped her throat as he circled it. Liquid heat met his fingers as explored further. She was hot and wet, more than ready for him.

His cock twitched in his pants. It would be so easy to push that satin aside, free himself and slide into her here and now. Seat himself to the hilt and fuck her right there up against his car.

*

Oh god, she was going to come. Right here and now. In a car park, up against the side of a car with a stranger's hand in her panties. She tried to hold back her moans as his lips paid homage to her breasts. He moved from one to the other as his clever fingers circled her clit in erotic little circles. Unbidden her hips rocked against his hand. A silent demand for more, far more.

Teresa opened her eyes and tried to focus through the sensual haze that had enveloped her. She couldn't believe this was happening. She didn't normally do things like this. Not impulsive, seat of the pants, dangerously erotic things like practically having sex with a guy she didn't know within an hour of meeting him.

His eyes caught hers as he straightened up, his handsome face set into grim lines. It was the sort of look she would have quailed at before. Would now, if not for the smoldering desire she could see in the peacock blue.

"Come for me." His deep voice urged her on, his breath fanning the soft skin of her neck in hot waves. Out of sight under her velvet skirt his fingers continued to work their magic. Stroking back and forth across her clit; each stroke making her pussy clench tightly. She needed something more, her body yearning, needing something more, her pussy desperate to be filled by the hardness she could feel pressed against her belly.

"Come and I'm going to fuck you," he promised, his voice hypnotic. "Not here, but on the way home. I'll stop somewhere quiet, dark. I'm gonna to spread your legs and eat your sweet pussy until you scream my name. Then, when you think you can't take any more pleasure, I'm going to take you. Hard and fast, like the bad boy you wanted."

Teresa shivered, unable to stop the tremors that racked her body. She pushed her hips against his hand again. "Yes…please," she begged, willing to do anything to get what she needed. To hell with being sensible, to hell with tomorrow. Right or wrong, she wanted more. An early Christmas present to herself.

He moved and slid a finger inside her. Teresa couldn't breathe. Her pussy clamped around the invading digit as a wave of fire rolled through her veins. He pulled back and then a second finger joined the first, his thumb pushing up against her clit as he thrust inside her.

"You feel fucking great. Hot and wet…tight. You like that, don't you baby?" he murmured, fucking her with his fingers as he leaned down to suckled on her tits again. All Teresa could do was moan and hold on. The coil of tension low down in her belly grew tighter and tighter. Any moment now it was going to snap—

"Yeah, that's it baby…let it go. Come for me, I want to feel you come." His whisper in her ear was a dark temptation. Teresa shuddered and turned into him, placing a clumsy kiss on his cheek as she panted in need. Her body ached, the familiar waves pushing her closer and closer to the edge. Cy groaned. "That's it. I want you to come. God, I can just imagine sliding my cock into you. Your cunt…so tight and wet."

The dirty words just did it for Teresa. With a gasp her world shattered apart and became pure, sparkling pleasure that filled her core and radiated out to every cell in her body.

Chapter Four

Holy hell, could his luck get any better? Sat in the small front room of Teresa's house Cy tried not to lounge on the comfortable couch but sit respectfully instead. Trouble was Pixies didn't do respectful well. In fact disrespect was pretty much coded into their genes.

He still couldn't believe what had happened back there in the car park and—when she'd asked him afterwards if he wanted to come back to her place—you could have knocked him down with a feather. In all honesty, once she came around from the shattering climax he'd brought her to, he'd expected her to tell him to get lost.

She hadn't. Instead she'd muttered something about an early Christmas present. Somehow Cy didn't think she meant for him but it was as near as dammit so he wasn't going to argue.

Sighing Cy gave up on the not lounging and rested his head back for a second and closed his eyes. Desire and anticipation throbbed through every inch of his body, creating a symphony of need that had him as hard as a rock. Things like this didn't happen to him, not with nice women like Teresa. Oh, he got the come on's from club-goers but the bosses tended to frown on fraternization, even though they had been the worst ones for it at one point. Even if they hadn't he didn't want some pissed up twenty-something who was just interested in a good time and alcohol. He wanted someone...

Cy opened his eyes and looked around. The scene that met his eyes was that of a typical family home. Battered and well worn couches surrounded a large fireplace and a television was set off to one side, tucked out of the way rather than the central focus of the room like in many houses.

The wreath trimmed mantle was overcrowded with photos. Teresa and two children—a girl and a boy. Cy's sharp eyes scanned them again, just to be sure. No man, no husband.

He released a deep breath, a sigh of relief he hadn't realised he'd been holding. No husband and no competition. He didn't think she was the sort of woman to cheat on her partner but it was nice to be sure.

The rest of the room followed the Christmas theme. Tinsel adorned the tops of the pictures and enthusiastically-made paper-chains were anchored in the corners of the ceiling and festooned along the walls. To top it all a large Christmas tree stood in the corner of the room, its decorations a riot of colour and, underneath it, waited a pile of presents.

Cy gasped as a wave of longing hit him hard again. Home, family, all the things missing from his life. All the things he'd kill to be able to turn the clock back for...to stop Marcus before he'd gotten tangled with the kyn. Lesson learned—never mess with Vampires, they made ruthless enemies.

"Yeah, they're both in bed. Sound asleep—"

The voice warned him an instant before Teresa and another woman walked into the main room. The babysitter. The one Teresa had to get rid of before he could strip that infernal dress from her delectable body and get her where he wanted her. Whether that was under his tongue whilst he ate her pussy or under his body as he fucked her slow and deliberately—he didn't care.

By then end of the night he planned to have taken her in every way possible. She might have borne two children but she still had a haunting aura of innocence. The wicked things he wanted to do to her, with her, it didn't stand a chance.

"—oh my. You're gonna do it. Actually gonna do it!" The babysitter squeaked, looking from Cy sat on the couch to the blushing Teresa and back again. Cy unfolded himself from the clinging embrace of the couch and offered his hand.

"Hi. I'm Cy..." he offered, trailing off so she'd introduce herself. If there was one thing he'd realised about women it was to endear himself to the friends as well as the woman he was pursing, it made things so much easier. She took the bait with a broad smile.

"Pleased to meet you Cy. I'm—"

"Just leaving," Teresa broke in, a new note of jealousy and impatience in her voice that Cy found he liked. She snatched her friend's hand from his and hustled her towards the door. "Thanks for tonight Joanie, I'll see you tomorrow. Have a great night's sleep," she said as she bundled the other woman through the doorway.

Joan just laughed, not appearing to take offence at Teresa's rude behaviour and waved over her shoulder. "Nice to have almost met you Cy. You make sure you keep her up all night, you hear?" Then she was gone as Teresa slammed the door in her face.

"So..." She leaned back against the now closed door, a sexy little look on her face. "Where were we?"

Cy smiled a dangerous little smile as he sauntered over. One hand reached out and slid around her waist to pull her hard against him. Her breath left her lungs in a little 'whoosh' as she landed against his broad chest. Her fingers weren't idle, initially hitting his chest but then spreading out to explore the solid muscle under the thin T-shirt. Cy had already shed his jacket but, at her touch, even the light material seemed too heavy and constraining.

His fingers spread out over the back of her hips as he cupped her ass, admiring the sensual curves before yanking her hips up against his. Her breath stuttered and those beautiful eyes widened again as she how much he wanted her. Cy hid his smile at the look of surprise. He was a pixie and, like most paranormal races, they were bigger built in the cock department than humans.

"Ever been with a paranormal?" His question was whispered a mere hairsbreadth from her lips but he knew the answer. She'd been too surprised to discover he wasn't human to be familiar with the night-races.

The tiny shake of her head confirmed his thinking a second before he leaned in and claimed her lips. He'd wanted to be slow and deliberate, wanted to take the time to savour this, but the instant his lips touched hers all bets were off.

All the need and passion that had been building up since the night of the auction, tempered and simmering since the incident in the car park on the way home, boiled over the top. Cy growled. His lips kissed, licked and nipped at hers. A demand she open up to him and give him what he wanted, what they both needed.

The growl turned to a groan when she did. His tongue thrust past her lips and tasted her, exploring the sweet recesses of her mouth ruthlessly. He urged her backwards until she was pressed against the closed door, his larger body pressing insistently into her.

"You want this?" he broke the fevered kiss for a moment to whisper against her lips. He was rough, tough and dangerous...he knew that, it was the pixie way...but unlike some of the others, he'd never taken an unwilling woman. "Say no now...or I'm going to fuck you."

"What? Here?" Her voice held a note of surprise but Cy felt the tremor that racked her body. Saw the way her eyes darkened with need. She'd probably never had sex anywhere other than a bed before but he'd bet his bottom dollar she'd fantasised about it often enough.

"Here...now." His lips grazed down the silken skin of her throat. As he kissed her his hands slid the straps of the gloriously stretchy dress off her shoulders. Whoever the designer was...Cy wanted to kiss him. He wound the straps around his fingers and dragged it down. The red velvet inched lower and the pixies eyes followed it every inch of the way.

It caught for a second on the swell of her breasts, then dropped to her waist. A waist so narrow Cy could span it in his two hands. His mouth went dry, his cock raging at the mere sight of her revealed to his eyes. Impatient he yanked on the fabric.

"Take your bra off," he ordered, hearing but unable to do anything about the pleading note in his voice. He needed her naked and naked now. As she slid her hands behind her back he pushed the dress over her hips and let it drop. It hit the floor at the same second her breasts were released.

Cy lost the ability to breath, his peacock blue eyes swirling dark with need as he looked at her. Stood against the door in just a thong, stockings and heels with her hair falling around her shoulders like a dark cloud, she was an erotic fantasy come to life.

"Uhmmmm..." He managed which, even Cy had to admit, wasn't him at his most eloquent. He reached out to roll one rock hard nipple between his thumb and fore-finger. She gasped, lips paring as her head fell back against the door. The half-lidded sultry look she gave him snapped the remainder of Cy's control.

With a small groan he moved in. Pressing her against the cool wood he gathered her leg over his hip, fingers of the other hand sweeping the satin between her legs aside as he took her lips. He didn't bother with preliminaries, thrusting two fingers inside her pussy at the same time his tongue slid past her lips.

The dual sensation almost unmanned him. Her sexy little whimper and wiggle were the most erotic thing he'd ever experienced. Her tight channel was hot and wet, slick with her arousal. He pumped his fingers twice, his thumb pressing against her clit, then scissored them to test her readiness. She moaned again and thrust her hips against him. She was ready, more than ready if the greedy clutching of her cunt on his fingers was any indication.

Unable to hold off any longer Cy pulled from her. It was the work of a second to drop his zipper and free himself. His rigid cock sprang free eagerly, aching to be inside her willing body. He dipped his knees and, using his hand, ran the broad head up and down her slick, wet cleft. He gritted his teeth at the sensation, rubbing his cock-head against the hard nub of her clit until her moans devolved into mindless whimpers. Then he moved, fitted himself against the slick entrance to her cunt and filled her in one hard thrust.

  *

Teresa's world stopped as he slammed his rigid cock home. A short panted gasp escaped her lips as her body stretched, pussy lips parting to accommodate his thick length. She'd never had a lover quite so big. She felt stuffed—almost uncomfortably so. The fit of their bodies was so tight she could feel blood pulsing through the thick vein on the underside of his cock.

Her mouth watered at the thought of it. She had always liked sucking cock and it had been a long time since Mario. A long, lonely time. But she was already too far gone to suggest it. She needed him inside her, needed him to fill her. Next time she promised herself, a small whimper in the back of her throat.

Cy reared back at the sound. His nostrils flared and he held perfectly still. Worry shadowed his eyes as he searched her face in concern. "You okay baby? I didn't hurt you, did I?"

Something inside her melted when she heard the tension in his voice. So much for the bad boy he pretended to be, she knew better. Inside he was as soft as marshmallow.

"No, you didn't hurt me..." she whispered, her voice gaining strength as she spoke. "But, if you don't move soon I'm going to die of bloody frustration."

Her arms wound about his neck as her lips found his ear. She sucked and nibbled on the lobe, pulling it into her mouth to flick the earring there with her tongue. "Will you quit worrying and just...just..." She couldn't say it, a flush rising on her cheeks as she trailed off instead.

"Just what?" Cy's lips curved into a wicked little smile. "This?" he asked as he rolled his hips. Pleasure exploded through Teresa's body. She'd climaxed earlier and normally, a release that explosive wiped her out for the night. Not this time. All the way home her body had thrummed with awareness of the lean, muscled man sat next to her.

"Yes, oh yes."

The look in his eyes grew more wicked at her soft plea. He pulled back, until he was almost out of her then slid back into her in one powerful slide. His thick cock stroked nerve endings which had been neglected for far too long. Pressing her back against the door he hauled her leg higher on his hip. Crowded against hard wood by his larger body Teresa realised how much bigger and stronger he was. For the first time in years she felt delicate and feminine rather than plump and dowdy.

Then he stopped. Teresa pouted in disappointment and bit back the urge to demand he carry on. She rocked her hips in impatience, trying to urge him on without words.

"Oh no sweetheart, you want it—you beg for it," he ordered. As if to punctuate his point he rotated his hips, pressing his cock against the slick walls of her pussy in all new and interesting ways.

"Beg," he demanded. "Tell me you want me to fuck you and I will. I'll fuck you so hard and in so many different ways you'll never...want another man." He said the last few words with a hint of surprise in his voice. As though he couldn't believe what he was saying himself.

Heat rose in Teresa's cheeks. At the same time her body insisted she needed more. She needed him to move. Needed him to fuck her. Now.

"Yes, yes! Fuck me...please. Oh please god, just fuck me," Teresa begged, wriggling on his thick shaft. Impaled as she was she couldn't move far but the movement provided a delicious friction which had her moaning all over again.

"As my lady commands," Cy murmured, his breath hot against her throat. Teresa jumped as his tongue flicked out, the rough, wet rasp swiping directly over the spot on her neck that made her go weak at the knees.

He surged into her again. And again. Each time pulling out of her with a sexy little liquid sound as the skin of his cock dragged against the tightness of her hot, wet cunt.

Teresa felt herself grow wetter which in turn made his thrusts easier until he was fucking her with long, hard strokes.

"Bet you didn't think our date would end up like this, did you?" he taunted, easily holding her pinned against the door with the force of his movements. "Getting a good hard fuck up against your front door with your pussy rammed full of pixie cock."

He pushed into her again, rotating his hips on the last few words. Her eyes rolled back in her head in pleasure. It was all she could do to breathe, never mind answer him.

"Look at me." His demand was harsh and dragged her out of her sensual haze. Blinking, Teresa forced herself to focus.

Reaching down Cy hooked a big hand under her other leg and lifted. His lips claimed hers in a quick erotic kiss before he leaned back. "Look," he ordered, nodding to where their bodies joined. "I want to watch you watching me fuck you."

Lightening arched through Teresa at his words. Her gaze dropped down. His cock was buried to the root in her pussy. As she watched he pulled out and her pussy lips parted, clinging around the rigid shaft that emerged, the skin glistening with her juices. Fascinated, she couldn't tear her eyes away, watching as he pushed back inside her—her body engulfing the thick veined cock.

"This is all I've been able to think about, ever since that night at the auction," he admitted, working himself back inside her with a series of quick thrusts. "I saw this amazing woman—you— and I had to have you."

Leaning down he sucked a pert nipple into his mouth and sucked hard. Teresa cried out and clutched him too her, her hands holding his head as she offered her full breasts to him. With his mouth on her and his cock deep inside her she was nearly there, almost ready to come. Something about his growled admission got to her but she couldn't concentrate on it. Not with what he was doing.

His cock filled her again, her clit throbbing as it was pressed between their pelvic bones. Her release throbbed just out of reach and the strong muscled of her channel tightened. A rhythmic clenching that made Cy grit his teeth.

"Oh fuck—I'm gonna come."

"Yes..." Teresa panted, adding an extra wriggle every time she slid down his engorged cock. It felt so good. She'd forgotten just how good sex could be. But then, she hadn't bothered much since Mario. Just hadn't felt the urge, at least until her bad, boy pixie here had turned up.

Then, without warning, she was there. Time slowed almost to a stop as the tension in her belly, the ache deep in her pussy, wound to an unbearable level and then...snapped. She cried his name as pleasure rolled her over and under like a swimmer caught in a wave. She heard but couldn't process his answering curse.

He thrust once, twice, three times more then slammed his cock home. As his body went rigid she felt his cock swell within her, pumping his seed deep within her.

Pleasure expanded within her like a million brilliant shards of light, each one perfect as they swirled out from her core, colliding with each other as the light filled every cell of her body. A perfect and endless firework display of sheer ecstasy.

Panting as the feeling began to recede and some semblance of brain function return Teresa blinked and then smiled at him a little shyly. Why the hell she should be shy after what they'd just shared she didn't know...but she was.

His face held such a look of surprise and intense erotic satisfaction that there was no question he'd enjoyed it as much as she had. But, despite that, there was a hint of wariness in his eyes, coupled with a resignation that yanked on Teresa's heart-strings. As though, now they were done, he expected to be thrown out.

She wound her arms around his neck, wriggling again and relishing the feel of his still hard cock within her. "That was fantastic," she purred. "But it seems to me that I got the better end of the deal here...How do you feel about round two?" She yawned widely, realising how late it was and how much she still had to do before the big day and Santa arriving.

"Or," she added, going out on a limb. "If you wanted to stay, I could give you your Christmas present after the kids go to their Nanna's in the morning...?"

Cy started in surprise, his peacock blue eyes searching her face. Eyes Teresa wanted to see waking up beside her in the morning, and not just once. Then he smiled, the slow, happy smile of a man who'd just been given the best Christmas present of all; the chance of a family again.

About the Author

Mina was born and raised in the East Farthing of Middle Earth (otherwise known as the Midlands, England) and spend her childhood learning all the sorts of things generally required of a professional adventurer. Able to ride, box, shoot, make and read maps, make chainmail and use a broadsword (with varying degrees of efficiency) she was disgusted to find that adventuring is not considered a suitable occupation these days.

So, instead of slaying dragons and hunting vampires and the like, Mina spends her days writing about hot shifters, government conspiracies and vampire lords with more than their fair share of RAWR. Turns out wanna-be adventurers have quite the turn of imagination after all...

(But she keeps that sword sharp, just in case the writing career is just a dream and she really *is* an adventurer.)

The boring part: A full time author and cover artist, Mina can usually be found hunched over a keyboard or graphics tablet, frantically trying to get the images and words in her head out and onto the screen before they drive her mad. She's addicted to coffee and would like to be addicted to chocolate, but unfortunately chocolate dislikes her.

Website: http://mina-carter.com
twitter: @minacarter

Other Titles by Mina Carter

Made in the USA
Lexington, KY
02 November 2014